Secondhand SECRETS

HARLOW SERIES BOOK THREE

KATERINA SIMMS

One

ALLY EGAN GAWPED at the wayward baseball shooting across the field toward her head, her eyes instinctively—and perhaps, nonsensically—clenching shut against the eminent impact.

"Whoa, Ally!"

A hand yanked her off-balance, and she re-opened her eyes just in time to land on Emilia Bonacci; Emilia's fiancé, Blaine, catching both women before they hit the ground.

The moment of collision passed, and Ally turned to Fred Harding in the bleacher behind, the sixty-year-old doing a little jig while waving his wrinkled-leather mitt in the air, the ball inside.

"You okay?" Emilia's voice cut through again, and Ally set about straightening and brushing stray locks of cropped blonde hair from her eyes.

How embarrassing. Still, she couldn't exactly complain about being spared an excruciating meeting with a hard, white orb, so she twisted around to Emilia—her friend of just a few months—and offered an appreciative smile. "Yeah, thanks for the save."

The fuss over the stray ball settled, and she tugged at the crooked hem of her baby pink cardigan, the bitter scent of beer wafting around her. Next, she steeled her focus back to the pitch where an early summer game played out between the home team, The Harlow Braves, and neighboring rivals, The Marston Giants.

The next batter stepped to the plate, some new guy she'd never seen in Harlow before, much less *play* for Harlow... *How odd.* She cupped her hand over her brow and squinted for a better look, struggling to figure how this person had joined the team so fast, much less without her notice *or* any mention in this gossipy town.

I guess this is what I get for avoiding Maynard's Tavern or, more precisely, the owner, Sarah Overton...

With Harlow being a middle-of-nowhere Minnesotan town, everyone knew everyone else, and word of fresh blood travelled fast. She sized this new guy up against the others that she *did* know on the pitch and guessed him to be about six foot, his shoulders wide, his build lean, but strong. Though she couldn't see his face all that well, he had the air of someone around her age of twenty-three.

Yep, definitely new blood.

Then again, I made a vow to stop looking, remember?

The pitcher threw the ball, and she loosened her posture, resigned to indifference. The new guy swung and, in all his admitted beauty, left a hefty metallic *thunk* reverberating around the two-hundred-strong crowd.

Unexplainable tension gripped low in her tummy. She followed the ball's trajectory far across the park, which allowed time for him to take all bases home.

Cheers roared around her. Almost everyone stood. Not her, though. Her mouth slipped open, while she peered up at all the people bouncing about and clapping hands, her ears stinging from all the hollering voices until her legs worked of their own volition and lifted her to join them.

Talk about the bandwagon effect! She twisted back to the stranger strolling casually across the bases, his body angled away and his blue baseball cap obscuring any distinct features. All she could really discern was the patch of dark blond hair protruding from under his cap.

Why am I still looking?!

Her heart fluttered, and her hand rose to the base of her throat, those actions providing her answer. *How familiar.* As was her problem here. A problem too many young women in these parts suffered. The complexities of living in a small town. Especially when confronted with a man the slightest bit handsome *and* physically capable.

His feet met the home plate, and the cheers around her peaked. She pressed her hands over her ears, but not so much that she didn't catch Emilia's next raised words. "Maybe I'm still too new in town, but I'm sure I've never seen that guy around."

A quick break in play was called, and Ally waited for the noise to fade before lowering her hands to reply, even though she didn't want to *look* at any hot young men, much less discuss them…

"That's because he *isn't* from Harlow. And I'm just as clueless as you."

"Now, that's different." Emilia's dark brown eyes glittered, and she settled back down on the bench, her hand quick to wrap around Blaine's. "Ally Egan is usually the first to know about these things. In fact, she's usually the first to knock on a newbie's door and invite herself in with her classic opener… a personally delivered breakfast."

Usually. Yes. But not anymore. Not since her fallout with Sarah two months ago. Though tightness pulled at her chest, she pinched her lips together and sent Emilia a benevolent scowl. Taking the hint to drop the subject, Emilia let out a sigh and turned to speak with Blaine.

Meanwhile, Ally stared ahead, where she unfortunately caught a glimpse of the new guy running up the stadium steps. Maybe he had people here watching him. A distant cousin or something. With any luck, his presence in this sleepy town would be limited to a super brief visit before he disappeared back to wherever he'd come from.

Really, after months of upheaval, all she wanted to do was enjoy her first fun day out. She didn't want any reminders of her more flirtatious past. A past based on nothing more than words and very little action. At twenty-three years old, she was as single as she'd ever been, and perhaps, her singledom was for the best.

Maybe all I'll ever be is a small-town girl, but there's got to be more to life than trying to fall in love. Art. Dreams of travel. Who knows, maybe one day I'll finally find it in me to leave this place…

So long as she stuck to her new plan—look but don't touch *or* even speak—she'd be fine. Just fine.

The man she meant to avoid side-stepped his way through a nearby row. The first feature to draw her focus was his strong and clean shaven jawline, then the habitual-seeming smile lighting his face. Perhaps a man light on worries.

Still some rows away, his eyes seemed not quite brown, but not as light as her own pale blue. Hazel, maybe? Though as far as total strangers went, he was a tall glass of cool water on a hot day. Even if this summer had just begun, and the weather still remained kind of mild.

"Ooo, look!" Emilia nudged Ally's arm. "He's talking to Sarah."

Of course he was.

Ally did her best to maintain her new vow of maturity and not roll her eyes, especially as Sarah Overton jumped from her seat and hugged the new guy—a peculiar gesture given the woman's general stoicism.

What was her connection to the dreamy newcomer? Definitely not romantic. Not since Dean Holloway stood beside her, a man who'd flatly rejected Ally not all that long ago.

Think positive. The connection with Sarah only puts Mr. Dreamy even more off my radar.

Though she averted her gaze, Mr. Dreamy's warm laugh sailed the distance to her ears, and an unwanted heat flooded her body, her heart giving a taut pang as a hush washed over the crowd.

"I think Dean's proposing." Emilia's voice barely filtered through. Ally's senses disrupted as her heart kicked again, all eyes turned to Sarah.

Or more so, Sarah *and* Dean.

Dean knelt on one knee.

"But they've only known each other three months"—the hard lump in her throat turned her voice into an incredulous rasp, and her head did a slow and unintended shake—"and he spent half that time lying about his sketchy past."

Which he'd spent time in jail for, after the truth came out…

Emilia's reply wasn't forthcoming, so Ally turned to her friend, the woman's sidelong glare fixed on her—narrowed eyes and tight lipped. *Oh, that's right!*

Emilia had been with Blaine just a month when he'd proposed.

"Oh, you and Blaine don't count." Ally swatted a hand and refocused on Sarah's gape-mouthed expression. "You two had history long before you got back together."

Emilia gave a reluctant growl, prodding at Ally's guilt. "Yeah, well. Just like the rest of us, Dean didn't have much say on his past. So, maybe it's time to cut him a little slack?"

Ally didn't reply, the tension in her throat drawing tighter. Emilia's comment pointed at the fact that Ally had lived a sheltered life and had only just come to learn she had a problem with relating to others.

Yet another reason to stay chained to this little town.

That said, she wasn't low enough to outright discount a man like Dean—raised in a dysfunctional home, then abandoned to foster care —a life of crime and misfortune unfolding thereafter.

Heck, she didn't even care so much that he'd picked Sarah, either. Those two made more sense together. What she didn't love was that Sarah had been her best friend. A best friend who'd hidden her relationship with Dean while allowing Ally to make a fool of herself.

Silly girl, too bright-eyed and immature for the truth...

As if Sarah—and everyone else, for that matter—figured they knew what went through her head.

The crowd burst into cheers again, awakening her to her wandering thoughts and the inevitable fact that Sarah had said, *"Yes."*

The Harlow High School Marching Band flooded the field— trumpets blaring, drums like thunder—followed by a small troupe of cheerleaders.

"Just perfect." Ally pressed her fingertips to her eyes, giving them a short break from the Sarah and Dean show, only to then lower her hands and lock stares with Mr. Dreamy.

Of course. Of course that would happen. The lousy timing fit, just as his easy smile did, as well as the thrill of recognition shooting up her spine.

Why did he even smile at her? And why did he seem so suddenly familiar?

That's not familiarity. It's hot-blooded attraction.
Jeez Louise, girl. Run. Just run.
Oh no, don't start that again.
Art. Dreams. Travel. Financial freedom…
A man is not a plan. A man is NOT a plan!

Was it possible for her heart to clench so hard it might actually pop? Either way, maybe it was best to do as her psyche ordered and leave.

But she didn't want to do that. Didn't want a man to dictate what she did, ever again. And quick relief came at the stiffening of his smile, as though he read her doubts before pushing his attention from her to the on-field ode to Dean and Sarah.

Crisis averted. New breath refreshed her lungs, and she crossed her arms against any future man-attacks. Since she and Sarah had grown up together and, therefore, knew the same people, maybe this guy was connected to Dean in some way?

"Well, that's a chilling thought." Her quip was loud enough to gain a raised brow from Emilia, but Ally gave her a dismissive shrug.

"Right. Well, Blaine and I are leaving to get drinks. Want anything?"

Ally shook her head and went on pondering, her stare pinned to Emilia's back as she left.

Hopefully this new man differed from Dean in that he had no connection to the Syndicate, a crime ring that kept finding new reasons to unleash terror on Harlow.

But she had to give Dean some credit. He was a bright man. Cautious, too. He wouldn't allow an active Syndicate member into town. Besides, if stereotypes were in any way true, this new guy looked way too clean-cut for a career criminal. Come to think of it, he was also way too young to be one of Dean's former army buddies.

"Ally?"

She jolted at the male voice calling her name, only to turn and find Mr. Dreamy squeezing past the people in her row and his undeniably brilliant gaze pinned her way.

Oh, no.
No. No. No!

"Ally Egan, is that you?"

Two

ALLY'S HEART sank before taking on a wild beat, Mr. Dreamy's smile growing to reveal two predictably perfect rows of shiny, white teeth. And his eyes. They *were* hazel. And even more heartbreakingly beautiful up close.

Though her previous self would have literally fallen over at his attention, the hard pounding in her chest told a different story, one conceivably not too dissimilar to the time-halting seconds one experienced before their car hit a pole.

Still, she took a sharp breath and blocked out the crisp scent of cologne wafting from his general direction. "How do you know my name?"

More than the man before her, she wanted to dance at her new ability to maintain an even tone; but then, in a sign this battle wasn't won yet, the golden flecks in his eyes flared like fanned embers in a low fire.

To add insult to injury, he shuffled past and claimed the empty seat beside her, her mouth drying at his sudden close proximity.

"You don't recognize me"—the skin at his cheekbones crinkled above his grin, like he held some revolutionary secret—"do you?"

Her insides flipped. *Nausea or anticipation?* She couldn't tell. But then, attraction wasn't clear like that. Not for a quick-to-fall woman like her. A woman now at the center of this gorgeous man's focus.

Think, girl. Think!

He's with Sarah… He seems to know you… So, how do YOU know him?

Her heart lost its solid beat, seeming to plunge lower into her body right along with the rest of her insides.

"No." She shook her head through her splintered and hollow whisper, the inside of her throat suddenly prickly. Maybe she *did* know him. "No way…"

His soft lines eased some more, a man both concerned and pleased with the outcome of his surprise or, in this case, her shock.

A brittle creak worked its way up her throat before she finally succeeded to speak his name. "Chip?"

His eyes lit up, and he gave a quick nod, forcing her to hastily tuck her trembling bottom lip between her teeth as well as fight the sting behind her eyes.

"*Chip?*" Her voice pitched upward, the sound akin to a confused parrot. Though he gave a quick laugh, his swift confirmation of his name solidified his identity.

Her heart climbed to another gallop, the tension from earlier evaporated, even as she lunged forward, throwing her arms around him.

Chip—Sarah's brother, and Ally's boy-genius best friend from her childhood—was back.

She leaned away, a million questions rattling her brain as she looked him over anew, less conflicted about his presence now, more just plain excited.

His lips curled into another smile, small and boyish, bringing back decade-old memories. Of them sitting side by side, just like this. At school. On her front lawn. Down by the Mirabella River after a summer swim… and it was summer once again, wasn't it?

"Jeez Louise, you look…" Though she failed to finish her sentence, her focus bounced all around him, remnants of the old—or more precisely, younger—Chip still there amongst his stark changes.

Gosh, that wiry kid now had broad shoulders. And his jawline. So defined. With the light shadow of bronze stubble. A slightly manic giggle escaped her.

Chip Overton has stubble now?

She searched for more semblances of the Chip she'd known. Something she could cling to. Something to dull the disorienting din inside her head. After all, he'd already stirred emotions she didn't want to associate with anyone, much less her sweet and geeky childhood buddy.

"Last time I saw you, you were—"

His slow smile revealed those perfectly straight teeth again, his once-gappy grin completely gone. "Fourteen."

"No." *Though, that too.* She shook her head. "Skinny… and pale… really, really pale."

His shoulders shook with an unrestrained laugh, and he reached out to her. The action from any other man would have resulted in her instantly reeling back, but all she had now was her own laughter taking over and her hand slipping into his long and nimble-looking fingers.

Relief drowned out her confused hormones, and a light sensation drifted over. Suddenly, the hand holding wasn't enough, and she extended her arms, pulling him in for another embrace.

Shock had drowned her appreciation of that first hug, but this time, *this time,* she breathed him in, making up for an entire decade of absence.

Another laugh disappeared into the curve of his neck, and she held him long enough for his crisp scent to reveal deeper tones of amber and musk. When she finally did pull out of the embrace, she looked him over again, all while ignoring any tight, fluttery feelings within her body. "You grew up on me!"

"Like you can talk." A slower, thoughtful expression swept his face. "What happened to the reedy, thirteen-year-old I left behind?"

She opened her mouth to offer an answer, but his reminder about "leaving" dried her reply. He *had* left. And suddenly, too. All the way to Boston in the wake of his parents' divorce.

Now, shame snaked through her torso.

What *had* happened to her?

Nothing. Absolutely nothing.

She'd stayed right here in Harlow while Chip—though not his fault —had been the first of many her age to either settle down and have kids or embark on adventures far, far away.

"Chip!"

The loud clap of Blaine's voice had her startled and sucking in a sharp breath, the man wading down the row until he sidled up to Chip, her solo moment with her old friend gone.

"How you doing, buddy?" Blaine dropped into a neighboring seat, one hand balancing a newly bought beer, the other snapping out to give Chip a quick pat on the back. "Finally decided to visit the old stomping grounds, huh?"

Though Chip flicked his gaze back to her, it didn't hold the same unabashed light as before. As though the new company had him hiding any overt signs of joy.

"Just taking a break from Boston." He turned back to Blaine with a tight nod. "I brought work with me. With Sarah moved in with Dean, I figured I'd take over her house and get more done in Harlow."

Blaine leaned over and latched his gaze to Ally at the same time. "Back when Sarah and I were a thing, we'd occasionally visit Chip over in Boston." He tilted his head to Chip. "You've only just graduated, right?"

"Yep." A muscle twitched along Chip's jaw before he rose quickly, the twist of his body indicating he wanted to leave. "Looks like your lady's here."

Sure enough, Emilia did make her way toward them. Not that Blaine noticed, his brows still pressed together in a quizzical stare. "What did you study again? Computer something…"

"Computer science."

Though Chip's attention kept bouncing between Ally and Blaine, Blaine snapped his fingers and pointed to Chip. "That's right. At MIT. And I hear you finished top of your class."

Now Chip's focus clung to Ally, his stiff gaze unreadable, while the bell to resume play now rang. Somehow, that tight expression pulled into a tiny smile, just as confusing as his previous look. "I better get back out there."

Even though he spoke to the group at large, his message seemed meant for her alone, and then just like ten years prior, he turned and walked away.

And just like ten years ago, he stopped and peered over his shoulder to her one last time. Except, *unlike* ten years ago, there weren't any tears. Only his renewed smile and a quick wink. His unspoken promise to see her again.

Three

"Must have been weird seeing Ally again."

Chip turned from the stove in his home—once Sarah's home, and before that, their childhood home—his sister's steadfast amber gaze now holding firm from her position at the pale-wood dining table.

Oh, right, she wants an answer.

"Yeah, it was." He poked at a steak sizzling in the pan, limiting his reaction to those three understated words. This was his first sit-down dinner with his sister and her new fiancé in his three days back in Harlow.

And even in those three days, he'd figured he'd see Ally eventually, but no amount of mental preparation had slowed the racing of his heart when he'd finally met her.

Just the first lock of gazes hit him with an onslaught of emotion, then came the pure ease of speaking with her again. He'd clung to her every word and reaction. Yearned for hours together to reconnect, instead of those mere few minutes.

What still baffled him now was how one short conversation could obliterate an entire decade of absence. Even more confusing, he hadn't thought about much more than her in the long hours since…

Dean wandered into the bright, open-plan dining area, his added height and piercing blue eyes, turning all "wandering" into a somewhat intense stalk.

"You and Ally still haven't ironed out your differences, have you?" He peered at his new fiancée and took a seat at the table beside her.

Sarah toyed with the carrot stick in her hand, her gaze falling to the tabletop while she shook her head.

"You two are fighting?" Chip switched the stove off and turned his full attention to his sister.

Even with Sarah's perpetually prickly personality, he couldn't imagine Ally being all that combative.

Maybe she's changed…

"I wish we *were* fighting." Sarah let out a rough laugh and met his gaze. "That day at Maynard's, you know, the one when Emilia realized Dean was a Syndicate member, and he got arrested? Well, Ally said something about being glad she's a wallflower, and she hasn't spoken to me since."

Chip frowned. Ally instigated this rift?

He couldn't imagine her holding a grudge against anyone, let alone Sarah. They'd been friends for years. And why would she call herself a wallflower?

His past perceptions of Ally as mischievous, but harmless, took a hard dent. Now, he stared at Sarah in her fitted, white tank top, looking about ready to leave for a run, even though she wasn't. As usual, the act of sitting still seemed unnatural on her. "What happened?"

"Let's see, aside from the fact that our friendship began after you begged me to hover around Ally and keep her safe in your absence?" She shrugged and bit into her carrot stick, sending him a taunting sort of stare.

"Now, that's a copout." He shook his head, turning to the steak's savory scent on the stove. "Every time you visited me in Boston, you had some funny story about Ally. Promises aside, you both got along just fine."

He pierced a steak and dropped it on a plate, soon ferrying it over to his sister.

She held a hand out and took the food offering, her gaze pinned up at him. "Well then, I guess when you've known someone long enough, you're bound to hit some trouble eventually…"

"No." Dean let out a sigh, his attention falling to his fingertips already drumming a steady beat on the table. "Ally's outright pissed at you. What did I say about letting that whole charade of us not being together run on too long? You let her believe that I was free to date, leading her to a humiliating attempt to get my attention. She thinks you lied."

"Hey"—she swatted out a hand and gave Dean a weak tap on the bicep—"you lied too!"

"I was just some blow-in from L.A." He didn't return her offended glare, his perpetually unaffected gaze somehow more impactful. "*You* were her best friend."

The tension on her face slipped away, the closest Sarah would get to an admission of guilt. "Well, 'the charade' was your idea."

New light entered Dean's eyes, and he reached out, bumping a knuckle to Sarah's chin. "Only because you wouldn't commit to going out with me."

Something about the soft moment between these two brought a heaviness to Chip's gut. Not an unusual feeling since his return.

"Whatever." She half-heartedly rolled her eyes and turned back to Chip, who distracted himself with delivering the remaining plates. "Anyway, back in the day, you two might as well have been conjoined twins, and it looked like you both got along great today too. So… I guess that means you'll be a married man by the end of this week, and Little Ally Egan's wedding dreams will finally come true."

"Hey!" Dean's voice was a low warning. "Too far."

"What?" Sarah gave an oblivious shrug. "You wouldn't think it possible to be both clingy *and* flighty, but somehow, Ally nails it."

Chip took a seat, albeit slowly, his sidelong stare held to his sister. *So much animosity.*

Sure, the friendship had soured, but Sarah's "joke" edged on cruel, as though she sought to one-up Ally's rejection.

That was the way with close relationships, wasn't it? The arguments were uglier. The hurt, deeper. He'd seen that in his parents' divorce.

None of this would have happened if I'd been able to stay.

And maybe he'd been wrong to ask his sister to look out for Ally…

Speaking of Ally, what did Sarah mean about *"Little Ally Egan's wedding dreams"*? That, plus the wallflower remark, painted a confusing image.

Come to think of it, so did Ally's anger over Sarah's secrecy—partly justified—but for this long and with this level of lingering friction? There had to be more to their fight, his concerns stuck less on *what* caused the discord, so much as his failure to understand who Ally Egan had become over the years.

Sarah was the type to keep most pertinent details private and he couldn't count on asking her, but he had three weeks in town to uncover the truth, so he'd drop the subject of Ally for now. Maybe focus on forming his own opinions of her.

"How are you settling in?" Dean's question knocked Chip from his musing; the man's steady stare seeming to register more than he gave away, perhaps a symptom of his military past.

"It's strange being back in our childhood home, that's for sure." Chip embraced the change in topic and pitched a genuine smile to his sister. "But thanks for the great timing, Sis. I've set up my computer, and the quieter setting means I'm powering through my project."

She laughed and kissed Dean on the cheek. "We're happy to help."

"So…" This time Dean spoke. "I keep hearing that you're kind of a big deal?"

Chip gave a tight laugh and peered down at his plate, using the pretense of scooping up potato mash as an excuse to not look anyone in the eye. "Sure, if being a big deal means keeping good grades and having an idea with *some* potential. Other than that…"

"Still way more than most 'round these parts." Sarah nudged his leg under the table—just like when they'd been little and his mind wandered—once again succeeding to shift his attention to what she had to say. "You're working on your own idea straight out of college. If not now, then when, right?"

Except so much rode on his success, his latest idea for an encryption program named *Stonewall* being the difference between proving his dad wrong and having to live out the frivolous life he'd otherwise planned for Chip.

"While true, Sister, I probably do need to start earning some money one day." He pointed his fork at Sarah, a square of steak still on the end. "Unless Stonewall secures some funding, that day might be sooner than I'd like."

He couldn't keep living under his dad's sway forever, and finding people to hand over large wads of cash wasn't all that simple either. He needed investors who understood what his work meant for the global information security infrastructure. People with money *and* technical knowledge. People who could give him the financial security to be free of his dad.

Thanks to him, who I am, and who everyone thinks I am, are two different people.

"What exactly is Stonewall, anyway?" Dean's gaze bounced between Chip and Sarah.

"Oh, that's right, I heard you're a bit of a tech fan." Chip lowered his fork, still hungry post-baseball game and wondering when he'd get another bite in. "Stonewall deals in information security. I'll start with email encryption, but the program's scope could be much wider. That said, working with sensitive data means Stonewall needs to be flawless, and with a host of bugs to iron out, I'm slammed with things to do. Which brings me to Harlow. So quiet. So little distraction."

Sarah scoffed, making a show of fake-choking on whatever food sat in her mouth. "Yeah, right. Don't be deceived. This town is way more dramatic and distracting than it lets on."

She had a point. What with her failed engagement to Blaine, then meeting Dean, plus all the Syndicate's carnage through town, Harlow had delivered some major upheaval. Which brought him to his other *secret* reason for returning.

Two months ago, Dean's past with the Syndicate had come to a head with Sarah being taken hostage. Though Dean saved her, the whole saga helped Chip to see past his sister's constant strong act and be the one to visit her... for a change.

Once again, his mind wandered, and she nudged him under the table, sending forth her bright smile. "Either way, I'm proud of you."

Not used to praise, he set on a silent retreat to his meal, reveling in his reducing hunger and his ability to cook a juicy steak while occasionally glancing back at his sister.

In so many ways, she looked like him. Her general facial features plus her tall, lean build. Except for her hair, which was much longer, straighter, and honey toned to his deeper bronze.

"Who'd have thought"—he shook his head and speared some salad from his plate—"Sarah Overton, falling head over heels, much less for an out-of-towner."

She picked up a paper napkin, scrunched it, and then tossed it at his chest. "Like you can talk, Mr. Perpetually Single."

He laughed and tossed the napkin back at her, the thing quick to land just shy of her plate. "Perpetually Single? Settling down straight out of high school is more a Harlow thing, remember?"

"And you're out of college now, twenty-four and still a bachelor, which makes you a geriatric single by local standards." She tossed the napkin back, a white blur through the air that he caught a moment before it hit his face.

"And you only got engaged today." He threw the napkin again. "And older than me. That makes you a bonafide old maid."

A slow smirk took over Dean's face, his focus directed to Sarah clutching the napkin in her palm, her lips parted in a stupefied stare. "Do I need to remind you I was engaged to Blaine for a moment there? No need to put me out to pasture just yet."

"No one's doing that." Dean outstretched a hand, collecting the napkin before it could make another trip across the table, a solid chuckle belying his amusement. "Now, you two settle down. And Sarah, let the man have his fun while he can."

Her eyes narrowed toward her fiancé before she unleashed a series of playful pinches to his shoulder. "You saying I'm not fun? I'm plenty fun."

Dean laughed and tried to swat her away, abandoning that idea for pulling her onto his lap and covering her in a spate of kisses.

Genuinely happy for his sister, Chip averted his gaze and allowed her time to enjoy the cozy moment. She no longer had to battle life in Harlow alone. A life of running the old family business—Harlow's one and only bar, Maynard's—where she'd parleyed her dreams of playing international tennis so that those with limited work options here could keep their job. All while he'd been whisked away to live with his dad in Boston.

Meanwhile, Chip never engaged in much more than a few short-term flings, his focus set on his studies and not wasting his chance at a world beyond what Sarah had. He owed her. Owed himself. And he wasn't totally free from the trauma of coming from a fractured family. Nor his desire for a future that looked nothing like his past.

But Sarah and Dean's relationship offered hope. She'd survived. Found contentment. Maybe Chip would get there too.

His thoughts inexplicably slipped to Ally. Maybe because of their recent encounter. Or because he'd never been so close to anyone as he'd been to her. Or because the age-old pain of being pried away lingered in the ache now filling his stomach.

But other things endured beyond those more bitter memories, like the ease with which they'd talked today and his instant calm in her presence.

That said, maturity brought complexity and understanding, and he never made a big decision without doing a little research. So, he'd find out more. More about her. More about how they fit together *now*. Or even whether they fit together at all.

Four

The very next afternoon, Chip began his fact-finding mission on Ally. The majority of his day had already been spent trying to untangle a particularly complex algorithm at home.

Now, the low sun exuded its orange glow across Harlow's Main Street, the surrounding smell of dry earth and summer grass rising up to reward his hard-fought victory in escaping his work.

That smell. This street's century-old stores. The lack of foot traffic. Every contrasting detail to Boston pulled at his childhood memories of Harlow.

There'd been skipping down this brickwork sidewalk. The regular pursuit of candy at Frank and Maureen Cooper's general store. And of course, Ally always at Chip's side.

Though a few unfamiliar shops now lined the strip, one thing that hadn't changed was the late afternoon closures. As always, Harlow lived and worked at its own pace. No twenty-four-hour convenience stores. And forget about buying anything on a Sunday.

Not that he'd left his house for the shopping, anyway.

"Chip?"

Bingo. That bright, feminine lilt, and her tone twisting his name upward into a question. Ally's voice was already imprinted on his memory. He didn't need to redirect his gaze off the storefront to his side to know who spoke.

Though she wore a frown and pulled the doors to Oak Tree Furniture closed behind her, he leveled a smile and waved, the jovial ting of the door's bell conspiring right along with him.

"Hey, Ally." He played casual and strolled closer, a light sensation working through his muscles at the chance to speak her name. To the woman herself. After so many years.

Her open surprise faded, and a slow smile spread over her face. Like she was genuinely glad to see him. *Good. Very good.* Especially now he stood close enough to indulge in the faint scent of candy and sunshine floating off her skin, her perfume matching her look and energy. *Delightful. Sweet.* As did her silver blue eyes shining up at him.

Like new cut crystal.

"Ten years of nothing, and now two run-ins in as many days." Her smile weakened, and she narrowed her eyes. "That's some strange karma, dontcha think?"

"I was bound to return eventually." He brightened his expression to balance hers.

"You were?" Her lips turned flat and disbelieving, like she'd never once believed he'd come back to this town, only for the naturally mischievous glimmer to return to her eyes.

His hands ached to reach out and hug her, just as they'd done yesterday, his palms recalling the sumptuous heat of her body and the firmness of her narrow frame. But the shine had dimmed from that introduction, and her gaze held more questions today. More doubt.

Not that he blamed her. He had doubts and questions too.

He ran his attention over her again, her hair so much shorter these days, her scraggly long locks exchanged for a sharp do that skimmed her chin—a carefree look that suited what he recalled of her personality. But the color. The color shone the same, not much different to the platinum hue of sunbeams breaking through cloud.

A little shocked at that observation, as well as his desire to reach out and sweep a wayward lock from her cheek, he shifted back, saving them both from an awkward moment.

Still, her gaze flitted about his face too. A sign that she sensed the weight in his pause, her sudden turn down the sidewalk confirming his theory. "What brings you to Main Street, anyway?"

"Just wanted to visit the old stomping ground." He fell in stride with her. "I definitely didn't come here hoping to see you."

Despite his frolic with sarcastic flirting, his better judgement told him to remember Sarah's warning. *Clingy and flighty. What had she meant by that?*

Ally glanced at him, a child-like excitement rising in her eyes again, the equally jubilant long flow of her rainbow-colored skirt fluttering in her wake. "Really, you came to see *me*?"

"I figured you might let me walk you home while we got reacquainted." He took in more details. Her hot-pink tank top under a sunset pink cardigan. The woman sure wore a lot of pink, although she wore it well. And the turquoise bangles clanging at her wrists said more about how quirky femininity had replaced the ragtag fashion of her girlhood. "Sarah mentioned you usually close for Blaine around now."

Ally flinched at Sarah's name, seeming to confirm the rift.

"I, ah… well…" She halted her stride, and so he did too, her focus on him erratic. "I actually drove today."

Despite the rebuff, she held a new stillness, and a moment passed where they seemed to ponder each other.

"That'll teach me to make assumptions." His focus snagged on her cupid's bow, her upper lip sitting slight fuller than her lower, followed by the pronounced set of her pout. One he now suddenly recognized as part of her "confused" look.

That look harked back to their classroom days, forever his cue to step in and help her. So just like back then, he helped her now, allowing a tension-breaking smile to run full-reign over his face.

Her head tilting back, she let out a shaky laugh. "I mean, I guess I didn't drive when you last knew me. Maybe your brain needs a minute to disconnect from the past."

An inescapable lightness filled him and overrode his need to harness his enthusiasm. "No. No, you didn't. In my mind, we're still gangly pre-teens stomping in muddy ditches and trying to soak each other on the walk home from school."

Her laugh cut through clearer now. "All while Sarah outpaced us by about a mile up ahead."

"Ditch stomping does eat up a bunch of time." He shrugged, recalling the sensation of cold, damp clothes against his skin, neither set of parents happy for the extra laundry. "And you'd always start it, remember?"

She laughed again, joy seeming to backlight the blue of her eyes. "Hell yes, and I'd do it all again in a heartbeat. Remember those summer afternoons when Sarah would be too busy with her tennis practice? We'd take a forbidden detour to the river instead?"

"Yet another thing you almost always started." He laughed, forcing his attention on her face, because his heart's increased beat pushed him to do more than stand here and talk.

"Got you away from your books, didn't I? Without me, you wouldn't have any fun childhood memories." Her focus left him, and he followed her line of sight to a small, electric blue car, the eccentric hue a big hint the vehicle was hers.

"Yah know what?" Her gaze flicked back to him, and she tugged the strap of her huge, patchwork shoulder bag higher. "This is too much fun. Let's walk, after all."

His jaw wavered a beat while he scrambled to recalibrate in the wake of her surprise change in plans. "W… what about your car?"

Shut up, dude. You wanted this, remember?

"I'll get my car in the morning." She tilted her head sideways in a gesture for him to follow. Not wanting any regrets, he did so without any further protest. "I need to walk more, anyway."

So they fell into step, arm in arm, like old times yet somehow, not at all like then.

But just like then, he reached out, took her bag off her shoulder, and slung it over his. "This thing's heavy. What do you keep in here?"

"Never question a woman on the contents of her purse." She turned to him, her brow raised. "Besides if I told you, I'd have to break your legs."

He noted the spring in her step and the defiant lift of her chin, actions denoting lighthearted strength. "I'd like to see you try, but maybe you could first fill me in on what you've been doing for the last ten years?"

Her lips parted as if ready to speak, only for her to press them together and pause. Soon, she turned her attention to the road ahead. "Just a typical Harlow existence, I guess. I did a short general art course over in Marston after high school, then floundered with not much to do for a while before Blaine offered me work at Oak Tree."

"You took an art course?" *Of course, she'd be an artist.* But then… "So, why are you working at Oak Tree?"

"Oak Tree pays my bills. Art… well, I guess it's cheap therapy." She gave a quick shrug and kicked at the rocky track below her bright red and purple flat shoes, the rocks making a light skittering sound. "Anyway, what about you? I hear you're a hotshot software developer now?"

She lifted her gaze, her question, along with her new focus on him, indicated reluctance to talk about her stuff.

She's not happy.

"People round here keep saying that." He gave a tight chuckle and glanced to the open field to Ally's right, black and white Holstein cows grazing farther away. A very Harlow scene. "But much to my dad's disapproval, I've foregone a well-paying job to work on my own project."

"Oh, he *must* be pissed." Her eyes lit up again, like she remembered his dad—more precisely, his overbearing nature. "You said something at the game about being here for work."

"Yep, but use that term loosely because I'm making literally no money right now." Though he forced a light expression, he pushed his hands into his pockets and pulled his attention from her. Even being a "poor artist," she had a job and, therefore, more than him. "Since Sarah moved in with Dean, I figured I'd make use of having a house all to myself. It's free on space *and* rent."

She gave a light chuckle. "Boston not quite enough for yah?"

Her Minnesotan accent prompted a new smile, his accent having mostly faded some time ago. "I still live with Dad. Let's just say, things are never easy there."

"Ahuh" She peered over at him, another hesitant pause before speaking again. "He still with that woman?"

"If by *that* woman, you mean, *the* woman he left my mom for, then yes. He's still with Kelly."

Focusing on the summer breeze *whooshing* in his ears, he hoped for an end to any more talk on Kelly. Though he'd never held much against her, her emergence had broken his already dysfunctional family and left his relationship with his dad splintered.

Now, all three merely tolerated each other and only because Chip needed his dad's money to survive. Meanwhile, his dad had an unyielding drive to see Chip prove something to the world. Though never once had Chip gotten the impression anything he did, or might achieve, would be enough.

So of course, he wanted to end this shallow alliance as quickly as possible. Preferably in exchange for Stonewall's success.

If that didn't happen, then he'd have little choice but to yield to his dad's vision. To sacrifice his aspirations in return for a secure job, wheeling and dealing to climb corporate ladders, making other people's ideas and dreams come true.

"How long are you in Harlow?" Though she stared at the ground, the previous silence hinted that she cared about his answer.

Or maybe it's just wishful thinking.

He squinted at the sun, soaking in the landscape once more and drawing out his reply, perhaps on the off chance his hunch about her affection might be right.

"It's hard to say. I have no hurry to return to Boston, although I've applied for a few funding programs. So if something happens with those, I might need to go back."

If he wasn't mistaken, her expression dimmed at the hint he might not be in town for long, although that too could have been his wishful thinking. At least, the low churn in his stomach said as much.

Even if his future could never be so far from a major city, leaving Harlow again would undoubtedly hurt.

"Knowing you, Chip"—her smile returned, though a little twisted and forced—"you'll get that funding, and there's gonna come a day when a whole bunch of people will fall over themselves to throw money your way."

He let out a laugh, and she joined him, hers milder with a slight bend.

"Ally, are you okay?" He stopped walking and waited for her to do the same.

Her attention lifted to him, one corner of her lip ticked upward while she swatted a hand through the air in a dismissive gesture. "Just that I seem to be a dying breed in these parts."

Hoping to soften the mood, he gave a light chuckle. "You look far from dying."

She rolled her eyes. "You know what I mean. Most people our age have moved away or gotten married. Sometimes I have visions of being the last person in Harlow altogether."

Moved away or gotten married?

Did that explain Sarah's comment last night about "Little Ally Egan's wedding dreams"? As in, marriage was Ally's ultimate goal? Even her means of escaping Harlow? Or at least, joining the status quo with the other younger people around here?

Either way, maybe the outcome of his mission to learn more about her was that he wasn't on the same page as her. Though not totally opposed to settling down, he had no plans of doing so in Harlow. And then there was the matter of establishing his career ahead of any personal commitments. So maybe, when it came to Ally Egan, keeping a safe distance would be his only choice.

Five

CHIP STARED at Ally while trying hard not to narrow his eyes, as if that would aid his desire to read her thoughts and bargain against her hints at wanting different things than him. Instead, he scrubbed a hand over the back of his neck and set about breaking the standoff. "You know, you could always move away for yourself or even just travel?"

The earlier spark returned to her eyes, and she spun her focus back to the long country road, recommencing her springy steps. "Oh, that's the dream. I've been saving for a while now. When I have enough, I'll jump on the first plane to Paris or Italy... Ooo, I've always wanted to go to Prague! Prague sounds beautiful and fun, dontcha think?"

She shot him another wide beam, a clue for him to extend the topic of travel. "Prague?"

"Yep." She swung her hands out in the breeze, her walk seeming to now involve an element of dance that made him almost want to join her. *Almost.* "I met this woman reading cards at a beachside festival over at Lake Superior once. I was a kid, and my sister was there too, and Momma had me sit with her while the lady read her fortune. The woman's accent was so far from anything I'd ever heard, and she wore the most colorful and flowy clothes. When she mentioned she was from Prague, I made a mental note to find a way to get there one day."

"That explains where you get your fashion sense from, as well as your theories on karma." He made a point of eyeing her eccentric outfit, jangly bangles, floaty skirt, and all.

She let out an exuberant laugh, another eccentricity that proved his point. "I guess you scientific types don't believe in karma?"

"Karma. Fate. Voodoo…" He shook his head. "Fun to read about in fantasy novels, but no, no, and no. I can't believe in something so unproven."

"Hmm…" She stopped and put her hands on her hips, the slight upward curve to her lips giving her stern stance a touch of cheer. "Life must be easy when you're so sure of yourself."

Though he spluttered a habitual laugh, a hard weight pressed on his chest and cut him off from any further reaction. Once more, he bought time by squinting at the road, the silhouette of a bus stop and an old bench his new distraction.

Remembering this view and the bus stop, his shoulders sagged. Her house was near and he could already envision her yard. The giant maple that turned gold in the late fall, them as children huddled in the dirt, building bug villages. Mrs. Egan's sandwiches and cold lemonade, her lemonade recipe using lemons straight from the tree out the back. But first, she'd insist they run inside and wash their hands.

That memory brought a smile to his face. More so, the times he and Ally would then spend polishing off their meals on the front porch, wild and aimless, the Egan's home a refuge.

A lump in his throat had him turning back to Ally. "Most times, I'm far from sure."

His voice held an unintended soft rasp. One that said more about his insecurities than his words did, his heart now clenching that he'd diverted from what he'd hoped would be a lighthearted catchup.

"I only mean that you've always been clever." She extended a hand and patted his arm, the slight pursing of her lips conveying sympathy. "You're the one with all the answers, remember? Take it from someone who's never had any of that, you've got more than most."

The strain around his heart increased, suspending his next breath while he weighed her support against the corrosion of his father's criticisms.

Always demanding. Never satisfied.

Maybe Chip *did* have more than most, yet it was never enough.

But rather than dwell on that, rather than bore her with any kind of denial, he asked another question. "So, if you did travel, would you return to Harlow afterward?"

"Of course, where else would I go?" She gave a carefree shrug. "Harlow's home."

His stomach inexplicably tensed and he stared at her a while, to some extent searching for any signs of doubt where there appeared to be none. Releasing his unwarranted disappointment, he nodded to the bus stop. "Seems we're here. I should let you go."

He slipped her bag from his shoulder and held it out to her, but she merely blinked at him, the bag left dangling in his hand.

"Chiiiiipppp!"

Her stare snapped to her right and in the direction of whoever called the elongated version of his name. Meanwhile, he wasn't so quick to look away, his focus held to the touch of orange sunset on her skin, that same light setting her eyes to a sparkle.

Time wasn't his friend here, and so he switched his attention to Mrs. Egan advancing his way on a wobbly sort of jog.

"Oh, boy. Look at you!" Velma Egan outstretched her arms, quick to wrap him in a tight embrace, her strength impressive given she wasn't much taller than 5'1".

Even when she did let go, she stayed close enough to extend a gentle pinch to his arm, her light-brown eyes glinting up at him to express her desire to check that he really did stand before her. "Why, when Ally told me you showed your face at the ballgame, I practically kicked myself for staying home that day, dontcha know. Just *look* at you. Such a strapping young man."

Heat rose in his cheeks, although the earlier weight from his exchange with Ally slipped away. Seeing Mrs. Egan brought nothing but good memories. He turned to Ally, her palm pressed over her eyes as though too embarrassed to witness this scene.

Since Ally wasn't an option, he focused on Velma again, a woman who'd spent about as much time with him as his own mother, the moment more poignant given his move to Boston meant his mom had all but disappeared from his life.

"Great to see you, Mrs. Egan." He offered a genuine smile, hoping his appreciation showed.

"Now, none of that 'Mrs. Egan' stuff. Velma suits me just fine, boy." She took his hand and tugged. "Maureen called and said she saw you on Main Street with my Ally, so I figured you might be headed this way and came out to invite you to dinner."

"Mom, no"—Ally's hand fell from her eyes, eyes that now pulled wide—"you're embarrassing him."

He flicked his attention to Velma, to the distinct drop of her grin and her shoulder-length bronze waves pushing in the light breeze, that small movement highlighting her stunned stillness. "I… I just thought, what with you living in Sarah's house on your own… you might need a good feed."

He might have laughed at her presumption that he'd never learned to cook well enough to survive, but the deepened lines between her brows spoke of genuine worry that she'd somehow caused him discomfort.

And sure enough, Ally only meant to let him off the hook, to allow him the exit he'd planned on. But in the wake of all his years away, and after her treating him as one of her own, Velma Egan really did deserve more than his hurried escape.

So, he conjured his old knowledge of basic Minnesotan values when it came to dinner invitations and reshuffled his plans.

"You know, Velma, I've always loved your cooking." He held Ally's bag out to her and waited for her to take it, his smile not moving from her mother because she'd also handed him the chance to relive yet another bright moment from his past. *Dinner at the Egans.* "Nothing could keep me away from joining you."

Six

ALLY HUNG BACK on the porch's edge, her shoulders slumped, and her fingers chilled as her mother pushed the front door open and allowed Chip into the house.

"So sweet seeing you two back together again." Her mom peered over her shoulder and beamed back at Ally, who did her best not to pitch forth an annoyed scowl. Her feet took her inside, although her mind longed to run in the opposite direction. Just so she wouldn't have to witness whatever happened next.

Suddenly, she inspected her home with new eyes. As if she were Chip, viewing this place for the first time in a decade.

The homely beige walls and wood paneling. An average-sized dwelling with a large couch and T.V. The two oversized furnishings made the place seem even smaller than "average."

Not much had changed in the decade since Chip's last visit, while so much about him seemed so evolved. She still didn't know how she felt about his "evolution," either, though the high ache in her tummy spoke some indelible truth on this latest exchange.

Their twenty-minute stroll from Oak Tree to her house had been a quick joyride through the past. One she'd wanted to end maybe less than him. *And that right there was her problem.*

A far too large part of her rejoiced in his return.

She grumbled past her mother and uttered a deflective, "You make it sound like we're married."

The door clicked closed, and she went about kicking her shoes under the cushion-covered bench along the entry's side wall.

"Well, you never know, dear." Her mom patted Ally's shoulder and strolled past.

Soon after, Ally spun around to mouth an apology to Chip. The outer corners of his lips pulled into a slow smile, even though his stare seemed less jovial, more analytical—like he sought to discover what she *really* felt about her mother's innuendo.

Delightfully barefoot, she shook her head and went about dumping her bag onto the same bench her shoes now lived under, the bag's heavy thud a satisfying statement on how much she *wasn't* into this whole setup.

Setup. What a great description of how she felt, and she'd no doubt have to endure more as other family members discovered tonight's visitor.

"Holy crapola!" Right on time, her older sister by two years, Laila, bolted down the stairs on a thundering gallop. "What happened to Chip?"

While Chip laughed and made a point of looking Laila over in her cashier uniform of black chinos under a white shirt and burgundy vest. "What happened to *you*?"

She threw her arms around him, the action muffling her next words. "Too much, Chip. Way too much."

Ally pulled her focus from the way Chip's white t-shirt stretched over his back muscles and expended her energy on tugging aggressively at her cardigan sleeves, then tossing the removed garment on top of her bag. *Bare feet. Bare arms. Much better.*

Meanwhile, Laila's four-year-old daughter, Whitney, padded behind her mother, her blinking brown gaze pinned on Chip. "Who's this?"

"Just an old family friend, Muffin." Laila scruffed a hand over Whitney's curly auburn hair, turning her focus back to Chip. "I'm grabbing a bite to eat, then I'm off for the long drive to my overnight shift over in Marston. Mama and Pa look after this one while I clock up the hours."

Laila gave him a stiff smile and shook her head, maybe because the years had been kind to him and less so to her.

Though Laila had always had a certain classic appeal that Ally didn't—these days, now that Whitney's dad wasn't around—Laila toiled double-time, working odd hours at the nearest twenty-four-hour grocery store while studying sonography, just to fill the financial gaps.

Ally could barely remember when her sister *didn't* look overworked.

Meanwhile, the last time anyone in Harlow saw Chip, he'd been a skinny fourteen-year-old, with limbs too long for the rest of his body, his nose often buried in a book. By some freak of nature, he'd grown into his height, and his narrow features filled out to a striking "boy next door" sort of appeal.

And as if to mirror Ally's thoughts on his changes, Laila chimed in with, "What about you? Married? Kids?"

"Too much to do first." Chip was quick to laugh and shake his head. "Marriage and kids are a long way off."

Despite Ally's recent vow to also stop caring about settling down, his air of finality brought a pang to her chest... Not that she had all that much time to dwell on her feelings.

"Chip, buddy!" Ally's father rounded the kitchen counter, likely fresh from tinkering with something in his tucked-away den. "Vel tracked you down after all."

"Surprise." Chip accepted her dad's strong handshake. "I didn't plan on an entire Egan reunion, that's for sure."

"Well, you should've." Her mom squeezed in and pushed Chip toward the kitchen. "We've been waiting for ten years to have you back at our table. If only your sister were here, too."

"We don't have enough seats." Instantly regretting the quip and what it revealed about her feelings on Sarah, Ally bit down on her lower lip and promised to shut up for a while.

Chip turned and stared at her, his narrow-eyed skepticism stirring a nervous energy within her, prompting her focus on pulling out a chair and ignoring him altogether.

Did he know about her problems with his sister? And why did the mere awareness of his gaze make her tummy lurch, flip, and flutter?

"Ally?" The abrupt sound of her name dragged her focus to her mother. "Not there, you sit over here. Next to Chip."

Ally frowned down at the chair beneath her hands, her fingers curled around the top of the brown wood frame. "But I always sit next to Laila."

"Not tonight." Despite being the shortest person in the room, her mom pressed down on Chip's shoulders and strong-armed him into a seat before eyeballing Ally and stabbing a finger at the chair next to him. "*Sit.* You and Laila can chin-wag together any other night."

Ally groaned and shuffled toward her designated seat, once again apologizing under her breath to Chip. "Mom likes to come on strong."

She sat next to him and tried to escape the electricity seeming to ping within the small space between them. Did he feel it too? Or did that energy exist only in her mind?

Not the first time I've imagined a connection.

Given this was Chip, her "imagining" came with a strong edge of terror. Especially since his trace of body heat on her arm made her skin tingle, leaving her with regrets over removing her cardigan.

"It's okay." His low whisper—light but somehow molten—had her peering at his hazel stare, fluttering about her face. "I *remember.*"

She snatched her focus away and dug her elbows into the table, the reluctant tension in her belly giving way to her shoulder's slight tremble. Though she tried to contain her burgeoning snicker, Chip did no such thing, his chuckle loud enough for everyone to hear.

"Oh, see, now look at you two." Her mom lowered a bowl of salad to the table, her smile practically glowing.

Unchecked laughter cracked past Ally's lips, and she clapped a hand over her mouth, which only forced her humor to escape through the tears gathering in her eyes. Chip's amusement grew louder, drawing her attention back to him and an exchange of mutual elbow nudges played out at the private joke.

His familiar levity overrode her confusion, and she relaxed a little. With everyone now seated and Whitney already chomping on a bread roll, the prospect of food added another welcome diversion.

So, Ally whiled away dinner by dipping out of the chatter and allowing her parents a chance to grill Chip over his years away while pinning her mind on slipping more and more food into her mouth.

Unfortunately, Laila's repeated sidelong stares from across the table reduced the places Ally could look, her sister's scrutiny a gut-churning clue she suspected something.

The harder Laila stared, the hotter Ally's cheeks got, her pale complexion already known to make her emotions all too easy to read. Especially for someone who knew her as well as Laila.

Even though Whitney's birth meant they didn't hang out alone much anymore, Laila had witnessed every one of Ally's wild misadventures. Her years of perpetual singledom. Her failed crushes. *Dean's rejection.*

No doubt Laila already predicted Ally falling for Chip too. Heck, Ally could see it happening as well—but maybe, just maybe—this one time, she'd succeed in letting things be.

He's not here long. I'll ride this one out and be okay.

Lots of men and women are just friends, right?

Besides, in light of our past, his rejection would downright crush me.

I'm NOT doing that!

The meal drew to a close, and Chip pushed his plate away, his bare arm brushing hers, though given the tight seating, not for the first time. She leaned away from his touch and tried to settle the solid thud of her heartbeat in her ears.

Her mom stood and clapped her hands, new excitement lighting her eyes. "Well, Ronny and I have a surprise for Chip, but we need him to leave the room for a few minutes while we set it all up."

Chip turned to Ally, his eyes wide, while he mouthed the word, "What?"

She shrugged to indicate she had no idea what her parents planned while her dad now rose, quick to collect his plate and ferry it to the sink, while addressing her mom. "Where should we put him, Vel?"

Laila dragged her all-knowing stare over Ally, again. Not a good sign. So, Ally twisted to her mom and pitched a deflective joke. "Maybe we could fold him up and slide him into the utensils drawer?"

"Oh, Ally." Her mom shook her head and *tsked*, pulling more plates from the table. "So silly."

"Maybe he can wait in Ally's room?" Laila raised a brow at Ally, her saccharine smile posed above the rim of her water glass. "It's upstairs, outta the way, not littered with Whit's toys."

Ally opened her mouth to protest, but her mom got in first. "Great idea!"

"No, it's not!" Ally's voice shot free and high, her hard glare on her mom a hollow threat over what she'd do if this plan went ahead.

The woman just rolled her eyes. "Oh, Al, ease up. It's only for a few minutes."

"Yeah." Laila stood, the conversation-ending move yanking this choice even more out of Ally's hands. "You two spent enough time up there as kids."

Her sister strode toward her thick work jacket hanging on a hook by the front door, soon jamming her arms through the jacket's holes. "Maybe you can show him the pottery you've been working on these last years. You've got some talent there, Al."

"What about my privacy?" Ally threw her hands higher and peered around the room at all her treacherous family members. "It's not like I'm *still* a child."

"Yeah, about that"—Laila threw Ally a wink and wrenched the door open, quick to call out from the landing—"you can thank me later, Sis."

Seven

Chip only ever set out to walk Ally home from work, never once expecting his entire evening would be taken hostage. First, to an Egan family dinner, and now, with this journey upstairs to Ally's room, while her parents worked downstairs on some secret surprise.

Each step left him with an increasingly twitchy feeling all over, like he'd bitten off more than he could chew, and that this day would never end.

Then again, this is Harlow. They might not set me free before morning.

Oh, Lord Vader. Please, help me!

Ally turned at the top landing, and he tried not to pause while she waited for him to catch up. "As you probably remember, my room's not the biggest space in the world."

He met her at the top, her close proximity a reminder of *why* he wanted this day to end. Being this close to her was dangerous, especially since he still hadn't learned much about who she'd become in the years apart. Only that old feelings died hard, and even those feelings likely remained one-sided.

Her parents' voices floated from the living room, Vel Egan muttering, "Oh, sugar. Where did you put it?"

Next came the sounds of rummaging, which inexplicably left Chip more concerned about their surprise.

"I don't know, woman." Ronny's gruff tone followed the light slam of a wooden cupboard door. "You had it last!"

Ally's eyes widened, although they held a habitual brightness, and her lips curled upward. "We should go. Otherwise, we'll be stuck with the soul-crushing decision to ruin whatever plan they're hatching in order to break up the squabbling."

She stepped away and opened the door to her bedroom, guiding him through the threshold and onto another trek through the past.

Just like in the past, an assault of color hit him, less the pink and lilac "teenage dream" from those days, more a mature palette of rose, violet, and magenta—those vibrant colors and the slight clutter announcing that a woman and artist lived here.

A fluttery sensation filled his stomach, his words lost with the slow wander of his gaze. *This place.* They'd spent so much time here together. On so many occasions back then, he'd insisted they hang out at her home over his.

He'd wanted the escape. Wanted to experience a functional family. And the Egans had delivered that in abundance. Then at some point, that need for escape evolved into something else altogether.

His attention fell to the jewel-toned rug over the bare floorboards, his body recalling the rug's distinct spring as they'd sprawled across those thick, woolly fibers. They'd played board games, listened to music, and finished homework; his later visits were punctuated with the extra effort of shutting down his desires to stare, or worse, to lean in and kiss her... *At least there's one upside to the awkwardness of youth.*

"I've changed some things in here." Her voice pulled his focus to her slight shrug, her hands gesturing out to the room at large. "Some, not so much."

"There are some noticeable differences." He strolled over to an array of ceramic vessels lined along her deep windowsill and picked up a bright orange vase with muted-pink polka dots, the quirky collection a nice contrast to the hyperclassical theme inside his dad's home. "This is one of yours?"

She gave a small nod and joined him, taking the vase from his hands and turning it over in hers—her fingers long and thin, her nails short and painted in a happy shade of watermelon red. "Just a side project. Yah know, something to do with my boredom, which I guess I have a lot of being here in Harlow."

Her gaze flicked up to him, one cheek tugging in a repressed hint that this was more than just "something to do."

Having grown up around her hours of drawing and crafting while he'd studied, he leveled his focus on her, not accepting her attempt to minimize her talents. "You'll have to explain your process. Your work is beautiful, and I wouldn't know where to start with making anything like that on my own."

Her brows lifted, allowing new light to catch in her eyes, her lips parting only for her to startle at a celebratory holler from her parents downstairs.

Clearly, they'd found what they'd been looking for, although their sudden joy broke the moment between him and their daughter.

As if to snap out of some daze, Ally shook her head and blinked down at the vase, slow to eventually extend an arm and return it to the window shelf. "Well, Aggie let me set up a studio in a spare shed out back of her nursery. Right now, I aim for functional pieces over anything purely decorative, which makes it easier for her to upsell vases, plant pots, occasional outdoor wall hangings, and the like to the nursery's customers."

Her attention slipped from one piece to the other on the ceramic-filled shelf, as though seeing each one anew. Her side profile, with her hair tucked behind one ear, highlighted the small diamond studs in her lobes as well as the subtle shift of the long tendon running down the side of her neck.

A soft prickle ran over his skin, a lighter sign of attraction paired with the sinking weight in his chest. *Hello, regret.* He'd spent years berating himself for missing her. For his grief over leaving. He'd dismissed so many emotions as no more than the vapid imaginings of a hormonal boy… but maybe that boy *had* been on to something.

Not wanting her to catch him staring, he peered over to a dark wood makeup table against a farther wall, where an array of pink glass bottles sat around a bundle of makeup brushes sticking out of a turquoise earthenware jar. A jar he'd bet she'd made too.

An easy smile pulled at his lips. Those feminine touches. The handmade art. He'd entered alien territory and loved every second of being in her space.

He turned back to her watching him, her unexpected beam soon coupled with a laugh. He responded with a sidelong stare, certain he'd missed something. "What? What is it?"

Her laughter stopped, and her lips bent into a thoughtful frown. "It's just… every time I get to thinking on how much you've changed, you throw some little reminder of what's the same. Like just now, you flash that same old geeky smile of yours, and I'm back to being thirteen again. Those were good times, weren't they?"

The slight lift at the end of her sentence pointed to her experiencing a moment of reckoning—the clash of murky memories and the equally confusing present. They still got along well enough, past ties maybe pulling them closer still… but… what to do with it all?

So, he narrowed his eyes and made sure to leave out any real malice, certain she would understand his lighthearted attempt to ease her concerns. "How does one smile 'geeky'?"

She laughed again, heartier this time, her head tilting back to expose the creamy-white skin of her throat. "I don't know, you just do. It's this big geeky grin, like everything is right and fascinating in the world, and you're all sweet as pie and full of innocence."

He gave an amused, huffing sort of laugh, although the weight on his chest pressed harder. Sweet and innocent? Not the description he wanted from her. Still, he picked up another vase—a green one this time, with teal stripes and a wavy rim—leaving room for her to fill the conversation.

"You used to shoot me that same smile back in class, yah know?" True to form, Ally Egan took up the offer to add more words. "Remember? Like when you'd let me copy math work fresh out of your book?"

"Yeah, I remember." Rationing the moments he got to eye her, he inspected the vase, maximizing another chance for humor. "I also remember the day Mrs. Davis caught you cheating."

"*Me?* Cheat?" Her rising pitch pulled him back to her, her arms now crossed in a fake show of attitude. "*You* helped me cheat."

He put this vase down and turned to her fully, leveling an unruffled expression. "Not my fault you got so confident with your copying that you went ahead and wrote my name at the top of your test."

"Oh no, you remember that? How embarrassing!" She gave a weak shriek and buried her face in her hands, her shoulders shaking from a new wave of laughter. "Oh, and then I had to go to the principal's office and explain."

"I don't think I've ever seen your face turn redder." He chuckled along with her, only for another memory to dull his joy. "Remember how you spent that last summer pining over Gerry Gibbons?"

Though he pitched forth a smile and delivered the question like some kind of joke, even he couldn't deny the rasp to his tone or the long pause while Ally's expression dimmed. "Yeah."

The silence continued, thick, oppressive, and hard to escape. He picked out a new vase in a dramatic wine shade, once again pretending this conversation mattered less to him than it did. *Gerry. A typical football player type. Muscle as thick as the brain in his head.*

And then there were her feelings for Dean. Another alpha male, though, with far more working for him than Gerry ever showed potential for. Surely, she'd never thought of either man's grin as geeky. So, maybe she had a type. One that excluded Chip.

Another memory washed him over, just days after he'd arrived in Boston, when his father prodded at his skinny, fourteen-year-old biceps. *You'll have to work on these. That brain of yours is an asset, Son, but it's not enough.*

A week hadn't passed before he'd been enrolled into every local sporting team his schedule would allow. Smarts *weren't* enough. *He* wasn't enough.

She took the vase from his hand and proceeded to trace a thumb over the etched-in, geometric details. "If it makes you feel any better, I'll introduce you to Gerry next time we're at Maynard's. He married

Darleen Hayes fresh outta high school, and they have three kids together with another one on the way. You wouldn't know it though, not with all the time he spends hiding at the bar, chasing any new female unfortunate enough to catch his notice."

Chip kept a straight face but raised a brow of mild interest, even though he wanted to laugh at the recap on his unofficial high school rival. "So, Gerry found his niche?"

"And he quit being a pretty boy in favor of questionable personal hygiene. But of course, he still thinks he's all that and more." She shrugged before reaching out and patting his bicep, the heat of her hand warming his skin. "So, let's just say, you win, Chip."

Her stare held him, and he could have sworn his heart skipped at her apparent awareness of his insecurities. "Is that your way of saying you've developed a preference for geeky smiles?"

She took her hand back, her laugh turning tight as she rolled her eyes. "These days, I prefer nothing over nothing. I'm good being single, thanks."

He waited, but her gaze didn't meet his. "Sounds like you've been through some things."

Her eyelashes fluttered through a quick, stunned pause, only for her to flick hair from her eyes in a seemingly self-fortifying move. "Nothing major. In fact, I have a lot to look forward to. Seems you do too."

But the husky dip in her voice once again contradicted, as did her sudden flurry of steps toward her bed, where she sat on the edge and patted the spot next to her for him to sit also.

The muscles over his face tensed, and the rest of him failed to move. He took a moment to gather his bearings and play casual about joining her. *On her bed.*

"So, want to tell me what your family's planning down there?" His heartbeat drummed loud in his ears, even as he leaned back and propped his hands into the white faux fur blanket behind him.

Despite all stereotypes about geeks, he'd learned to hide his eccentricities well enough to be with other women and even turned down a few over the years.

He also never really got nervous about being around any of them, his take on physical intimacy being that it was little more than an act to satisfy biological urges. Fun? *Sure.* Still, nowhere near the magical experience so many of his fiction books described.

Only Ally hinted at rebutting this theory. And they'd never engaged in anything more than a plutonic touch.

We just have history, that's all.

The red vase still in her hand, she lowered it onto her lap and lifted her face to him, her sudden bright expression akin to a cheerful cloudless day. "I'm about as clueless as you are about what my parents have planned, but we're in my house, and they are *my* parents, so I have more reason to worry here. I'm just hoping they don't pull out an album of embarrassing childhood photos."

"Oh, I don't know." He refocused on her makeup table again, a piece of furniture not there years ago. "Your folks don't do things by halves. At least give them the credit of having *multiple* big albums of embarrassing childhood photos. Hey, what's that?"

He pointed at a matching chair tucked under the table and squinted at some garment draped over the top, distinguishing the details of filmy lace and midnight blue shiny satin, his teeth clamping down on his inner cheeks the moment he discerned what he looked at.

Ally's gaze hit the same spot, and she drew in a quick gasp. "You're *not* allowed to check out my underwear."

She grabbed his face and wrenched it toward her, only for him to jokingly fight back, even though he preferred the view of her wide blue eyes over any inanimate set of underthings.

Either way, he ticked one corner of his lip upward in a disappointed gesture. "I would have figured you more a sensible tank top and cotton panties type."

Her face stilled before a distinctive and alluring deep blush bloomed up her neck and into her cheeks.

"Chiiip?" She dragged his name down to a low warning. "Why are you even figuring anything about my choice of underwear?"

He gave an easy shrug, although the heat trekking through his body likely had him mirroring the rosiness of her face. "I didn't until I was confronted with your stray wardrobe. You may want to tidy up occasion—"

"Do you want me to boot you from this room?" Her deliberate stare dared him to let loose with another joke, but the dry scratchiness in his throat kept him from doing that. Meanwhile, his smile fell at her hands still touching him.

He liked a joke as much as the next guy, but he liked *this* more. The delicate banter. The sudden shifts and uncertainty. Time alone with *her*.

So, he held her stare and shook his head, offering a rough, "No."

Her gaze danced about his face, as though she too could feel her blood coursing at the constant push and pull between who they'd once been to each other and whatever seemed to linger now. "Chip?"

Her gaze dropped to his lips, and his heart damn-near burst. She offered a clue on where her thoughts went, but he had no words. All he had was the slight lean of his torso toward her and raw hope.

But her impossible stillness shot holes through his hope, at least until her pupils expanded into wide, black pools, and her next words poured out on a breathy exhale. "I want you to kiss me."

Electricity shot through his arm, and he lashed out a hand, hooking his fingers to the back of her neck and pulling her in, her eyelids snapping shut in an open invitation.

He closed the final distance and brushed his lips over the silkiness of hers, that tentative first caress already pushing his heartbeat to an erratic thunder. Suddenly, ten years of suppressed emotion surged through every inch of his body, and he gave in to unspoken longing, deepening the kiss.

After a lifetime of her in his orbit, no time or distance could dull this thrill.

Where she offered a sense of gentle femininity, he countered with his hard and shameless need. Though she took a moment to join him, her fingertips soon curled either side of his face and she demanded more of him on a low and hungry moan.

Impulsive. Impossible to contain. She, and this kiss, surpassed everything he'd imagined. The exchange didn't live only in his head but existed as real as the heat off her body and the warm wetness of her mouth. Every time he penetrated her with his tongue, her taste seemed designed to increase his yearning, so lush and addictive.

And yearn he did. With a mind skilled at conjuring possibilities, he grew desperate for relief, hot need rushing his veins so that his length hardened.

Though her mother's voice called for her from downstairs, he didn't let Ally go, and she didn't pull away either, so he dared to take this further. Dared to grasp for what he wanted most right now. *Her in his lap.*

But his quick tug at her body brought the sharp sound of shattering clay. She broke the kiss, leaping from his hold and onto the mattress at his side. Her gaze fused down to the wood floor beside the bed, her glossy stare quick to hit him next.

Sure enough, the red vase she'd held in her lap, lay in a cluster of broken pieces.

"Ally?"

She shook her head silently, her tongue darting out to lick her red and kiss-ravished lips, as though she sought to confirm what had just happened.

Never wanting to destroy one of her pieces, he wished to apologize. But truth be told, his only true regret was that the kiss had ended. So, the only honest thing he could think to extend was an offer to help clean up.

"Have you got cotton in your ears, girl?" Her dad burst through her closed door, his presence forcing a metaphorical gulf between them, one that had Ally leaping back even farther away from Chip.

Her dad's brows dipped in the middle, and he passed his gaze between Chip, Ally, and the shattered clay, his voice momentarily stammering before he spoke again, "You two come on down, the surprise is waiting."

His attention held for a moment longer, and then he slowly turned and padded out the door.

Ally's incredulous stare dropped to the mess on the floor again, then sprung back to Chip, her mouth hanging agape. "Oh God. That shouldn't have happened."

The shock in her eyes indicated she spoke of more than the broken earthenware. As in, the kiss shouldn't have happened.

If hearts could sink, then his most certainly did—along with his instinct to reassure her—since reassuring came close to convincing, and he sure as hell wouldn't do that. Not now. Not ever.

Besides, her silence spoke volumes. It said that they'd been apart too long to call each other friends, and one kiss didn't make for lovers.

"Come on." Burying the internal sting from her regret, he stood and reached for her hand. "The mess can wait. Your parents won't."

Eight

Mark Farro settled into the brown leather chair in his new home office. His scowl landed on the mahogany bookcase to his right before he trekked his gaze along the leather-bound tomes, intersecting with the occasional antique alabaster bust or brass armillary globe.

Just as he preferred, everything he'd carted over to Boston from New York screamed luxury and expense. Only his beautiful setting didn't at all fit with the video call he was set to take.

He would have liked to visit his cousin Luciano in person. They'd lived apart for close to a decade, their branches of the Syndicate stretching opposites sides of the country, but now that Luciano resided in a Minnesota prison and would continue to do so for the foreseeable future, Mark had new priorities.

Though Luciano's arrest struck a genuine blow, Mark would deal with his anger in the best way he knew how. Productively. With research. With a plan. Hence his move to Boston, where his presence would make a far bigger difference to Luciano's problems than any fleeting prison visit.

A notification appeared on Mark's open laptop browser, Luciano's call connecting. Within seconds, the man's joyless face appeared on the screen, his complexion gray and the skin beneath his eyes wrinkled and wary.

Mark fought an unfamiliar battle to find words, but then Luciano spoke first. "You gotta plan?"

Mark nodded through the weight of a heavy frown, his attention sliding from his cousin's once meticulously slicked black hair, now sporting an inch of silver regrowth. Mark's own image mirrored back to him in a smaller window on his screen—his thick, bronze waves and his tailored, navy-blue oxford shirt—a styled contrast to his cousin.

"Nice to see you too, Cousin." He cleared his throat and told himself to get a grip.

"Now, that's a lie." Luciano gave a soulless laugh, the small jolt of his shoulders bringing focus to his bright orange prison suit. "What are we gonna do about this?"

He motioned to the world around him, to the fluorescent lit room behind him with sickly, mint-green painted walls. Two other men stood in the background, also busy on video calls, other men lined up on a long bench behind, presumably waiting on their turn.

Though Mark knew full well who and what he was—a professional criminal motivated by money—few people got his compassion like Luciano did.

Luciano Conti, a decade older, with a head-start in the Syndicate, had made countless sacrifices for his family. Though his money wasn't from clean or legal dealings, what he'd done with that money was provide for Mark in ways his parents couldn't.

Unlike Luc, Mark had a college education and abilities and vision that outstripped his cousin's. One day, he would break from the Syndicate but not until it was safe. Not until his obligations were fulfilled. Not until he had reinforcements strong enough to keep the Syndicate away.

Despite Luciano's assumptions over the years, Mark didn't look down on him. He *owed* him. Now Luc's skinnier face, compared to the past, came as a cold reminder of what the stress of being incarcerated had done to him. That Mark should have taken better care of his cousin. Or at least, taken Luc's troubles in Harlow more seriously.

But Luc's famously heavy-handed approach didn't always work, especially not against someone stealthy like Dean Holloway, which was why Mark had no choice but to get involved.

For payback.

For his own damn freedom.

"I can't bust you out of prison." Mark paused to replace the hollow edge in his tone with something more substantial and stoic. "But yes, I have a plan."

Luciano gave a tight nod. "I'm not safe in here. Not until we make things right with the boss."

Luc couldn't mention Rudolph Manzinni's name from inside prison, but he didn't need to.

"I'm keeping the boss informed." Despite the tension drawing at his muscles, Mark plastered on an unmoved expression. "I closed a deal today that will make everyone more money than ever. Better yet, this deal will leave the entire town of Harlow suffering."

Appease Rudolph. Avenge Luciano. Make a ton of money… Get away from this entire clusterfuck altogether.

Mark wanted to smile but wasn't the type to get ahead of himself, even if he had stumbled upon an ingenious means to hurt Dean Holloway and make truckloads of money in the process.

This job was only just getting started, and he had a lot of lost ground to reclaim with the Syndicate. Luciano—and therefore, Mark—had already failed twice. First, there'd been the botched mission to blackmail money from Emilia Bonacci, which resulted in Anthony Stucco's death. Then there'd been the ensuing national news coverage. Amongst it all, Dean Holloway had escaped the Syndicate, the recovery mission to stop him then leading to Luciano's arrest.

If Mark failed again, the consequences would be lethal.

So, there was no boundary he wouldn't break. And not just with Dean. Mark would crush them all. Emilia, Blaine, the sheriff involved in Luc's arrest… Dean's woman, Sarah Overton.

Mark's move to Boston was just the beginning, and one day, only when the job was done, he would celebrate.

"So, don't you worry, Luc." He smiled for the first time this conversation, feeling at ease. "I'm not stopping until we hurt every person who hurt us. Not until every last resident leaves Harlow, and that entire malignant town is leveled to the ground."

Nine

ALLY PLASTERED on her brightest smile and stood before the couch, hovering like a weirdo above Chip's sleeping face. In typical Minnesotan fashion, her parents had kept him from leaving last night, surprising him with the Star Trek board game they'd once reserved especially for his visits. Only last night's rematch also included the pointy Vulcan ears and flight crew outfits they'd bought as his Christmas present that final year in Harlow but never had the chance to gift him.

Smile waning, she rolled her shoulders back and straightened the hem of her loose hot-pink t-shirt. Not that a wonky hem mattered all that much when teamed with the disarray of her t-shirt's two fluffy, white kittens on the front, plus her bare feet, *and* her short gray pajama shorts.

"Still a fan of banana pancakes?" She startled a little at her own overly cheery tone just as Chip jolted, and his eyelids flung wide open.

He blinked at her awhile, like he needed a moment to remember where he was. "Ahh, yeah."

He shuffled and groaned into a seated position, the green wool blanket at his chest slipping to reveal a strong set of shoulders and pecks. "I could do pancakes."

A good few seconds passed before she noticed her attention still stuck on his far-too-appealing torso.

"Great." Her voice shot up as fast as her gaze. "Just great."

She spun away to hide the heat quick to engulf her face, although at least he couldn't hear the panicked beat of her heart. "I'll... ummm... get to cooking, then."

Jeez Louise. That man. He's just too beautiful...

Did I really kiss him last night?

My childhood best friend... also... a fudging amazing kisser!

Fearing her thoughts might somehow escape her mouth, she cleared her throat and went about disappearing behind the kitchen counter.

"Don't you ever wear shoes?" Blankets rustled from Chip's general direction, but she refused to look at him just yet. Not while her lips still tingled every time she recalled that kiss.

She glanced down at her watermelon colored toenails and shrugged. "Why would I? I'm in my own home."

Forgetting her vow not to look at him, she peered up and was punished with a view of gently defined back muscles, her racing pulse forcing her next blurted rebuttal. "Don't you ever wear a shirt?"

He pushed his feet into the brown plaid slippers borrowed from her dad and merely chuckled, the man far too comfortable in her home, much less his semi-nakedness.

She pressed her lips together and hid behind an open cupboard door, her stream of uncharacteristic shyness less about immaturity, more about the searing need still winding through her body. That need screamed at her to get way too comfortable right back at him. Perhaps in his lap. Just as he'd wanted her to do last night.

"Better?"

She startled at his voice and poked her head out from the cupboard door. Chip now stood in her kitchen, too close, albeit with his white t-shirt from yesterday now on.

Abandoning her attempt to hide, she pushed the cupboard shut, careful not to brush him as she squeezed past on her way to deposit a bag of flour onto the dove-gray counter.

"Here you go." She reached into a drawer and passed a glass bowl to him before pointing to a small bunch of bananas in the nearby fruit basket. "You can help. Get mashing."

His gaze shifted from the bowl, to the fruit basket, and then onto her, his attention holding for a beat too long. More a question about last night than the task she'd just lumped on him. He wanted to talk. She did too. But what to say exactly?

At least her parents had taken Whitney out early, first to the morning markets and then back to Laila's house for lunch. No one would be around to witness the awkwardness of what would be said.

She had regrets over that kiss. Still, for once in her life, she'd choose the grown-up approach and put friendship over impulse. She loved having Chip back. Loved the plain and simple fun of having him near. But he'd be leaving soon, and she didn't want to ruin this rare and close bond.

"Got many plans for today?" She opened another drawer and pulled out a masher for him, quick to dodge any more eye contact in favor of retrieving eggs and milk from the fridge.

"Just ironing out bugs in my current project."

"Oh, yeah?" She retrieved her own bowl and got to work on the counter beside him. "What exactly does this program do, anyway?"

"Encryption."

"Encryption?" She frowned down at the batter slowly thickening before her, the sweet-milky scent a nice diversion from the oaky, crisp peppermint that always tended to waft from his skin. "You mean like emails and stuff?"

"Yeah, protecting sensitive information." He stepped closer and tipped the now pulpy bananas into her bowl, his long fingers seeming a contradiction of nimble and strong. "I'm starting with email encryption with room to expand."

He took the spatula from her hand, and she stepped back, reclaiming some breathing room and accepting his silent offer to fold the remaining ingredients together.

"So, does your program have a name?" She lowered a pan to the stove and turned on the heat.

"Stonewall." Again, he drew near, stealing her space, this time to offer the finished batter.

So, she covered her need for distance with humor. "You mean, like when someone is acting all cagy and weird?"

Kinda like I am now…

"More like a nod to the limestone fortresses used in centuries past to keep the enemy out, but sure, caginess works too." Again, his easy chuckle blanketed her with a soft and tingly sensation all over.

He leaned back against the section of counter next to her, his fingers curling into the stone edge.

The stance highlighted his long torso, igniting her desire to draw closer and press her body against his, maybe because she sensed he wouldn't reject her if she did.

She pried her focus off him and onto dropping batter into the hot pan. Though she could have asked more questions on his work, she figured he'd just end up saying a bunch of things she didn't understand, so silence seemed the better option.

Last night, he'd brought up her old crush on Gerry Gibbons. Truth was, as part of Harlow's salt-of-the-earth population, she *did* have more in common with jocks like him. Uncomplicated. Average in most every way. *Her* people.

Chip on the other hand. His quick wit and super intelligence labeled him as too much. Too talented. Too clever. Way above her understanding.

How in heavens did we ever get along as friends?

She peered over to him, his current position drawing her focus to his powerful looking biceps, his physicality still a shock, and yet another thing that was *too much*.

Brains *and* that body.

Then there was the shiny future ahead of him while she was little more than a scatterbrained artist, who failed to make an actual living out of her art, whilst harboring pipe dreams of leaving her smaller-than-usual town, even though she knew she really could.

"Plates?"

She snapped her gaze up to his, not aware she'd been staring, all while her brain scrambled to filter his question on where her mom stored the plates.

"Just over there." She turned from the soft crackle of butter in the pan and stabbed a finger toward an overhead cupboard. "I'll have these done soon."

Though she spoke of the pancakes and pointed in another direction altogether, his gaze stayed on her, gliding down her body, as though returning the favor of her earlier stare.

Her skin warmed in protest at her decision to stubbornly maintain the normal by wearing her usual tiny pajamas. Maybe full-length winter flannels would have served better?

Her eyes inexplicably prickled because, as usual, she had no freaking idea what to do. In the past, she would have thrown herself at him. At anyone, really. But disappointment had a way of birthing caution, and her old patterns just didn't add up anymore. Especially not with Chip.

So, breaking the stare-off and opting to let him drive the conversation, she turned back to the pan.

"What happened between you and Sarah?"

She slammed her eyes shut and held back a need to swear.

"Nothing." Though what *had* happened with Sarah was yet another warning on Ally's old patterns of behavior. How invested she tended to get with any man of interest. How easily she was hurt. Why Chip should remain off-limits. "Just your typical case of two squabbling women."

She flipped pancakes and withdrew her attention.

"Really?" His voice, of course, still found her. "You're playing the 'two squabbling women' defense?"

The flat disbelief in his tone spoke of the cheapness of using that tired stereotype, the one that said women in close proximity were doomed to episodes of jealousy and cattiness.

"Chocolate spread still your favorite?" She directed an oblivious smile his way, but his analytical stare didn't budge, so she used his failure to gather tableware and turned for the plate cupboard in lieu of answering his question.

"Ally?"

She kept busy again, this time with shifting cooked pancakes to a plate and then dropping more batter into the pan. "Yep."

"What happened between you and Sarah?"

She shut her eyes again and shook her head. "Can we just enjoy breakfast, please?"

"Sure, we can." Despite the casual term, his tense voice suggested he wouldn't let her escape this topic so easily. "But Sarah is my sister, and your squabble kind of makes a difference to what happened last night."

"Our squabble makes no difference to last night." Ferrying the plate to the table, she strode past him but steeled her focus ahead. "Last night isn't happening again."

Even with her back to him, the stare she imagined he leveled her way burned the space between her shoulder blades. "It makes no difference, huh?"

Her heart squeezed, and she peered at the sheer curtains opposite the table, the yard outside seeping through on a hazy impression. Her evasion hurt him, and still, she gave a small nod. Her problems with Sarah had nothing to do with him.

"You have a thing for Dean Holloway."

Cold shock ran through her, and she spun around, instantly regretting how the move revealed Chip's still expression, that stillness somehow more painful than the prospect of fielding his anger. "And you're hurt that Sarah got there first."

Her heart sank, and she wanted to be sick. "Wow… is *that* what Sarah told you?"

He shook his head, his earlier tension eased, while hers soared higher. "I inferred."

"Well"—she stormed over and flipped more pancakes, once again making sure to avoid eye contact—"you inferred wrong."

A quiet few beats passed, before Chip spoke again. "So you *do* have it bad for Dean Holloway?"

A small twist in his question denoted humor and filled her chest with a soft flutter, one that threatened to evolve into a giggle.

She rolled her eyes and put on a bored tone. "I *did* have it bad for Dean Holloway. He's a handsome guy and was new in town. Heck, in the single most embarrassing moment of my life, I even tried to corner him at his home." She switched off the stove and flicked her gaze to Chip, the rising heat in her cheeks prompting her to the fridge for condiments. "But I am capable of knowing when I'm not wanted."

She lowered the jars and tubs nestled in her arms to the table and then plonked herself into a seat.

Soon, he pinned her with a hard-to-read expression, and a dull ache grew in her tummy. Seeking relief, she stabbed a fork toward the chair next to her, gesturing for him to sit too, but he drew the silence out, perhaps still grappling with her brief crush on Dean.

"Ally…"

What was with the low hurt and huskiness in his voice?

She shot him a direct stare, frustrated she even had to justify her past crushes simply because Chip Overton waltzed into town with plans to stick his annoyingly proficient tongue in her mouth. "Does the story *you* insisted on hearing not match your mental image of me?"

Truth be told, back in the day, the months before his interstate move, there'd come a point when she suspected he liked her, that all the school yard teasing about their friendship edged on truth.

Perhaps old emotions influenced last night's kiss. Like he had a need to see her as the same innocent Ally Egan he once knew. The same bubbly and undemanding woman everyone else in town seemed to want too.

And maybe Sarah had shared stories about Ally's dating failures over the years, and Chip returned to Harlow with delusions of Ally just waiting around for him to claim her.

"Sarah, was supposed to be my friend." She let out a weary sigh and reached for the strawberry spread. "She hid an entire relationship. Let me, and everyone else in town, believe she and Dean were enemies. To think back on the chats we'd had about him. I'm so sick of people thinking I don't notice their condescension. So, no matter how you dress up Sarah's actions, she lied, and I don't *have* to forgive her."

"Hmm…" His gaze dropped to the table. "I want to say it would be nice for you two to make up, but I see your point."

She shrugged, nudging the jar of chocolate spread—once his favorite—toward him, his quick acceptance confirming that was still the case.

"I'm not ready to make nice with her yet." She sawed into her pancake, the action pairing well with her mood. "So as immature and ridiculous as it probably sounds to you, this is where I'm at. I'm not the one who should be breaking the ice, and we both know Sarah well enough to know she won't do it either. "

He maintained more silence, a silence that signaled his disappointment at the situation more than her, while he cut into his breakfast. At least he didn't try to persuade her to heal the rift.

And because he didn't try to persuade her, her trust in him as a confidant grew, and she spoke again. "About last night. I'm sorry, I didn't mean to—"

"Say our kiss shouldn't have happened?" He lowered his fork, his narrow stare boring into and then raking over her. "Just so we're clear, I'm not sorry at all."

For all her years of thinking him a harmless friend, he didn't seem so harmless right now. Not that she felt threatened, only his even tone stated his thoughts on the kiss as being simple and unrepentant—so contrary to her own raging emotions when she'd always been the free-spirited one.

She peered down at the table's wood grain. "We're friends, we always have been..."

A frown pulled at her lips. Maybe he didn't have regrets, but she still had boundaries to assert here. "What happened last night was... weird."

"Wow." He lowered his utensils and leaned back in his chair. "Of all the girls I've ever kissed, not one called the experience weird."

She lowered her own fork and shelved a perplexing desire to ask just *how many* girls he'd kissed. "You and I grew up together, and then we see each other again, and we're suddenly kissing? *That's* the weird bit. The kiss itself was great. Amazing even..."

And because he still scowled at her, she reached out and gave him a congratulatory clap on the back.

Good for you. Amazing at math. Crazy smart. Good looking... and OF COURSE you're a perfect kisser.

Chip, a man born with a glint in his eye. Someone destined to do good and great things. Whereas she, everything about her screamed literal mediocrity, with a smattering of chaos that followed wherever she went.

"I distinctly remember you making moon eyes at me." He leaned into the table, his unnerving stillness taking over once more. "And then you told me you wanted *me* to kiss *you*."

"Moon eyes?" Her voice pitched up, and she shook her head, momentarily pretending she didn't know what he talked about. "Okay, maybe I did."

He let out a sigh, his stare still burning into her, demanding something she either couldn't or didn't want to decipher. Like he wanted her to dig deeper to unearth what *really* held her back.

She slumped in her chair, allowing her shoulders to sag, forgoing her will to pretend any longer. "You're returning to Boston in a few weeks."

His brow crinkled, and his softened gaze roamed her face, as though he sought to gauge her thoughts. "Yeah, I am."

And there it was. The *other* reason that kiss would be a one-time thing.

"Chip"—she swallowed at the thickness in her throat, a thickness that delayed her ability to explain *why* she held back—"I don't want to fall for someone who won't be around."

$$\mathcal{T}en$$

"Hello, is this William Overton?"

Chip sat in his office with his phone pressed to his ear, this new office his childhood bedroom while he'd taken over the main bedroom for actual sleeping.

This call now interrupted his latest attempt to debug the issues with Stonewall's network protocol stack. The easygoing voice on the other end of the phone seemed bright with enthusiasm. Still, the use of his formal name, William—just like his dad tended to do—had Chip sinking deeper into his office chair and frowning at his computer screen. "Yeah, that's me."

"This is Jay Evans. I'm senior management at Encode Enterprises."

Chip paused, before rolling his seat back and sitting taller, as though Jay could see him rather than just hear him. "Is this about my grant application?"

Though he did his best to sound unaffected, he'd been waiting weeks for this call, and his hasty delivery was hard to miss.

Jay gave a quick chuckle. "Certainly is. Firstly, hello, Mr. Overton. Secondly, I'm calling to say your application for our Graduate Fund has proceeded to the next round. A note from your screening interview states you're not currently in Boston. Is that correct?"

"I can return if needed." The speed of his offer brought a dull ache to his chest, springing to mind Ally Egan's words.

I don't want to fall for someone who won't be around.

She'd disclosed her limits just that morning, and he'd already proved her right. Then again, even without the news his application had progressed, an invitation to apply for an Encode grant alone was a big deal. Meanwhile, Ally had all but turned him down, and he didn't have the luxury of chasing dead ends.

"That's great to hear." Jay's voice brought him back to the conversation. "I've had a look over your proposal, and frankly, Stonewall sounds like a powerful program."

"Thanks." A relieved sort of chuckle fell from Chip. "It's nice to talk to someone who understands what I'm working on here."

Jay returned the laughter. "Oh, yeah, I get it. Though you'll find being misunderstood is less of a problem when you work at Encode."

"You mean *if* I get to work at Encode." And still, Chip's breath halted at Jay's mere implication that he *might* get to work at Encode.

"You're a step closer now, and if you do get the grant, you won't be *just* working at this company. Your idea will become one of our products with all the perks that come with being a product co-owner. Actually"—he dragged out a pause, one that suggested hesitation—"having looked at your project, I wanted to ask if you've considered what reverse engineering your technology might do?"

"To be honest, not really." Chip paused now, too, mostly because he worried that he *should* have thought about reverse engineering. "I've been too busy just getting the code to function."

"Well, your tech has unique capabilities. So, think about it now." Jay's business-like tone pitched a genuine request for Chip to do some on-the-spot brainwork.

"I mean, yeah." He took a moment to think, whatever his reply now, he'd likely spend days flicking through the many layers to Jay's question. "I guess a reverse-engineered Stonewall could potentially breakdown a number of security measures to allow access to otherwise protected data."

"Mr. Overton, this is where I would advise you to be very careful with which company you trust your work to." Jay held a low, grave tone, one that made the muscles over Chip's stomach harden. "Provided you get this grant, Encode has the capabilities to manage such a precarious project, but not every company will. So, back to the task at hand, remaining candidates need to put together a final pitch to present in three weeks' time."

A thick knot formed in Chip's throat, not just from Jay's gloomy warning, but because the pitch would be tied with the pressure of keeping his project on track. "I can manage that."

The statement hung as a lie around him, or maybe an attempt to convince himself as much as Jay.

"There are only two other candidates left, and you're all invited to Encode's Annual All Staff gala the night prior to your final pitch. The evening is an opportunity to build connections, regardless of whether you get the funding. Although—" As if mulling over his next words, Jay took a moment before speaking again. "I should also mention the grant's budget is far more flexible than what's stated in the application terms."

Chip's gaze clouded over, and he rubbed his fingertips over his forehead. "What exactly do you mean?"

"Nothing bad, Mr. Overton." Jay chuckled as though he sensed Chip's concern. "Only that our goal is to make great tech ideas happen, which means providing whatever capital needed to thrive."

But the budget on offer was already generous and well within the tens of millions. Still, Chip saw no use in overthinking Jay's bit of extra information. Not until Chip knew for a fact the grant was his.

One thing that made Encode's grant so hugely coveted was that the winner would essentially become a stakeholder in Encode itself. As in, Encode would create a salable product from the winner's project, the winner given a choice of sharing profits and continuing to manage the project into the future or outright selling the idea to Encode at a negotiated and life-changing price.

A sharp prickle formed over the base of Chip's neck and travelled down the rest of his body, stealing his words as he stared at the long chain of code glowing from his computer screen. All those symbols and commands held the keys to a world of financial and creative freedom he couldn't even begin to imagine being his. "I... ahh... thank you for the call, Jay. I guess I'll be seeing you in three weeks?"

"Sure thing. The board is looking forward to hearing what you have to offer. Until then, I'll have my assistant email the details. See you then."

Jay hung up, and Chip lowered his phone ever-so-slowly to his desk, his hand resting atop the device for the longest time.

After five years at MIT. His internships. The late nights at his desk. The risk of an unsightly blank spot on his resume while he worked on his own project. The risk in defying his dad's wishes—Stonewall being what his dad dubbed "a baseless dream." Chip now had a one-in-three chance at being the developer behind his very own multi-million-dollar product. A chance to live his life so far from anyone's criticisms and control.

His legs worked of their own volition and lifted him from his chair until he paced the room. He kept his fingers interlaced behind his head and blew out a flustered breath, needing to get back to work but too hyped to do so.

Now, his mind raced to Ally, to her admission that she didn't want anyone who would leave her behind. That she also had no plans of living anywhere but Harlow, while he still had little idea where his life was headed beyond pinning his mind to launching his career. Did he need to call her? Tell her what had happened? Was their relationship at the point of making phone calls? Or even sharing random good news? *Probably not.*

After all, she had a point. Even if he did want her more than what was healthy, it wouldn't be fair for him to drag her down a path of no return. There'd be two broken hearts. Rather than just the one he'd had that first time he'd left town. Besides, his connection with her was *way* too fresh and non-committal to ask her to consider following him anywhere.

No. For all his smarts, even he couldn't change his numbered days in Harlow. He'd have to focus on the next weeks. Ensure his future with Encode. Enjoy his short time with Ally before life pulled them apart a second time.

Eleven

THE NEXT DAY, the brass bell *tinged* above Oak Tree Furniture's door and shifted Ally's attention away from the receipts she tallied at the white glass counter.

"Is Blaine in?" Emilia power walked over, a standard-sized envelope clasped in one hand, her beautiful dark curls flowing in her wake.

"He's repairing a window fitting at a house across town." Ally waited for Emilia to reach her, glad that only one customer remained amongst the store's sea of dining settings and beds.

If not talking to Sarah didn't suck enough, Chip's home visit meant Ally now had things to say and no one to say them to. But with *Emilia* here, well, her presence changed everything. Besides, she wasn't Chip's sister so even better.

"Say, how 'bout you stick around for a cool drink?" Ally tried to offer a smile that didn't look calculated. "I don't think Blaine'll be much longer, anyway."

Emilia's warm Mediterranean complexion sported a rosy blush, and she fanned her face with the envelope. "You know, I could do with a break from running about town. *Sheesh.* Summer in Harlow is hotter than I figured."

"That's right, this is your first summer in town, isn't it?" She rounded the counter and hooked an arm through Emilia's, leading her to the back, past the living room displays of oak, maple, and ash furnishings. All Blaine's creations. The man was closer to a loveably annoying older sibling than a boss, the sale of his work enabling him to provide Ally some financial help. First with this job and then with the shelf he allowed her to keep filled with her own vases and handmade homewares. Even though it wasn't a huge source of sales in his store. "Give it a few weeks, it'll only get hotter."

The small table of complimentary iced lemon water stood along the back wall, Blaine's workshop hidden on the other side, even though Ally liked to leave the door open when he wasn't around, so customers had a glimpse of furniture pieces mid-creation.

If she had her way, the back wall would sport a giant sound-proof window, so everyone could watch Blaine work, but being on display wasn't his thing.

Now, she poured water from a bulbous, blue glass jug into two matching glasses. "So, how is everything?"

"I have a wedding to plan while building a new business." Emilia chuckled and lifted the envelope back into view. "So, a little hectic, to be honest, but I came today with good news."

"Ooo. What is it?"

Ally reached for the envelope, only for Emilia to snatch it back.

"*This* is my first cheque."

Ally laughed and handed Emilia some water, the glass's chill lingering on her palm, the sharp scent of lemon hanging between them. "Well then, can't say I blame you for being possessive."

"Exactly, but"—Emilia took a sip of water, her ensuing small sigh a hint that she'd really needed refreshing—"remember how I had you sweet-talk my friend a bit more than a month ago while Blaine was in the hospital?"

"Rochelle? Oh yah, sure." Ally paused, her insides churning at the memory of having to fill in because Emilia's ex returned to town seeking revenge, and Blaine had been shot trying to protect her. "She was nice enough to follow me from our display at the town fair and to the shop for a better look at our range."

"Well, she liked you too. You did such a great job talking up Oak Tree that Blaine landed his first wholesale order… and this first cheque." Emilia gave an excited laugh and tapped Ally's arm with the envelope. "Since I have another idea, today's good news isn't just for Blaine, it's for you too."

"Idea?" Ally's sole customer now headed for the door, leaving hope that the conversation she'd been eager to rope Emilia into would still happen. "What do you mean?"

"Well, during my brief stint working at the nursery, I got very familiar with your plant pots, and Ally, I think your work is something I can sell." She did a quick bounce on her heels, the strain in her wide grin begging Ally to reciprocate her excitement.

"I… I mean, sure." Ally closed her mouth out of fear she'd stumble on yet more words. She wanted to get all giggly over the offer, but just as fast as any joy surfaced, doubt came crashing in. What if Emilia invested a lot of effort, only to sell nothing? "But there are so many potters out there, why mine?"

"Why *not* yours?" Emilia laughed. "I mean, I'd been planning on asking if you'd make some glazed-heart favors for my wedding—"

"You what?"

Emilia swatted a hand as though the added request were no big deal. For Ally, Emilia's trust in her to deliver such a personal request, one that would serve as a gift to her guests, meant everything. Probably more than any vague chance to sell her work.

"I know people, Ally." Emilia lowered her voice, her heavier tone imploring Ally to listen, to give her first offer some genuine thought. And truth was, Emilia *did* know people. She'd been an L.A. socialite, after all. "The people I'm thinking of own a decor company that specializes in garden pieces. I just might be able to secure a deal to distribute your art on a larger scale, just like I did with Oak Tree."

A seemingly endless silence stretched out, and Ally stared at Emilia, her jaw loose, and her overly dry throat failing to form words. She was experiencing an artist's version of a near-death experience, the winding path to where she stood now flooding her brain with memories.

She'd first touched clay in junior high, her preceding time in art school giving her access to lessons from professional potters. She'd learned how to "pull" vessels into shape on a wheel. Had kilns and glazes at her disposal. So despite the huge expense, she'd returned to Harlow determined to save for her own equipment.

Oh, and bless Blaine and Aggie. They'd hatched a plan for her to work at Oak Tree and provided a rent-free studio at the nursery, also allowing her to sell her art through both businesses. This year included the go-ahead to run children's art classes at the nursery, with Harlow town council onboard, including Ally's classes in the town's official summer school holidays program.

"I... ahh..." As much as she wanted to back out, that she couldn't possibly be good enough, other people had invested in her, and they'd rightfully never let her live down rejecting this offer. "Yeah, okay."

Emilia gave a high, happy squeak and tapped Ally's arm with the envelope again. "Right decision. Just leave the rest with me. If things work out how I think they will, let's just say, your life will change fast."

As if that wasn't happening already.

Then again, Emilia didn't know about last night. About Chip and how things *had* changed. Fast and forever. Faster than Ally could keep up with. And still, she couldn't commit to that change being one she wanted.

The tension in her throat forced her to swallow, her eyes strained under the effort to keep focus on Emilia. "Can we talk?"

Emilia's smile collapsed, and she gave a hurried nod, like she read Ally's darkening mood. "What's happened?"

"There's this boy—"

"Another one?" Emilia slapped a hand over her mouth, her eyes moon-shaped with visible embarrassment and regret.

Ally laughed before rolling her eyes, unable to blame Emilia. There *had* been multiple crushes, and every single one of those a failure.

"I'm sorry"—Emilia lowered her hand—"please, go on."

Just to punish Emilia, Ally did a half turn and placed her glass down on the small, white table beside her, taking her time to wipe condensation from her fingers. Although the enlarged pause punished her more since she'd have to admit to something she'd never figured she would. "Well, *this* boy is different. Very different."

"Oh, you mean the guy from the ball game?" Emilia's smile grew into a full-scale beam. "Sarah's brother."

"You know?"

Emilia chuckled and gave a big and repeated nod. "Even Blaine noticed the energy pinging between you two at the game."

Cheeks turning hot, Ally veered her gaze, the muscles in her throat still thick and hard to speak through. "Was I that obvious?"

"When aren't you, Ally?" Emilia held a pause, her words and the ensuing silence prompting Ally to look to her. "You wear your emotions all over that beautiful face of yours, like right now. Why do you look so worried? Chip Overton is one cute guy and, by all accords, nice too."

A manic energy stirred within Ally, and a derisive laugh shot past her lips. "Because he's more than just Sarah's brother, which is bad enough now that we don't get along. Chip and I grew up together, were even in the same grade at school. Worst still, up until he left, we were best friends."

Emilia shrugged. "I'm struggling to see the problem here."

Ally spluttered another sarcastic laugh, thankful she'd lowered her glass. Otherwise, she might have accidentally spat water all over the shop floor. "We were too close. Heck, when we weren't in school together, he was at my house, and everyone in Harlow would call him my unofficial brother."

"Oh. Ewww." Emilia wrinkled her nose. "Wow, yeah, that *is* awkward."

"Right?" Ally bit her lower lip, delaying the next thing she had to say. "And seeing him again... He's *so* different... and then last night, I don't know how, but... but we kissed."

"Wait. What?" Emilia's voice shot higher, and she lashed out her hands, grabbing Ally's arms and tugging her in. "You *kissed* him?"

"Well, yeah, though he didn't much appreciate me admitting the whole thing was weird."

Emilia let loose with a series of stupefied blinks, her lips parted in a way that confessed an inability to know what to say.

So, Ally stared at the ground and spared her friend by offering further explanation. "But it wasn't the kiss that was weird, it's that I'm even attracted to him in the first place. And I know I've been here countless times before with other guys, but this one really does feel *different*."

"Because you two were so close?" Emilia's lowered tone indicated her shock had settled, but Ally shook her head again, still trying and failing to process her feelings.

"That, but there's more too. For so long, he was everything I *didn't* want." She lifted her gaze, catching the small and confused twist of Emilia's brow. "We've both changed so much, Emilia. And Chip, he's different *and* scary. As in, so smart and sure of everything he does while having this unexplainable intuitive grasp of what I'm thinking. I wouldn't know where to start with a man like that. Jeez Louise, even if I did, there's just no going back if things don't work out. I don't know what I'm supposed to do here."

A gentle smile played at Emilia's lips, her fingertips curling into a reassuring grip around Ally's arms. "Sounds like you had a solid decade to disassociate from whatever bonds you two had. Things feel different because they *are* different. You could start with getting to know the man he is today."

"I don't know if I want to."

"Why?"

"Because ever since I've known him, he's had this bright future mapped out. I, on the other hand—"

"Shine bright in your own way"—Emilia reached up and tapped the tip of Ally's nose—"and don't you forget that."

She released Ally from her hold and dipped her head, her stance denoting a moment of thought. "He's not in town for long."

"Yep, which is why I told him nothing can happen between us."

Emilia whipped her chin up and leveled a death stare Ally's way. "Not with that attitude, it won't."

"I don't need another soul-destroying crush."

But Emilia swatted a hand at Ally's husky admission, her attention dropping again, as though she returned to whatever plan she hatched. "Look at Blaine and I. We bridged ten years apart as well as my temporary plans in Harlow *and* my being fresh from my first marriage. Plus, don't forget, I even had my ex literally gunning to end me. So in comparison, getting you and Chip to work will be easy."

"Except if it isn't, then I'm lumping you with my therapy bill." Ally held a flat tone and stare, even though the light fluttering in her tummy said the woman's logic already took effect. "What if this goes all wrong? I'm not on great terms with his sister. If things go bad with Chip, she'll probably make friends with the syndicate just put a hit out on me ."

Emilia gave a light chuckle. "But you like him, don't you?"

Wanting to escape the weight of Emilia's scrutiny, Ally stared down at the white floorboards and offered a weak nod.

"Great." Emilia's enthused tone had Ally lifting her chin. "And are you tied to living in Harlow forever, or would you consider relocating for love?"

She scowled at Emilia for a bit, not happy to confront her old habit of throwing herself all-in for a man, much less consider sacrificing her ties to her entire family. "I want to see the world, but leave Harlow and my family altogether? That's a major leap of faith, dontcha think."

"And yet that's not an outright *no*." The woman's gaze swept over her. "Where's your phone?"

"In my pocket…" Ally pitched a frown. "Why?"

"Don't even stop to hesitate. Send Chip a message right now. Just tell him to meet you tonight." Emilia crossed her arms and gave a resolute shrug. "You haven't got all that long to decide how you feel, and the only way to do that is to spend as much time with him as you can… *while* you can."

"Nah-ah." Ally shook her head, pressing a protective hand over her phone tucked in her short denim skirt's only pocket. "That's not going to happen. I can't—"

Emilia shot back a hard scoff. "Yeah, well, you already have. You kissed him, and it was clearly good enough to leave you all tied up and confused. I'd even wager you've barely thought about anything other than Chip since."

Ally narrowed her eyes into a half-hearted glare. "No comment."

"Yeah, exactly." Emilia matched Ally's expression. "So, get your phone out of your pocket. Now."

For the first time ever, Ally saw what Blaine meant when he complained about his fiancée's stubbornness. Still, not quite ready to surrender, Ally slipped the phone from her pocket and clutched it to her chest.

"Damn it, Ally." Even as Ally shook her head and backed away, Emilia lunged forward and snatched the phone from her fingers. "Fine, I'll do it."

Stuck between wrestling this smaller woman, or allowing Emilia to take over where Ally lacked courage, Ally just gawped and muttered a weak sounding question, "What are you doing?"

"Saving you from regret." Emilia tapped away at Ally's phone, occasionally peering through her lashes to shoot Ally a stern stare. "Chip is all grown up now, so give the man a chance to prove himself. In a few short weeks, you'll know if he's your dud of the decade or the man of your dreams."

Twelve

ALLY KNOCKED at Chip's front door, a mild ache lingering across her knuckles as she eyed the pale, beveled wood plane before her. Footsteps grew louder from inside, signaling his approach and causing her to back away on the porch's crackling aged timber.

Before long, he appeared at the threshold, his lips the slightest bit parted while his gaze did a slow glide down her body. "I thought you were joking."

She peered down at herself, at her sheer blue wrap shrouding her orange and pink polka dot bikini. "You got my message?"

She lifted her gaze to him leaning a shoulder onto the doorframe, his arms crossed while an all-too-knowing smile curled his lips. "Yeah. I just kinda ignored it, though, because—"

"You thought I was joking." Her voice held an embarrassing huskiness, and she took to staring blankly at a side window. One she recalled led to his living room while she debated whether to tell him the message wasn't *hers* so much as Emilia's.

Still, I'm here, aren't I? I own this now.

She glanced back to him, a frown now dragging at those expressive lips of his, his narrowed focus bringing heat to her cheeks. Not a good sign, given his less-than-enthusiastic reception.

What did he see right now?

A famously desperate woman trying to get the attention of a man she'd already turned down?

"It's hot out." She swallowed the thickness coating the inside of her throat and gave a wobbly smile, vowing to dial down the desperation and revert to the charade of wanting to maintain nothing more than an old friendship. *What a wimp.* "I thought maybe you'd like to visit our old swimming spot at Mirabelle Falls."

He cocked his head to one side, his eyes giving little away. Though his gaze flicked down her body again, his acknowledgement of her swimwear sent tingling ripples over her skin. "You want to swim?"

"Yeah, yah know, escape the heat for a while?"

Her jaw hurt from all the forced grinning, but she powered on, at least for the long and painful moment where he said nothing, only to let out a sigh and push away from the doorframe.

"I guess no more work was happening today anyway. Come on in. I'll change and grab my towel."

He turned and wandered away, his cool scent washing over her as she took a few timid steps into his home, still too rattled to enter the living room proper. "I brought a cooler full of food and drinks, and I'm driving."

"Fine with me." His muffled voice coupled with the thud of his footsteps somewhere farther down the hall.

She tried not to analyze every detail of his house which, in all honesty, hadn't changed all that much since Sarah's move, as if she'd taken little with her to Dean's place. Within moments, Chip's footsteps returned, and he strode into the living area wearing a loose T-shirt and swim shorts, a towel draped casually over his shoulder.

He held both hands out to his sides in a silent request for her approval, that silence weighing on her as she eyed his ruffled hair, all-too-easy demeanor, his mussed-up appearance evocative of how he'd looked awakening at her house only that morning.

"That should do." She swallowed against the raspiness in her throat and spun around to lead the way out the door and to her car.

Each crunching step on the driveway's gravel had her cursing her nerves in what should have been a simple exchange. Cursing Emilia for her stubborn-headed meddling. Cursing herself again for going along with this ridiculous plan.

He's leaving. And I've already rejected him. What did I think would happen?

And sure, maybe Emilia had a point about not missing opportunities, but even captured opportunities had the potential to hurt those ass-backward enough to grasp for the near impossible.

Chip finished locking the front door and then jogged down the porch steps. Meanwhile, she wrenched her car door open and set about starting the engine. Within moments, he landed in the passenger seat, his face turned to her in her periphery, even though she pinned her focus ahead.

"Productive day?" She savored the pretense of being busy with reversing out, even as she dug her nails into the steering wheel's hard leather, and her muscles felt all weak and jittery.

"Yeah. You could say that." His warm tone ricocheted within her car's small cabin.

She made no sign of noticing. "Oh, yeah? Care to talk about it?"

"I guess you could say I didn't get much work done, but I'm somehow much further along than I expected."

An uncontrolled laugh broke from her, but she focused on turning the car down a seldom used lane, Mirabelle Falls so much closer to his place than hers. "You rarely make any sense to me as it is, but that would have to be a super vague and confusing response even for you."

His soft chuckle stoked the tingling over her skin again. "I had no idea I had that effect on you."

She glanced over to him, quick to look away. He had to know he had *some* effect on her. That she'd been the one to ask for his kiss. That she'd approached him today. Chip sure had an innocence to him, but he wasn't naive.

Her car drew nearer to what they'd once unimaginatively called their "secret hideout." The hideout, not much more than a narrow bend of river covered by a multitude of weeping willows that provided a decent amount of privacy.

Not that she or Chip ever did anything requiring much privacy, but the spot had been a welcome break from houses filled with annoying siblings and parents. One of many places he'd read to her while she'd scribbled on one of her many notepads or splashed in the nearby water.

She guided her car to an area just big enough to fit between a cluster of pines, then cranked the brake, and took a moment to send an unhurried glance his way.

A steady flow of memories of him and this place made her less shy about holding eye contact. They'd had something special. And a simple smile from him now was enough to settle her mood on this whole outing.

So, she mirrored his light expression, and together, they set about gathering bags and towels and heading down the small hill to the river.

Maybe friendship would be all that happened here. Maybe this *was* her answer. Far be it from her to put in all the effort chasing him. She'd already done a ton of chasing with other men and learned her lesson. So maybe, what they had now *was* enough.

The river flowed full but calm, and the light breeze shifted willow tendrils in a tranquil dance of green, dappled light. So many years had passed since she'd last come here, her days in this spot ending when Chip left town. She hadn't felt right coming here without him.

Now, he pulled the rolled picnic blanket out from under her arm, startling her from her daydream. She recovered enough to wait for him to lay down the red and white plaid blanket, then adjusted her towel on top.

"Right." He pitched forth a broad grin and whipped off his navy-blue t-shirt. "I'm going in."

All too fast, he turned away, practically running to greet the water. Meanwhile, her breath stuck in her throat at the vision of his tanned and toned torso—a reminder of yesterday morning and his seemingly sudden maturity and beauty.

Even as she squeezed her eyes shut and told herself to stop gawping, the tight sensation in her belly called her to race over and touch him. Instead, she settled on ripping her sheer wrap from around her waist and pretending his eventual astute stare on her semi-nakedness wouldn't at all lead to more unnerving reactions from her body.

So, the quicker she got into the water, the quicker she could hide. Except the short stroll to Mirabelle's banks revealed waters that inflicted a sharp iciness to her feet.

She scrambled back and wrapped her arms around her bare midriff, the air warm, but the water so frigid that she contemplated retreating to the blanket.

But the ache of cold toes faded when she lifted her gaze to the man in the river, Chip's stare holding her with an intense focus that had his jaw set in a hard line.

Oh, that's right, I've seen plenty of his body, but he hasn't seen this much of mine.

She wanted to say a hot blush rose to her cheeks, that would have been easy compared to the gaping hollow opening up inside her. The one that questioned what he saw. She'd never been shy about her body. In the right weather, she wore short skirts and midriff baring tops with no second thoughts. Heck, she and Chip used to swim in this very spot in little more than their underwear.

But that was then, and this is now…

That thought pushed her attention from him and onto the river's glittering surface, the water her overly crisp chance to hide from Chip Overton now being a man.

Don't wimp out. Just get in the water and don't wimp out.

Good idea. Be brave. One foot in. Then the other.

"Here, I'll help you."

She startled at him wading closer, his hand outstretched as though her two feet in the water wasn't enough. *Okay, it wasn't enough.* But still an achievement to her.

The sun illuminated the gold and emerald in his eyes and didn't exactly make her want to step closer. Nor did the fullness at the center of his lips. Lips she'd kissed… and *so* wanted to again.

Still, her dragged-out pause probably made her appear no better than a stunned fish—not a look she aimed for here—so she extended a hand and accepted his help.

"I forgot to ask"—he peered back at her, not at all a distraction from the electricity traveling from his fingers to hers—"how was your day?"

She smiled and did her best to escape her uncharacteristic silence. "Emilia thinks she can sell more of my pottery, and Oak Tree was quiet, so Blaine let me go early."

"Which is what brought you to my door at 3:30 on a Wednesday afternoon?" By now, the water reached her belly button, the cold still a bother, although the conversation helped. "Good luck with your sales, by the way, and thanks for dragging me out of the house. Now that I'm here, I missed this place more than most."

For once, her nerves stilled, and she said nothing, more out of comfort than jitters. "Really?"

"Really." His gaze held hers for a beat too long, and still, his smile grew. "I have some good memories here. Of the fun we used to have. And how sitting beneath the willows always felt like being inside a tent."

"They always had a way of making me wonder what it would be like to have my own place." She released an easy laugh. "Life seemed so hectic back then, but it was simpler, wasn't it?"

"*Some* things were simpler." His smile faded into a flatter line, and he pulled her along.

Right. *Her* life had been simpler. Her family a picture of stability while Chip's and Sarah's was a chaotic mess that ultimately left members scattered across the country. Gnawing shame had her peering down at her fingertips skimming the water's glossy surface.

Sometimes I can be a total ignoramus.

"Ally?"

By now, the water covered her chest and had done so for a while. She lifted her gaze to him and his focus dancing about her face. Had she played a part in his past complexities? Well, the swirling in her belly said the tables had now turned.

But all he said was, "You're not getting your hair wet?"

She laughed and shook her head. Since when had she become an over-thinker? "I'm still wearing my makeup from work and the drowned-rat look isn't in this season."

He gave a soft shrug. "It's just me."

She bit her lower lip to keep from laughing. *Had he seen himself lately?* But a simpler excuse would lead to less embarrassment. "I like to be presentable."

He shook his head and sank backward into the water, letting go of her hand before he slipped under completely, only to soon rise in all his glistening glory.

No drowned vermin look for this guy.

"I still remember when a giggly and energetic Ally Egan would race me to the water just to be the first one in." His smile grew, although not enough to drown the pang of *something* that alerted her to yet another role-reversal. This time, when it came to being self-conscious. "Remember that?"

She laughed and dipped down to neck level in the hopes of appeasing him. Truth was, she hadn't become more self-conscious. What had changed were her feelings for the man before her.

Oh, hell!

"No, I'm good here." She waded back a little, trying hard to seem unaffected, but he lowered his chin, droplets of water trailing along his jawline, the challenge in his stare melting her from the inside-out.

"Jump in. Or I'm coming after you."

The low warning should have intimidated, and it did to some extent, but more than anything, his hollow threat left her skin prickling while a ripple of nerves stirred at her insides.

She kept her voice light but backed away some more. "No, you won't."

He laughed and drew closer all the same.

"Chip. I'll scream." But her scream was more a squeal of delight as she spun away, running—as fast as one could in water.

"Just dive in, Ally." His laugh trailed behind her along with the loud splashing sounds of him chasing her. "It will be over before you know it."

Sensing him closer, she shrieked and used humor to eke an escape. "That's what all the boys say."

His splashes stopped as did his laughter. She turned to find deep lines scoring the space between his brows, his stare unblinking, as though she'd stunned him.

A long moment passed before he folded forward in a roar of laughter, the sound bouncing within the grotto of water and trees. A small chuckle grew inside her, the crinkles at his eyes holding a familiar mischief.

"Chip." She shook her head at all the silliness. "I'm going back to the picnic blanket."

"No, you're not." He narrowed his eyes, although the rest of his face still smiled.

Before she knew it, a large wall of water flew at her.

That devil!

She ducked but too late.

Doing her best to cover her face, she spluttered out what water landed in her mouth. "You're such an ass!"

She ran at him now, not even caring that the water slowed her steps. The surface hit at just below his waist, and she launched herself at him, aiming to push him over, only for his longer arms to catch her first.

"Not fair." Her cry held an unmissable huskiness, the solid wall of his body meeting her bare skin as he pulled her into an all-too-coordinated embrace.

So much for pushing him over.

His warm breath stroked her cheek in an enthralling contrast to the cold air and water around her, one that made her heart race and her head dip in surrender, her forehead coming to rest on his.

Emilia's advice rushed in. That Ally was best to learn Chip as a grown man. A man—once, her dearest friend—now, maybe so much more.

She'd already had glimpses of his personality. Lighthearted, balanced with cutting intelligence. A man who maybe saw too much in her. Then there were moments like *this*.

When nothing else mattered but the breath-taking sensation of his body against hers. The musk rising from his damp skin. Or the sharp adrenaline shearing her veins as her eyes drifted shut, and she rose to press her lips to his.

Thirteen

CHIP TIGHTENED his hands at Ally's waist and pulled her closer, the river lapping against him in calm discord to the desperation sweeping him over. *Her kiss.* A rare and sumptuous stillness to the noise that overran his brain. She tasted like fresh summer berries, warm and sweet, and so he crushed his mouth harder to hers, seeking more.

Her arms latched around his shoulders, and she pulled herself up, attempting to wrap her legs around him. His help came in the deliciously evil gesture of cupping her ass and lifting her.

Fire roared deep within him, swallowing every question he had about how they'd gotten here and whether he was right to let lust consume him. But her gentle moan in response to each hungry lash of his tongue obliterated his innate ability to stop and make a sensible choice. As did his muscles drawing taut with a need to explore her further.

Slowly. Slowly. He'd never wanted someone so much, but he didn't want to blow this with rushing. Then again, she'd been the one to instigate this kiss… and the last one.

Oh, but I'm not all that innocent, either.

Of course, he wasn't. And he didn't want to be. Still, he'd sensed her doubt time and time again, had a few of his own. Besides, this was Ally. *His Ally.*

She moved her hands so that her fingers raked through his hair, simultaneously pulling him to deepen the kiss. So passionate. So demanding. Tempting fate, he gave her what she asked for, not just with the kiss but in walking blind toward the river's bank, her still supported in his arms.

Willow branches brushed his shoulder, the water up to his calves while his skin tingled from the press of her sex against his already rock-hard excitement. He wanted her in every way a man could want a woman, and her legs at his waist made the prospect of taking her so much easier.

This isn't like me at all.

But his need for her only grew, giving him the distinct feeling a one-time romp by the river would never be enough.

He got her as far as the thick grass beyond the sandy banks, then lay her down beneath him. Could he even have her? Here, in the open? Her legs clamped tight around him, pulling him closer *down there,* crushing his doubts like a tidal wave to land. She didn't want him to stop. No. She downright urged him on.

He ground against her, and she threw her head back with a needy whisper, prompting his own possessive growl. Since when was he possessive?

I don't want to fall for someone who won't be around.

Those words bashed about in his head, and he slammed his eyes shut, wrenching his lips from hers. Taking her *would* be easy, but *easy* now would lead to *complicated* later.

"Chip?"

Her tone held a reassuring warmth, and he opened his eyes to her softened gaze searching his, her languid body sprawled beneath him, the creamy white of her tummy highlighting the gentle swirl of her belly button.

The sight of her had him hardening anew, that hardening excruciating given his position between her bare thighs—all while he burned to lean down and trek his lips over her exposed body.

"Chip?" New brightness entered her tone, bringing his attention back to the light smile on her lips.

Was he supposed to say something?

For a man with a vast vocabulary, he had nothing to say. All he had was a painfully sharp awareness of his desire. That her fingers now raked over his back, the rigid bite of her nails daring him to continue. To kiss her again. To—

Unwilling to finish that thought, he hissed and pulled back.

One little mistake with potential for so much damage. Not that he would ever consider Ally a mistake, but hell, he didn't have a condom. Maybe his desire burned hot enough for him to care less on that front, but he'd also gleaned enough of Ally to guess she *would* think this moment a big mistake. Maybe not now. But later.

Dark pools swelled in the pale blue of her eyes, and the twist of her brow hinted her sudden understanding.

So, seeking to comfort her, he opted for talking this out. "Last night—"

She squeezed her eyes shut and pressed a hand to her face. "I changed my mind, Chip."

She opened her eyes, the sensual haziness from before gone, while she pushed at his shoulder, gesturing for him to give her space. "This is so humiliating. I'm rushing things again, aren't I?"

"Again?" His stomach clenched, and he settled in beside her, pitching his elbows over his bent knees, his eyes battling the sunlit water's glare. "So, throwing yourself at men is just a normal afternoon activity for you, is it?"

She gave a light chuckle, even though he didn't turn to look at her, because heaviness still filled his stomach. Despite what others seemed to think, sometimes his brain was his worst enemy. Maybe he'd been wrong to stop kissing her long enough to think.

"Not in the physical sense that you're probably thinking. So congratulations, Chip." She gave him a gentle fist bump at his shoulder, not too dissimilar to when she'd congratulated him on his kissing skills, her new levity filling him with hope. "You're special in that department." Though he turned to her again, she gave a tight shrug and gazed at the water, as if looking at him directly was too much of a challenge. "For a time there, I thought that being less backward about coming forward would solve the whole *single in a small town* thing, but… well… let's just say that approach had its drawbacks."

Her lips pressed into a flat line, suggesting emotional pain, though he had the vague backstory on Dean and could understand love was hard to come by. Even in a big city, with a huge population to draw dates from, much less a tiny place like Harlow. That he would soon leave her for Boston only proved her point.

He had no soothing or useful advice to offer, so he simply reached out and pressed a hand over hers. She lifted her gaze from the water to their hands joined on the grass, her focus gradually drifting up to him, the sun turning the blue in her eyes a silvery hue. "I'm sorry, Chip. I just figured kissing you was worth a shot."

Ouch! A shot at *what* exactly?

Despite the thoughts rushing his brain, her rueful smile twisted with mischief, drawing from him a chuckle. "This isn't a game of darts, Ally. I didn't stop because I thought we wouldn't get along. I stopped because we get along *too* well, and maybe it's worth hashing some details out before we go ahead and break our own hearts."

She took her turn to chuckle and did so while shaking her head, the weak ache in his chest suggesting that broken hearts might be inevitable here. No matter what, Ally would play on his mind far into the foreseeable future.

"You always were the reasonable one." She twisted her palm and wrapped her fingers around his hand.

"Sure, but you're impulsive and, therefore, way more exciting." He reached out and nudged her chin with his knuckle.

She wrinkled her nose in a tease, and an unusual silence took her over, her focus returning to the water. He let out a sigh, suddenly spent, and lay back on the grass, making sure to keep his hand linked to hers.

Water droplets rolled from her wet hair and down her back. Those droplets, and her unwillingness to stop them, somehow gave her an air of vulnerability. That she also sat with her legs folded beneath her, almost childlike, only added to the effect.

The years had given her something else, too, an element of idiosyncratic beauty. A beauty that extended beyond physical appeal, encompassing the little quirks even she still seemed to struggle to wear at all times.

She swiveled back to him now, and he didn't even care that she'd caught him staring; instead, he patted the ground beside him and invited her to lay next to him.

"I don't ever want to think of you with regret." He stared up at the cloudless sky, her head now rested on his shoulder. All those years he'd spent away from her were regret enough. "What happens when I go back to Boston?"

She'd talked about travel, but did he have a right to pitch the idea of her visiting him Boston? Even if she did, longterm, he had no intentions of staying in Harlow, and asking her to bridge the distance alone didn't seem fair.

She didn't answer right away, but when she did, her voice held a far too casual lightness. "I can handle it."

He eyed her, her pupils wide and looking far from carefree, while that same conversation about travel had seen her confirm how Harlow would always be the place she returned to. "You think so?"

She shook her head and let out a ragged laugh. "No. I'll be crushed, but I spoke with Emilia, and she said getting closer to you was worth the risk, so I thought—"

"So I have Emilia to thank for our little make-out fest?" He rolled over to his side and raised a brow, all while she turned to face him too.

"I don't regret kissing you last night. I don't regret what almost just happened now, do you?"

His heart lurched, and he reached out to sweep a strand of wet hair off her cheek. As much as he tried to summon the will to say he'd been wrong to touch her on both occasions, she lay close enough to kiss now, and the burn in his body called him a liar. So, the best he could muster was a weak shake of his head.

"Chip." She rolled onto her back, and the blue sky lightened the color of her eyes. "Do you remember the last time we came here together?"

He ran a knuckle down her upturned face, swishing willow

branches casting mild shadows over her skin, all while his memories slipped to their last visit to this river. The eve of him leaving for Boston.

The weather had been cooling and headed for winter, the overcast sky turning the choppy Mirabelle nickel gray when she'd asked him to kiss her. *Not because she'd liked him in any romantic way. No.* She'd just been scared that, with him gone, it might be years before she knew a boy well enough to get another chance.

Weird teenager logic, sure, and he'd made a show of laughing and pretending to be grossed out, her request only exacerbating his ache over leaving. But even back then, he'd known not to throw himself into something that meant the world to him and nothing to her.

Now, her gaze searched his, lips bent into a tiny frown. He needed to hurry and answer, even through the renewed misery of that past exchange. "Is that why you picked this place? Because of a fumbled kiss?"

"No, Chip. Because this spot was only ever special because of you and—" She shrugged, gaze veering away. "I mentioned that last time because I sold you *way* too short. I tried to rope you into helping me tick off some dumb milestone, and I'm sorry."

She returned her attention and hit him with a smile so big that it pushed aside any lingering bitterness, prompting him to joke back. "I'm still pissed at you, by the way."

She gave a light laugh and reached out to stroke his jawline, her soft touch encouraging him to turn his head and kiss her palm. Her smile grew some more, and she added, "You were here for so long, yah know? A huge part of my everyday life until you weren't. Suddenly, everything I did, I did alone. And I know this is way over the top, but a part of me has been kinda adrift ever since."

For the longest time, the river's lapping and the rustle of willow overtook every sound but the hard pound of his heartbeat in his ears. All because she'd said everything he'd wanted to hear. Everything he'd felt back then and still, now. But he'd be leaving again soon, and had other priorities beyond her and this small town. What comfort did her admission really offer outside of dangling the illusion of something that could never be real?

So, he clamped his jaw shut to keep from reminding her not to get too invested in him, only daring to speak once he had something positive to say. "Ally, you've got time."

Time for what? To find someone else?

What a ridiculous thing to say.

A lump formed in his throat. Maybe his words *were* ridiculous, but they offered more to her than anything else he could suggest. She wanted stability, and someone who could at least stick around. He possessed neither.

"Yah know, I tell myself that a lot." She paused, her strain-filled gaze shifting about his face as though she thought twice about what she had to say next. "But I've been rejected so many times now, I can't help but wonder what's wrong with me. Am I too much? Not enough? Maybe you can tell me, Chip. Just once… just once, I want to know what it's like to fall in love. Even better, to have someone love me back. Is that too much to ask?"

Fourteen

ALLY FORCED her stare to hold Chip's, her heartbeat thundering like a thousand wild horses charging dry ground. She'd exposed her deepest wish. *To love. To be loved. And all her insecurities over having neither.* Now, even though she lay comfortably beside him, the Mirabelle's burble colluded with the sun's soft flicker through the trees, painting a calming scene that laughed at her misery over not being able to read his thoughts.

For so long, she'd worried there was something wrong with her. Something everyone else but her could see. Like she missed some crucial piece that made her strike out on love time and time again.

So maybe Chip could provide some answers. He'd be leaving soon, so what risk did he have in telling her the truth?

Or maybe he'd offer more of the same. *Rejection. Indifference.* Her vulnerability in this moment once again amounting to nothing.

His attention drifted over her face before he leaned in and kissed her forehead. "There's nothing wrong with you."

His gentle delivery lingered in her ears, and he went on to stroke the pad of his thumb over her cheek, giving his words more weight than any hollow platitude. "You're perfect, Ally. To me anyway."

Her breath stilled, and she blinked at him. Numb. Stupidly silent.

Her muscles warming at his sentiments while her fingers coiled into the soft grass beneath her hand. "Well then, maybe there's something wrong with you too?"

He gave a soft laugh, and though she told herself he might be just like the others—only meaning to be nice—the slow smile at his lips didn't say nice. Nor did his steady eye contact. All signs of emotions he refused to utter out loud.

Or maybe that's just my wild imagination again.

He blew a hard breath and rolled onto his back, his stare pinned to the sky. "Okay, let's figure this out. Why do you think relationships just aren't happening for you?"

Though his diversion snaked cold reality through her body, the fact he blinked at the great blue yonder, his Adam's apple bobbing as he swallowed, offered some comfort that he too felt heartsick at not being able to simply suggest himself as the remedy.

"I don't know." She rolled onto her back, too, once again using his arm as a pillow. "Despite what you've seen from my quarrel with Sarah, I generally avoid conflict and try my best to be the fun girl. I'm not *that* bad to look at." She peered up at him and shrugged. "Fun and at least a little attractive, shouldn't that be enough?"

He stroked a hand over her hair, returning his focus to the sky. "On a surface level, sure, but maybe the timing just hasn't been right?"

She spluttered a small laugh and shook her head. "I doubt it. Look at Laila, twenty-six and already divorced with a kid. Meanwhile, I never even left the starting block."

"Don't tell me you're jealous of Laila?" Through his flat delivery, his attention returned to her with a raised brow. "Sarah's told me a little about your sister's troubles and—"

She laughed again, fuller this time, and she gave him a light shove in the ribs. "Not jealous in *that* way. Laila's had a rough time, that's for sure, but there was a time when she and Mike were unmistakably in love. I look at her with Whitney now, and on a personal level, she still has so much more than I do."

"I still think she'd trade places with you in an instant."

The gleam in his eye held an air of confidence that compelled her to concede. "Maybe."

Meanwhile, despite her list of confessions, she still seemed to know so little about him.

"And what about you?" She nudged her chin at him and tried not to think about how he'd ravished her not that long ago. How she still wanted him to ravish her. "Any past significant others?"

He twisted his focus back to the sky. "Nope."

She kept her attention on him and frowned, even though he likely couldn't see. "I would have thought you'd have your pick of women."

He shrugged again. "It's not that straightforward. Besides, having a *pick* only helps if you're looking for nothing in particular, which is nice enough, sometimes. But there's something to be said for quality over quantity."

She nodded at the sky, burying the sting within her chest at how much she didn't want him to expand on his indiscriminate picks.

"We should go." The words fell from her without much thought, although those words made up one of her few mature decisions in living memory.

She and Chip only tortured themselves here. If recent months had taught her anything, she needed to keep her feelings to herself, especially when the odds pointed to disappointment.

She sat and dusted loose grass blades off her legs, ignoring the way his stare burned into her, giving him her back as she left for the picnic blanket and her sheer blue wrap.

Chip followed and soon helped clear the blanket, her heart twinging at the reminder that they'd never even gotten around to having that picnic.

So she set to filling the sorrowful silence. "If you could be anything in the world, what would you be?"

He straightened and stared at her, the bend of his brow denoting confusion though his glower soon lightened, and a smile graced his face. "That's easy. A mantis shrimp."

He shrugged and went about shaking out the plaid blanket, folding, then rolling it into submission, as though his answer somehow came with an implicit explanation.

Willing to put her usual ignorance on display, she tugged her fat beach bag off the ground and onto her shoulder, then spoke again. "Why would you want to be a shrimp?"

"Not just any shrimp." He chuckled, turning toward the car though his attention lingered on her. "A *mantis* shrimp."

"Yeah. I'm sure that makes all the difference." Having expected a more meaningful answer, she rolled her eyes at his turned back.

"Hey, a mantis shrimp is the meanest sea creature there is." He slowed, bringing his stride level with hers.

Meanwhile, she pressed a button on her car keys, the indicators flashing in reply, the vehicle now unlocked. "Somehow I doubt that."

"Hear me out, okay?" He ran in front of her and pressed his hands to her shoulders to stop her stride, although the pure joy on his face alone could have done that. "While human eyes have only three color receptors, the mantis shrimp has *sixteen*. Not only can that badass see colors we can't even conceive of, but they have these two raptorial appendages at the front of their bodies that enable them to strike their prey at a velocity equal to a bullet."

"Reptile appendages?" She wrinkled her nose and reeled back a step. "Eww."

He held a stunned silence, then laughed, and swatted in a dismissive gesture. "*Raptorial appendages.* Never mind. Anyway, they strike with so much force that they can set off a process called *supercavitation.*"

His unmistakable joy didn't fade, but his persistence hinted that she should have understood his line of thought here, all while she tried not to gawp, because she most definitely did *not* understand. "Super what now?"

"Supercavitation." His smile softened, as did his tone, as though he found her confusion endearing. "Mantis shrimp move so fast and with so much force, the water around them boils and sends a shockwave strong enough to, even if they miss, still kill their prey from the resulting shockwave alone."

She blinked and shook her head. "Wow. Okay."

Her breathless answer had less to do with mantis shrimp and more to do with Chip unleashing full geek-mode on her, an ability she'd forgotten about over the years, which still carried the power to leave her in his intellectual dust.

His smile faded, and new shadows formed below his eyes. "That wasn't the answer you were looking for, was it?"

"No, it's fine." She cleared her throat and forced a reassuring smile. "I just didn't expect mantis shrimp to be your answer."

Nor did I expect being left in his intellectual dust to be so arousing this time around.

His eyes narrowed as though he analyzed her reaction, his shrewd stare only deepening the wild flutter blooming low in her tummy. So, she did the one thing that would save her and stalked around him, only stopping when she reached her car.

"What about you?" His voice followed her before the man himself appeared at the passenger side door. "What would you be?"

She took her time tossing her bag through her door and onto to the backseat, *umming* as though she hadn't considered her answer a million times before. "A drop of water in the ocean, I guess."

"Water?" He slid into his seat, and she followed into hers behind the steering wheel, his focus holding while they buckled seatbelts.

"Yah know, so I could travel to lots of places?" She played at casual and started the engine, commencing the short drive toward his house, even though her nails dug into the steering's leather, once again. At this rate, her car would soon be sporting claw marks. "Every time I made it to a river, I'd see different lands. That's kind of cool, right?"

"Or you might just evaporate." He sent forth his endearing smile, and she chuckled as she refocused on the road.

He probably figured he had her there, but she'd accounted for evaporation too. "Even better. I'd float to the sky and become a part of the clouds. For a while, I'd be closer to the stars before turning into rain and falling back to earth to start the adventure all over again."

"Wow." She didn't look at him, but his voice had a breathy and bright edge. "Miss Egan can science."

Laughter burst from her, and she caught him chuckling back.

"But seriously, is Harlow really so bad these days?"

His long silence signaled a genuine desire for an answer. So, she stifled a frown at the sight of his driveway and gave him what he wanted. "No, and that's the problem. Nothing's changed since you left. *Nothing.* Literally everyone I know and love is here, and my family is so great that separating myself from them, in any way, feels like betrayal. So, apart from a few short trips around Minnesota, I've never really been anywhere else."

Despite the ache of offering that admission, she pulled into his driveway and set the handbrake, turning to get a full look at him. "What was it like, Chip? Yah know, leaving?"

He squinted against the glare through the windshield, his face otherwise lax and heartbreakingly still, as though he contemplated all that she'd said, along with his answer.

"It was tough." He pressed his lips together and gave her a weak frown. "Everything was unfamiliar. The people in Boston had a completely different way of doing things. The pace was fast, and no one ever had time. I guess that's the thing about Harlow. Home was always less about the location and more about the people, and that's what I missed most."

She tried to ignore the muscles bunching in her throat and offered him a joking sort of smile. "Did you miss me?"

His gaze didn't leave her, and he didn't blink, his face not at all mirroring her humor. "More than anyone."

More silence took over, heavier than before while neither looked away, and her heart pounded hard against her ribcage.

What to say next? What to *do*?

She knew what she *wanted* to do, but they'd already decided against that, hadn't they?

Though she could barely breathe, she focused on her hand resting on the center console and searched for more words. Words being the safer option.

"I missed you too." Her voice cracked a little, and so she fought to distract from that small weakness by meeting his gaze, the depth of what she had to say growing with every second. "I guess that's how I ended up latching on to Sarah. Every conversation with her returned little pieces of you. I wish I could have gone up to visit, but you just seemed so far away."

"You could have called." He held a pause that wrenched her heart.

"You could have asked to swing by anytime. I would have found a way to get you to Boston."

She shrugged and gave a tight laugh. "You coulda called too."

But she understood that the years had a way of escaping. That imposing on another person, even just to say, "Hello" wasn't always as simple as picking up the phone. "Anyway, I guess the years got away from me too, and I figured you'd moved on from everything to do with this little town. Can't say I blame you."

"Ally"—the heat of his hand caught hers, and she blinked down to where their palms met, his fingers now interlocked with hers—"you were always welcome."

Her lips parted, but for the longest time, she couldn't speak through the deep ache just begging for him to pull her close. She wanted to drown in the details of who he'd become. To lose the fear of what would happen if she did. As well as the fear of what would become of her when he inevitably left.

"It's not fair." That whisper crumbled past her lips, but his hand clasped hers a little tighter, like he understood. Like he wanted her to explain further. So, she scoffed and continued, "Up until a few days ago, you were just some kid from my past. Someone I learned to live without and merely thought on from time to time. And just as I'd come to figure I'd survive fine on my own, with my feet planted firmly on the ground, here you come along again, changed, and still a little the same. All too quick to turn my world upside down."

"That was never my intention."

"I know."

His brow dipped lower, even though she couldn't decide what emotion ran through him. Guilt? Annoyance? Maybe he still figured she blamed him for upending her life? Maybe, despite her assurances, she did and he had.

"We're in the same boat, Ally." His fingers slipped from hers, and the lost connection gouged a hollow high in her tummy—none more so than when he turned and pulled himself from her car.

She stared out at his stalking gait across the dry rock of his driveway and onto the short wooden steps of his front porch. Stunned into silence, her body moved of its own accord, hands shoving at her car door, her legs storming after him.

She didn't know what she would do when she reached him, but that decision fell out of her control as he spun around and captured her in his arms.

The satisfying crush of his lips gave her no time to gather her senses. He cradled her head in his hands, deepening and directing the kiss until she went with what he offered, only stopping so long as to utter what she'd yearned to say all along. "I don't want to miss out on you."

He pulled away, his stare darting about her face—his breaths exploding, hard and punishing. "What you said back there, it isn't true. I never moved on from *everything* to do with Harlow. I didn't move on from you."

Fifteen

ALLY'S MOUTH DROPPED OPEN, as if she wanted to reply, only for her to snap it shut again and say nothing. Though a weighty silence hung between them, Chip had zero regrets about admitting his "forever like" when it came to her. That he left her stunned and speechless only added to this moment's gratification. Hell, he wanted her stunned and speechless in more ways than one. Wanted to be the one to leave her all scattered and adrift for once.

Prolonging her uncertainty, he studied the details of her pale smooth skin, the flutter of blonde wisps about her face out here on his front porch, the soft pout of her lips—extra red and lush because he'd just been kissing them—all while her watery gaze shifted to a startling and bewildered blue, searching his face for answers.

How could it be he felt in control of this moment while, at the same time, somewhat lost?

Because this can't last.

For once in his life, he didn't want to think. Not about that. Not about the consequences. So, he removed all chance of second thoughts and drew closer, ready to kiss her again, his heart skipping at the quick widening of her pupils. A clue this shift was as monumental to her as it was to him.

Her eyelids drifted shut, giving him permission, and he plunged himself into the distinctive taste of her, heat radiating wherever he touched. Her mouth. Her torso pressed to his. His hands sweeping through her hair and the silk of bare skin around her waist.

This kiss was by no means a dance of coordinated movements. Not while he shoved at his front door, ushering her back with him, stumbling at the step leading inside, the situation worse when his phone began to ring.

He growled and pulled the thing from his pocket, still kissing her and clicking a side button to hang up on whoever called, his next action to toss the obnoxious device somewhere on his couch.

She was like no other woman he'd ever been with or would likely be with again, and impulse urged him to rush, another part of him craving to slow time by even just one more damn minute.

Her hands now clasped the sides of his face, pulling him close, nipping and sucking, and kicking off her shoes. Amongst all the movement, her sheer wrap fell away, and all that stood between him was the minuscule fabric of her polka dot bikini.

He chuckled at that, polka dot bikinis being a very *Ally* thing. Though his chuckle also came from the flurry of elation, this moment itself, so very *Ally*. Fun with an edge of frustration. And just to prove his point, she laughed back, and he scooped her up, her legs almost reflexively wrapping around him, causing the bulge of his sex to nudge hers.

A gentle moan escaped her, and she tipped her head back. He wanted to groan in response, but so many needs clashed all at once, and he dropped his lips to her neck instead, charging with her toward his bedroom.

In no time at all, he had her on his bed. Though there would be regrets here, no matter how much either of them wanted more from his short stay in Harlow, there was one regret he insisted on eliminating.

Her brows furrowed from beneath him in an unmissable question, and he leaned back a little more, giving her space. "Are you sure about this?"

The tension on her face eased, and she offered a fast nod. "Yes. Heck, yes. I want you."

His heart jolted at that unequivocal answer. *Her* answer directed at *him*. He caught her lower lip for another quick kiss, then drew back again, shaking his head. "This is a bit bananas."

Laughter shot from her, and she pressed her forehead to his, speaking through a series of chuckles. "This is A LOT bananas." Her laughter settled to her habitual wide beam, the crinkles at her eyes softening. "But it's nice, isn't it?"

Her voice's light wobble at the end hinted vulnerability. That he might reject her. Perhaps as those who didn't quite understand her had.

The weight of what was about to happen pressed on him. The scars of all her past rejections. That he, too, would be a source of her pain. That he, too, would feel that pain in the weeks to come. So now, all he could offer was a rain of kisses that told her not to worry.

Nothing in life was guaranteed, right? They'd passed enough regrets between them, but he would not regret this. A short summer fling with a woman who'd always, in some way, meant something to him.

So, he allowed her hands to explore his body, to push his shirt over his head—that unveiling rough and hurried—like she, too, ran from what wouldn't last, preferring to cling to what she had right now.

Her palms warmed his chest, and he kept his eyes closed through another hard and needy kiss, shutting out what would hurt him most. The meeting of gazes. What he would find in hers and she in his.

Her delicate fingers traversed lower to his abdomen, her pelvis grinding against his and eliciting a sharp hiss as her fingers curled around the band of his shorts. He stopped. Eyelids flinging open. If he didn't maintain control, if he let himself fall too far here, she'd break his world into pieces he would never be able to pick up.

So, he took his lips from hers and sat, catching her hand and relocating it to a spot beside her head. Uncertainty filled her eyes, but not so much that she didn't seem to catch his message. She should lay still. Allow him to set the pace.

Next, he slipped the straps of her bikini down, then pulled the knotted string between her small breasts. The dart of her gaze warmed his face, but he didn't return her stare, his focus caught on this gradual reveal. The push of one bikini cup aside, then the other, his length growing at the sight of her radiant skin and two perfect, pink nipples calling for his attention.

For this brief moment, Ally Egan was his. *All his.* Beautiful, sprawled, and ready beneath him. Though he didn't want to wait, he made himself savor this image, to file it in some deep and impenetrable corner of his mind, one that might survive anything life and old age would impose on him one day. He drew his hand down to the last of her clothes, again taking his time in another sweet unveiling.

The bend of her legs helped him, and his vision soon filled with the dusting of light blonde curls at the juncture of her sex. He reached out to her now, her breath catching as he placed his palm over her right breast, his gaze finally hitting hers, though he failed to move his lips to comment on her perfection.

No words seemed enough, so he set about making her *feel* instead, leaning to capture a nipple between his lips, teasing her with his tongue until she arched into him and sighed out her pleasure.

He swept his arms under her ribcage and pressed her into him, intensifying his hold and the pressure on her breast. Her hands were quick to find the back of his head, her short nails rewarding him with a mild and gratifying ripple of pain.

He wanted to take her quickly, but this moment seemed so fleeting, and so he kept his mission to preserve her in his memory. He'd already captured the sound of her moan in his brain, the sheer arousal in having her laid out before him. Naked. Hair fanned over his pillow. Each heavy sigh demanding more.

He logged it all and searched further, to the gentle resistance of her tummy calling for his lips, his kisses there filling his senses with her soft scent. Before long, he slid his hands under her to the dip of her back, proceeding lower still until she once again moved through reflex and opened for him.

He paused to appreciate her there, all glistening and pink folds belying any secrets she might seek to keep on her state of arousal. *And she wasn't alone.*

His every nerve ending prickled and stung for her, but he dared to meet her gaze again, her wide-eyed bewilderment returning as though she read his thoughts before he even formed them.

He could have touched her some more, but this first time—perhaps his *only* time with her—was about holding on to as much as he could, and his mouth was far more sensitive than his hands.

So he drew lower and landed a tentative kiss to the center of her arousal, the instant shuttering of her eyes and her ensuing low purr, spurring him on.

Her supple sweetness caught him as did her taste, and he pushed her wider, intensifying his pressure. His heart near exploding on her drawn-out moan.

If molten silk could be a thing, as well as a person, then Ally Egan would be it—hot, sleek, and oh so responsive—the sound of his name on her desperate cry, shattering his last intention to hold her back. Compelling him to use his hands as well as his mouth.

Once again, his name tore from her, ragged and raw. Though her legs fought to close around him, he held her pinned and challenged her not to run from the sensations he drew.

In time, she eased and seemed to redirect any strain to her fingers clawing at his sheets, the unbroken pace of his touch within and around her turning her cry to an unmistakable, full-body shudder.

He pulled away only long enough to shuck off the last of his clothes and retrieve a condom from his bedside drawer. She arched against him, her climax still pulsating in time for him to enter her on one firm and unapologetic thrust.

Though he would have loved to go slower, the firm clench of her around him forced him to drive into her hard and fast—his movements wild and his breaths bursting from him about as quickly as this moment passed by.

And even as his climax rose and swept him under, his awareness of Ally didn't fade. She embodied his pleasure and touched his soul. *As if he even believed in souls.* But then, she had that effect on him. She colored his world and made him want to believe in the unbelievable— even as his lips claimed hers in a search to cling to something real.

Soon, he rested his forehead to hers, their breaths intermingling while he delayed the inevitable as long as he could. He didn't want to leave. Not now. Not ever. But unfulfilled dreams led to resentment, and he'd gleaned enough evidence of that through his parents as well as his conversations with Ally. He simply didn't have what she needed.

So, he withdrew from her, rolling away and taking her with him until her head leaned on his chest, tucked beneath his chin.

"Never thought *that* would happen." Her flat, but joking delivery worked her usual magic of soothing him.

"Me either." He dropped a kiss to her head, pausing to breathe her in some more. "Though admittedly, it's the only thing I've thought of since first seeing you at the ball game."

She snapped her head up, almost taking his chin out with her, her eyes narrowed in a mischievous look. "You horndog."

A grin tugged at his lips, and he did nothing to stop its advance into a full smile. "Not until I met you. Besides, don't lie, you loved it."

The corners of her lips rose as did the glint in her eyes, only for her expression to freeze while she jolted up off him. "What's that sound?"

She peered around the room at large, and he listened as his phone's jaunty tune came into focus. All the way from his couch in the living room.

He growled and folded an arm over his face, wanting to shut out all reminders of the world outside this room. "Clearly, someone who doesn't know when to let up."

The phone stopped ringing, only to start again.

"You probably should get that." She tugged at his arm. "Sounds urgent."

"Fine." Despite his clear reluctance, he gave her a quick kiss through his shuffle out of bed.

Maybe it was another call from Encode. Or maybe some new emergency transpired. Not the Syndicate, again. Not his sister…

A loud bang came from his door just as he hiked his shorts on. "Hey, Chip, are you in there? I know you're home, there's a car in your drive. Open up."

He paused a beat and then swung around to Ally, her eyes taking on an instant wide panic. "What? Who is that?"

He shook his head, momentarily unsure, until the banging started again and along came the words. "Chip, it's Greg. Open up, dude. Jamie and Matt are waiting in the car."

"Who the heck are Greg, Jamie, and Matt?" Her voice lifted to pitchy panic, and she clutched the bedsheets to her chest, her knuckles white and gaze darting about. "Oh God, where are my clothes?"

But she'd entered this room wearing no more than her bikini. There weren't that many clothes to be sought.

More knocking, and his frustration grew. This wasn't how he'd wanted his moment with Ally to end. Hell, he didn't want it to end at all.

"Just hang on a minute, will you?" He yelled clear across the house and pulled a shirt from a pile of clean laundry in a basket by his window, tossing one to Ally too. Next, he lowered his tone and addressed her directly. "Just stay here. I'll handle this. They're college friends, and they weren't supposed to be here till tomorrow."

Sixteen

ALLY SAT ALONE at Chip's kitchen table, save for his three friends who sat across from her, all avoiding her gaze and fidgeting awkwardly with their unoccupied hands. Meanwhile, Chip did as she'd already done and finished his shower, washing away all traces of river water and the earlier lovemaking they'd not-so-secretly engaged in.

She stared down at the table's light timber for what felt like the millionth time, still not sure what to do here.

Did she get up and offer them a drink?

But this wasn't even her house.

Was digging through Chip's fridge even okay?

Where did he even keep his glasses?

The fact she didn't know, plus her frozen state, only drove home just how much she did *not* belong here.

Maybe I could escape out a back window.

Crapola, his friend's car blocked hers in the drive, so even an unannounced escape was out of the question. And to make matters worse, there'd been talk of everyone, including her, heading to Maynard's for the night.

She ran her right foot up the inside of her opposite ankle, pushing at the hem of her ill-fitted pants since she'd been forced to wear some spare clothes Sarah had left behind in the guest room.

Of course, Sarah was a few inches taller, and so Ally's current turquoise sweatpants were way too long, the borrowed peach t-shirt sagging a little low at the neckline too. Still, better than the t-shirt Chip had tossed her in his room.

"Sorry 'bout this." Chip's friend, Jamie—who unexpectedly turned out to be a Black woman with a short and skinny build, wearing a dark t-shirt with Japanese cartoon ninja bunnies printed on the front—cringed. "We planned on arriving tomorrow, but bad weather meant we had to cancel one of our stops. So we figured there'd be no harm driving straight here. We didn't expect…"

Ally closed her eyes against Jamie's trailing words. It was pretty damn clear what his friends had interrupted, and now Ally's cheeks burned, the skin over her neck taking on a hot prickle, her hair still wet from her shower and her makeup long gone.

Jeez Louise, I'm meeting his friends in the most embarrassing way possible.

"It's fine." She opened her eyes and plastered on what she hoped looked like an unbothered smile. "Chip says you're on a road trip and planned on staying a couple of nights to get a taste of where he grew up."

"Yep." Greg squinted his already small blue eyes at her, more a probing look than anything hostile, his focused look bringing attention to the thin and prominent bridge of his nose. "The whole trip ends in San Fran."

"San Francisco?" Ally tucked wet hair behind her ear, happy that at least some semblance of a conversation unfolded.

"Yep." But before she could ask what was in San Francisco, Greg jumped in with, "So, how do you know Chip, anyway?"

"Chip and I have been friends since we were little." Her skin burned anew, and she eyed Matt—with his somewhat squat build and light brown hair—the one friend yet to speak, although his overly still stare said what everyone here probably thought.

She and Chip were clearly something other than friends.

"Oh yeah…" Jamie's voice pitched upward, and she tapped Greg's hand with the back of hers. "Chip once told us about her. Remember that games night last year, playing Settlers of Catan? We all got drunk and started talking about our 'one that got away.'"

"That's right." A wide and goofy grin took over Greg's face, his pale blond fringe flopping over one brow. "Chip said this chick was the closest he got. And let's not forget, I told you all it was a stupid conversation. We're not even in our mid-twenties and don't yet have enough data to collate a worthwhile answer. So, I'm still right, by the way."

Matt burst into laughter. "No, dude. You're the only one who lacks any data."

Greg rolled his eyes, and Jamie just smiled, her dark brown stare on a glass saltshaker she'd swiped from the table's center and now twisted between her palms.

Hoping to stop any future uncomfortable silences, Ally peered around the table and retrieved her unanswered question from earlier. "So, umm… why San Fran?"

Jamie leaned back into her lemon vinyl seat and paused her saltshaker tinkering. "We're hoping to make it all the way to Silicon Valley to catch some tech conferences."

Greg shrugged his shoulders, his oversized cobalt t-shirt hanging off his reedy frame. "Yep, Michelle Ibanez is doing a talk on the next generation Haskell type system, and it's bound to be a life-altering experience."

Ally's face turned cold, and she looked to Jamie for support.

"No one in their right mind expects you to know who that is." This time it was Jamie's turn to roll her eyes. "I think if I hear him mention Michelle Ibanez one more time, I might whack him over the head with the lightsaber he insisted on taking on this trip. "

Matt shook his head, seeming to settle in Ally's presence, the upward tick of his lip directed at her. "As if my car didn't have enough people and stuff crammed into it."

"Hey guys, Chip really should be joining us on this trip, don't you think?" Greg leaned over the table and eyed his friend. "What with his big news, imagine the networking he could do in The Valley."

Ally peered amongst the friends again, confusion weighing heavy on her overly tight brow.

"Nah, dude, he's too busy getting his shit together in time to put on a half-decent show." Matt bumped Greg with his shoulder.

"Show?" Ally frowned, feeling even more the least intelligent person at this table. "Big news?"

"Oh, it's more than big news." Matt leaned toward her, his brown eyes wider and lighter than before. "It's—"

"Hey, guys. No." Jamie glared at Matt, then Greg. "Let Chip tell—"

"Chip got a call from Encode." Greg's smile grew, and the wild glint in his eyes made him appear almost manic. "He's a finalist for this year's Graduate Fund."

Jamie growled and threw her head back as though she wanted to nothing to do with Matt and Greg and whatever ensued next.

"Oh… okay." Ally's voice creaked while she searched for more words, her attention bouncing between the three friends. *Chip's friends.* Who knew more about his *news* and unintentionally made her feel about as bright as a beaten-up lump of coal. The more they spoke, the less she understood.

Matt tilted his head at Greg. "This guy works at Encode so got the jump on this year's finalists via the company newsletter. Chip's idea would have to be out of this world to make it this far."

"What's Encode?" She turned to Greg. "What's a Graduate grant?"

"Encode is one of the biggest tech companies our side of the country, and each year, they offer a grant for new graduates to have one of their ideas made into an Encode product." The wide excitement in Greg's eyes made Ally's tummy churn and a jittery pain grow in her chest. "Imagine that, fresh outta college and already in charge of a project *you* created. I've seen glimpses of Stonewall. I'd be lying if I said I wasn't jealous I didn't come up with those goods."

Jamie toyed with the saltshaker again, giving the impression she tended to fidget even without Ally's earlier clumsy introduction. "What did he end up doing with the buffer overflow problem?"

Though Jamie's attention stuck on Greg, Matt was the one to jump in with an answer. "Oh, maybe he rewrote the memory allocation code! He could have pulled it out into a separate library and then refactored the rest of the code. Might even be able to open source it all later. It's bound to be gold."

"Not a bad idea." Jamie nodded and pushed the saltshaker away as though she once again noticed her restless habit. "Although, I would have just rewritten that part in a memory-safe language. Instead of using C, maybe use Java or even Erlang for bonus fun. Write it as a daemon and then call out to it via RPC. It'll probably increase latency, but you won't need to worry about overwriting anything you shouldn't on the heap, so practically zero chance of segmentation fault."

Matt stared off into space before offering a mumbled, "Yeah, maybe…"

After that, everyone just fell into a confusing silence, where Ally couldn't tell if the conversation had truly died or if the others just puzzled through the current trouble-shooting related topic.

Meanwhile, she felt just about as clueless as ever, if cluelessness meant having a mind that worked double-time to understand, only to draw constant blanks…

Why hadn't Chip told her about making the finals of this grant thing his friends fawned over?

Maybe I mean less to him than I assumed.

Then again, what ARE we to each other?

Barely even friends. So maybe I don't have a right to assume anything.

"Anyway"—Greg's voice pulled at her attention, his chin dipping and his stare drilling into her—"let's just say, we're making Chip pick up the tab tonight. The man is on the fast track to becoming a multi-millionaire."

"What?" Her voice squeaked, and a sharp ache dug at the insides of her throat. Not because of the money, so much as the magnitude of how little she knew about a man she'd just shared a hugely intimate few hours with.

"That's highly presumptuous." Jamie reached out and patted the table between her and Ally, shaking her head as though she caught Ally's surprise and mild heartbreak. "Forget about what Greg said. As you can see from his obsession with Ibanez, he likes to get ahead of himself."

"Like hell, I do." Greg snapped his posture into an impossibly straight position, his chin near disappearing into his neck. "I see Olaf Garner, the Encode winner from two years ago, all the time. Not a day goes by when he doesn't pull up to the office in his yellow Ferrari, flashing cash, and dating supermodels like it's nothing. By the way, the Ferrari alone costs like, six hundred grand, only a fraction of what the guy makes since his project went public."

An icy shiver zinged up Ally's spine, and she tried not to visibly tremble.

Why didn't Chip tell me? Why didn't he tell me?

Had he simply forgotten? But as Greg had said, this *was* big news. Not the sort of thing someone as sharp-minded as Chip just "forgot."

Maybe she didn't know him as well as she thought. Maybe she'd held on to far too much of the well-meaning boy she'd once known. Maybe the man she'd been with today wasn't so innocent after all, his lack of transparency a testament to the distance he intended to keep with her. She'd voiced a desire to get out of Harlow. It wasn't a stretch that Chip might fear she'd see him as her ticket out.

Then again, his motivations for secrecy could be far worse. That he used her as a way to blow-off steam while he finished his work in this sleepy and otherwise boring town. He'd abandon her once again, only his path this time led to a far more glamorous destination—so far removed from anything anyone in Harlow could ever imagine.

"Okay. Ready to go?" The man himself entered the room, and everyone turned to Chip in another heavy and collective silence. He peered about, his bright and unassuming smile dipping to a small frown. "What? What did I miss?"

Her heart gave an uncomfortable and hard thump. She hated where her mind had gone with regards to this man. Hated that she had to hide her raging and raw emotions in front of him and his friends.

So she rose from her seat and tried not to wince at the pitchy scrape of those metal legs over the floorboards. "I think I'll go. This is a reunion between college friends, and I'm not one." She offered Chip a tight smile and mini wave as she powered toward the exit. "I'll catch you tomorrow, maybe."

Her heart lurched once more, the uncertainty behind her "maybe" literal in meaning. The front door loomed just up ahead, but the steady pound of Chip's footfall caught her all too soon.

"Hey"—heavy hands landed on her shoulders, and he spun her around, his gaze darting about her face in a probable search for reasons behind her hurried exit—"I'm sorry, my friends…"

His intimate whisper trailed, but his hand snaked around her waist as though he'd already figured her mood ran deeper than today's already unpleasant surprise visit.

But even as she reeled at her far-too-sobering brush with reality, the touch of his hand at her waist sent a small flutter through her tummy. *There he went again.* Literally. Figuratively. Pulling her in.

"This…" She paused, clearing her throat to distract from the hot prickle behind her eyes. "It's all too much."

The tension across his brow dropped, and his expression turned slack and incredulous. "Which part exactly? My friends showing up, or—"

Not wanting to hear him talk of their intimate moment, she squeezed her eyes shut and uttered, "Everything. It's *everything.*"

And as she opened her eyes again, she schooled her voice into something more defiant than a rough whisper, stabbing her finger toward the kitchen where his friends sat. "I have nothing in common with your friends. I mean, sure, there's one girl there, but she's—"

"A geek?" A smile wobbled the corner of his lip.

"Yes, a geek. And your friends intimidate me. So, I can't go to Maynard's with you. The conversation will get technical, and I'll have nothing to do but down one drink after another, which will only make you regret inviting me along."

"I doubt that."

She let out an exasperated sigh and leaned into him, tracing a finger along his hairline for no other reason than, at this rare moment, she still could. "Remember in sixth grade when our school ran a math competition? Not only did you beat the rest of the school, but you went all the way to place second at the nationals."

His brow drew, the new wrinkles there belying confusion. "Yeah?"

"Remember how I was like the third student knocked out in our class, just behind Paul Chester and Paolo Diaz—a kid who could probably still do math way better than me but for being only in his fifth week of living in an English-speaking country?"

His mouth curled into a small smile. Even back then, he'd found humor in her academic failure. Though to be fair, most times, she did too. "Yeah?"

"Well"—she eased back and out of his hold—"that's what it feels like when I'm talking to your friends."

"Ally." He took a few hurried steps and followed her hand pressed to his front door, set for her escape. "I can tell them to steer clear of any shop talk."

She gestured down at her outfit, which wasn't even *her* outfit. "Still a hard pass. Look at me. The patrons at Maynard's might not notice these are Sarah's, but she sure as heck will. And then she'll take one look at me with you and know exactly *why* I'm wearing her clothes."

His cheeks sank, suggesting he finally accepted her many reasons for leaving, even though he really didn't want to. "Greg's car is blocking yours, just let me get his keys, okay?"

Even though she nodded her understanding, he didn't move right away, his attention sticking like he sought to hold on to her just one moment more.

Perhaps he sensed it too. That she wasn't ditching him, but that an indisputable time limit still hung over this relationship.

So, she sought to help him out, already catching the double-meaning in her words before they even left her mouth. "Thanks for helping me leave."

Seventeen

DISPLAYS of potted flowers surrounded Ally at Aggie's nursery. Those full blooms mingling with the giggle of children. Ally's heart soared at the scene, a perfect mix of beauty, mess, and noise, where multiple small tables spread across the open space designated for her art class.

With the children here extra receptive to her bouts of goofiness and creativity, she felt at home. At least, so much more than yesterday when she'd tried and failed to fit in with Chip's friends.

Though her heart still sank at that memory, she forced her mind to the midmorning's brilliant weather, the gentle sun enhancing the earthy sweetness emanating from the nearby plants, then the chalky smell of paint from her table where children decorated mini plant pots.

Aggie McKey stood in a far-off corner, entertaining parents and offering refreshments, the older woman's joy at having so many people at her nursery evident in her beaming smile. Meanwhile, Emilia sat at Ally's table too, having volunteered to paint faces, her deep brown gaze snagging on Ally. "So, how did things go with Chip? Am I allowed to send him an invite to the wedding yet?"

"It's your wedding, you can do whatever you want." Heat rose in Ally's cheeks, and she kept busy passing a plant pot to a small boy to her right.

A beat passed, only for Emilia to speak again. "Sure I can, but we both know you were headed to see him after I spoke with you yesterday, and your evasive reply makes me think things didn't go so well."

"Wrong." Ally let out a tight chuckle and reached for the paint palette the turning child beside her elbowed off the table, thankful to catch the thing long before it hit the ground. "I can tell you from recent experience that things can get better *and* worse all at once."

"Oh no." Emilia lowered her voice, her expression suddenly pinched. "What happened?"

Ally let out a sigh. "Let's just say, things got more serious than either of us planned, and then Chip's friends staged a surprise visit, which is when I learned his life away from Harlow is far more prestigious than he let on."

"Hang on a minute." Emilia sent forth a sideward stare. "Serious, as in…"

That stare, along with her trailing voice, hinted she asked whether things had gotten physical between Ally and Chip. Given all the inquisitive minds around, the conversation needed to stay restrained, so Ally gave a slow and confirming nod.

Emilia's jaw dropped open, and she mouthed the word, "What?" before turning to gesture to the little girl she'd finished painting that she could go.

"You have to tell me how that all came about. I mean, not now because of kids, but…" She smiled at a little boy stepping up for his turn to have his face painted. "Eventually."

Ally chuckled, although the sound held a tight edge of bitterness. "Well, all you need to know is, he has a huge opportunity knocking at his door. Any day now, he'll be too busy being a super-star tech guru in Boston to show his face round these parts ever again."

"Well, there goes my chance of having him at the wedding." Emilia kept her tone flat, and her attention fixed on transforming her latest face-painting subject into Spiderman. "But *ouch*. That explains your vague answer. Let me guess, you like him too much already, and you're worried he'll be too busy for you?"

"You know me so well, it's scary." Ally scrunched the corner of her lip, not completely ready to admit her fears out loud. "But him being busy is the best-case scenario from what his friends had to say. I figure it's more likely his new life will take him places that will have him completely forgetting I even exist. Not that I blame him."

She checked the time on her phone. With just another twenty minutes left of today's program, the children needed to switch workstations one last time. So she clapped her hands to get their attention. "Okay, everyone, it's that time again. Stop what you're all doing and move to the next table."

The children's voices grew louder, the relative peace abandoned for pushing chairs aside and racing to new tables. A hard tug came at the waist of her lavender summer dress, and Whitney stared up at her. "Aunt Ally, can I stay at your table? I don't want to move."

Ally bobbed to meet her four-year-old niece at eye-level, her gaze skipping to the potting table Whitney was due to visit next. "You don't want to plant your own flower to take home to show your mom? I'm sure Jenna will help you if you don't know what to do. She's got a special way with gardens, yah know?"

She lifted her gaze and waved at Jenna, a waitress at Maynard's, who also dabbled as a landscaper through the nursery, her presence today an early attempt at returning to work following a recent accident. The woman paused shifting potted plants onto a cart and waved back.

"It's not that, Aunt Ally." Whitney's tiny voice had Ally peering down again. "I'm scared."

"Really, now?" She gave a trouble-free smile and offered Whitney comfort in the form of a pat on the back. "Want to tell me what scares you?"

"Spiders." Whitney scrunched her face, and her eyes turned watery. "Last time I played in Nan and Popo's garden, a big black spider jumped out of the soil. It tried to eat me."

Ally bit back a laugh but recalled her own childhood fears of spiders. So, she tilted Whitney's chin upwards and gave her a light kiss on the nose. "Well then, there's nothing to it. You stay at my station next to me, and since you've got a knack for painting, we'll get Miss Emilia to spare one of her brushes, so you can paint my face."

"Really?" Whitney's cheeks lifted with an exuberant smile, the glint in her eyes a good sign that Ally would come to regret the offer, even though her smile broke loose too. Whitney, like almost all children, had an affinity for finding joy in life's little happy turns.

Emilia, having heard the exchange, handed the girl a brush while lifting her brow at Ally in an, "Are you sure about this?" expression.

Ally nodded and reclaimed her seat, Emilia's sideways glance continuing. "You're at least a little happy for Chip though, right? It sounds like he's going places."

"Sure, I am." Ally shrugged, her face hot because she should have felt prouder than she did. "For someone from these parts to be so talented, that Chip is making an impact on the wider world…" She paused, distributing pots for this new batch of kids to paint. "I just wish we had more time, yah know?"

Spiderman junior finished, Emilia changed kids again. Soon, she dipped a wet brush into her dry paint palette and then went about applying a vibrant purple unicorn horn to the forehead of the new girl before her. "Time to figure out if your relationship has potential?"

"I don't know." Ally's voice turned husky, and she blinked down at her lap, the cold tip of Whitney's paintbrush hitting her cheek. "Our potential is there, but Chip wasn't the one to tell me about his new opportunity, his friends were, and I guess that leaves me with more than a few doubts and questions."

As well as a sense that an end between us is inevitable, because in the end, I'm not sure I want to leave Harlow forever, and I'm not sure he'd even want me to go with him.

So, inevitable and painful. So much worse than any other guy-related heartbreak I've experienced so far.

"But, I mean, you got to meet his friends, Ally. That's kinda big."

"Emilia, I met his friends by accident, remember? Now focus. What am I supposed to do about all this?"

Emilia laughed and wrinkled her nose at the girl in front of her, a smiley little girl who—aside from her purple unicorn horn—now had a black pirate patch painted around her right eye. "Look, I haven't had the chance to speak with Chip in any great way, but everyone keeps telling me he's a guy worth knowing. Maybe he simply didn't get a chance to tell you about his opportunity yet? Maybe he didn't want to get your hopes up, or down, depending on what happens?"

"Because, once again, he'll be leaving me behind." Ally scoffed. "Let down is just the tip of how I feel now that I know."

"Okay, well, that first time he left, you were kids. And this time, you already knew he'd be leaving. So, what's changed?" Emilia shrugged, her focus not on Ally as she painted away. "Why not stick with the original plan and give the guy a chance to explain?"

"I know. I know. I guess I just didn't want the truth quite so soon after, we... we... Yah know." She winced at another cold slap of paint on her forehead from Whitney, that cold slap a welcome excuse to pause and take stock of the conflicted emotions churning in her belly since yesterday. "Things are so new and changing so fast. I don't think I even have a right to confront him over what his friends told me, much less his leaving. He knows about my Dean dramas and is probably looking for signs of me being clingy. I don't want to scare him away. And about his friends, they're so... just so incredibly different. The years apart have turned me into an outsider. One thing's for sure, I'm nowhere near on the same level as Chip."

Emilia jerked her chin back in a look of surprise. "Well, now *that's* a broad statement if ever I heard one. I wouldn't know the first thing about building furniture or mending broken window fittings. Meanwhile, Blaine grew up far from the upper echelons of L.A. society, and still we get along great. You know, opposites attracting and all."

Emilia patted the girl she'd been painting on the shoulder, allowing her to run along and show her parents her new pirate-unicorn face.

Ally stopped to let the boisterous noises around her, as well as Emilia's advice, lift her spirits. "Maybe you have a point."

With no more children left in line, Emilia turned and gave Ally her full attention. "So then, maybe quit fretting about the what-ifs and talk to Chip? You'll have no answers until you do, so do it today before your doubts fester into something bigger." Emilia gave an unfazed shrug paired with a quick smile. "And in the meantime, I have some news that will keep you fretting over something else entirely."

"I'm not sure I like that idea of more fretting, but I'll take any distraction you can offer."

Emilia clapped her hands in a fast and excited manner, her shoulders bouncing in unison with her claps. "Remember how I wanted to find a wholesale buyer for your pots? Well, I did. I found someone."

"What?" Ally slapped a hand over her mouth, her sudden loud and high-pitched tone a surprise even to her. She peered around at the nearby children, but no one really looked her way, maybe because loud and high-pitched was normal background noise to this lot.

"Now, don't get too excited." Emilia held both hands up in a gesture for Ally to slow down. "It's still early days, but we have a foot in with Wanda and Stephanie Argyle."

"No way." Ally slipped her hand from her lips, regretting she hadn't taken Emilia's offer to find a distributor for her work more seriously, her voice now a rough whisper. "The Argyles? As in, the chain of boutique nurseries along the East Coast? I've seen their ads, but I've never had a chance to go far enough to visit one of their stores."

"Yep, same Argyles, and they liked the initial photos I sent. They've asked for some physical samples of your work to assess quality and suitability to their brand."

Emilia's words were slow to filter through Ally's excitement. She no doubt wore a wacky smile while her pulse maintained a steady thunder in her ears. "I mean, yah, of course! Take your pick from the pottery studio out back. Just let me wrap things up here, and I'll show you."

Ally stood and called time on the class, allowing the children to go find their parents. Almost as quickly, Emilia slung her purse strap over her shoulder and let loose with one final declaration. "Just so you know, I've decided I'm inviting Chip to the wedding after all. I'm sure it'll be a real hoot if he can make it."

Eighteen

CHIP SAT amongst his friends for one last night at Maynard's before their road trip recommenced in the morning. Though Sarah worked behind the bar, too busy to join the group, Dean wasn't, and Jamie held her wide-eyed stare on him, her mouth still agape. "So Chip *wasn't* joking when he said a crime ring kidnapped his sister?"

Dean shifted his gaze to Chip, his prolonged flat stare asking if he really *did* have to answer Jamie's question.

More awkward silence passed before he let out a sigh and turned back to Jamie. "The Syndicate were out to get me for leaving and hurting Sarah was part of their revenge. Except, she never had any real contact with the Syndicate."

Jamie frowned at Chip. "You said they held her hostage in a freezer?"

Chip shrugged and took another sip of his beer. "Sure did, but Dean's friend, Ramos, infiltrated the Syndicate and ended up being the guy holding her hostage."

"Ramos? So, he kept Sarah safe." Jamie's lips bowed further, and she focused on Dean. "Does he live in Harlow too?"

"No, Ramos is back in L.A., at least for now anyway. He does still sometimes slip Syndicate information to me, but that's getting harder to find since the showdown with Luciano folded the Syndicate's West Coast branch. Last I heard, the feds are now focusing on the East Coast arm."

Chip set his bottle down on the table with a light *thunk*, tension drawing high in his belly. "That sounds ominous."

"In that the Syndicate still exists? You bet." Dean, a real roll-with-the-punches-and-don't-sweat-the-rest type, showed no true concern on his face, although he did twist the brown-glass neck of his beer bottle between his fingers. "The East Coasters are harder to nail down. Far more sophisticated. Less blatant thug, more stealthy corporate shark. Even in my days at the Syndicate, the East Coasters already had plans to shift toward a more legitimate facade of making bank, buying up large companies and the like. Though, I doubt their hands will ever stay clean."

Dean's warning settled like a lead ball in Chip's brain, and he blew out a hard breath, the man's description of the Syndicate a million times more menacing and insidious than anything he'd experienced. Not that he had any experience with crime rings. "I don't know how you kept yourself and Sarah safe that day."

Dean shook his head, clearly still blaming himself for Luciano's inability to leave well enough alone. "All I know is, I'll do anything to stop something like that happening again. And believe me, knowing the Syndicate, I can't, in all honesty, say their beef with me is over now that Luciano is gone."

Silence befell the table, and Chip stared down at his drink until a bottle top *pinged* to a stop before him on the table. He glanced up at Greg, now jabbing his chin toward the entrance. "Isn't that your girl over there?"

Sure enough, Ally stood before the doors wearing a floaty, knee-length dress speckled with giant sunflowers, her gaze quick to meet his, her habitual smile slipping the moment her attention hit Dean. Still, she padded over, her fingers digging into the leather of a small, violet clutch that acted as a barrier between her and everyone else.

Jamie pulled out the empty seat beside her and offered it to Ally, while Ally's greeting to Chip was no more affectionate than a simple and overly safe "Hello."

He tilted his head to one side and sent her a *What gives?* look, although his actual words were far tamer. "I didn't expect to see you here."

The tension over her face faded, and she at least didn't shy from giving him a direct stare. "I felt bad about skipping out on you yesterday and wanted to see your friends again while I had the chance."

In an apparent peace offering, she smiled out to the others at the table, her joy once more drying when she got to Dean. His presence a seemingly sad reminder of what had passed between the two. Even if Dean made no sign of being bothered. Though, once again, not all that much bothered Dean.

"Hey, Ally"—Jamie nudged her with an elbow—"hope these two didn't upset you too much yesterday spilling Chip's news like that."

"News?" Chip narrowed his eyes at Jamie. "What news?"

Though Jamie opened her mouth, Ally's giggle interrupted any potential reply, and she swatted a hand in a gesture to let the subject go. "No, it's fine. It was just a surprise. That's all."

Her reaction, plus the fact he still had no answer, had him glaring at the guy most likely to defy all social cues and speak. Greg. "What news?"

"Dude." Greg gave a condescending grimace, one that said he thought Chip was slow on the uptake. "Your Encode grant."

Chip's world stilled, and he looked to Ally. Her quick exit yesterday and sheepishness today made a whole lot more sense.

"You got the grant already?" Dean's question pulled Chip's focus away.

"No, I've only—"

Ally's lips parted in Dean's direction before she spoke. "You knew?"

But her attention didn't stay on him long, her gaze flicking to Chip with a small and incredulous shake of her head. "*He* knew?"

Her clear disappointment brought a pang to Chip's heart, and he groaned, pressing his hands to his face and adding in his own head shake. "No. He didn't know any more than you. And no, there's no money."

Though he dropped his hands, ready to ask why his news even upset her, Matt took his turn to interrupt.

"Here we go again." Matt huffed out a big, exasperated sigh. "You're playing yourself down, Chip. Making these finals is a *huge* deal. If you get it, there's a huge target on your back as a tech genius in the making, and you're set for life. If you don't get the grant, well, pretty much every other tech company out there will at least be interested in looking at your ideas."

He flared his eyes at Matt, a non-verbal order for him to shut up before Chip's attention instinctively turned to Ally again, her lips pressed into a tight line and her bare shoulders rounded. The shift of her gaze away from his made his world slow, a new understanding taking over.

He *hadn't* told her. He'd slept with her but hadn't revealed this part of his life. *Why?* Right there and then, he wanted to explain, but any explanation would bring up personal details neither his friends nor Dean needed to hear.

"The way Sarah talks about you I'm sure you're a shoe-in, man." Dean gave Chip a congratulatory clap on the back. Chip jolted from the impact but couldn't pry his attention from Ally.

She still clutched at her purse in her lap, although now, her gaze drifted to Sarah behind the bar. He reached under the table for Ally's hand, her stare hitting his, only to bounce to Dean and then back to Sarah. Just before she pulled her hand away.

Maybe he should have questioned her move, but in that moment, he wasn't all that sure he deserved to. Or that he blamed her. What assurances had he given? Not that he had any to give, not with where his chance with Encode would take him.

He'd move up and move on. Meanwhile, she'd stay in Harlow and deal with the million-and-one questions and comments the townsfolk would have about this brief relationship.

He peered back at the bar, momentarily wondering how much of Ally's aversion had to do with her quarrel with Sarah. How much had to do with her past feelings for Dean?

Even if Dean was a decent guy, undeserving of jealousy, the

reminder of Ally's infatuation alone left Chip's stomach churning and an angry heat boring deep into his chest.

Focus on Ally.

So, he turned to her again and pretended he didn't mind her keeping her distance in public, even though he did. "Want me to get you a drink?"

Her gaze snapped from the bar back to him, the strain around her eyes only easing slightly with her small nod. "White wine. Thanks."

She moved to open her purse, but he left before she could offer any money.

Quick to make his way to the bar, Sarah soon leaned against the counter, her easy grin pointed at him. "What's your poison now?"

"Just a white."

An expected silence took over, her fading grin hinting at her recollection that white wine wasn't his usual drink. As expected, her stare skidded to his table, no doubt quick to find Ally.

"Oh, for Ally?" She blinked up at him now, new wrinkles forming over her brow. "She's welcome to come over here and ask for the drink herself, yah know? There's no reason to keep avoiding me."

He gave a light shrug, even though his sister's clear and lingering animosity made him feel anything but light. "Maybe for you."

Giving a small snort, she went about pouring the drink anyway. "Funny how she's fine to sit with Dean though. She hasn't been to Maynard's for months but—"

Halfway to sliding the wine his way, she paused, fingers still clutching the glass's thin stem, the lines on her brow returning. Like she didn't miss much, her mind already searching for reasons behind Ally's sudden visit.

So, of course, he made quick with trying to distract her. "Ally's being awkward around Dean too. You're not so special."

Sarah raised a brow and finished handing him the drink, one side of her lip creeping upward. "Why *is* Ally here tonight, anyway?"

Her attention washed over him, and all the lightness in her expression collapsed, suggesting he didn't need to answer. "Say it isn't so."

He gave another disingenuous shrug. "How about I just say nothing?"

"Oh, Chip." The weakness in her tone denoted concern over anger, concern the more unnerving emotion that prompted him to step away.

Whatever warnings or doubts she had, he already nursed his own. The last thing he wanted was to hear those doubts spoken out loud.

"I'll speak to you later." He swept up the wine glass in his hand and made to leave.

"Let me talk to her."

Sarah's offer left him pausing midstep before he eventually found the ability to keep his back to her and lengthened his retreat. "You're a good egg, Sarah Overton, but not today. Just not today."

Things with Ally already stood rocky. Maybe that rockiness didn't matter. He was leaving, after all. So, perhaps this latest issue was a good thing. Still, he didn't want issues, much less his sister enlightening Ally with her hot takes on life.

Back at the table, Ally leaned closer to Jamie, Jamie's backpack open in her lap and her laptop open on the table.

"What are you two doing?" He handed Ally her drink and sat beside her—yet more "fake casual" from him now that he also kept Sarah's knowledge about them a secret. On top of what he'd withheld about Encode.

Jamie spun the screen toward him, the laptop alight with her editing program and one of her Japanese style princess drawings on the screen. A princess striking a combat pose. "Ally showed me some photos of her clay work, so it seemed only fair I'd show her my anime art."

"She's amazing." Ally flashed her famous wide grin, and he felt like he could finally breathe again. "I've tried and failed at digital art many times, but Jamie here is a total gun."

"Well if you ever want to try again, you can always hit me up on the socials for help." Jamie pressed her laptop screen closed and peered over to Chip. "And while my art exists only to take my mind off coding problems, your girl here is the real deal."

A wicked smile pulled at Dean's lips. "That's the second person tonight to refer to Ally as *your girl*, Chip. You move fast."

Though Chip's jaw slackened from the shock of another person confronting him over private affairs, Ally cut in with the loud clearing of her throat, her nose crinkled at Dean in a playful expression. "I'm nobody's girl, thank you very much. And way to draw attention from my professional efforts and onto more personal stuff."

Dean held both hands up in surrender. "Well, sorry. Please do share more on your professional life."

While Chip scrambled to acclimate to the dissipated tension since his time at the bar, Ally laughed and sat a little taller. "Well, aside from me coming here to see off Chip's friends, I also wanted to celebrate receiving some potentially exciting news of my own."

Matt laughed and pulled a fry from the table's share plate. "Don't tell me Encode wants you on the payroll too?"

"Close, but not quite." Ally stabbed a finger in his direction, her eyes glittering and her cheeks holding a rosy glow. "My friend, Emilia, has a client interested in distributing my pots to an East Coast chain store."

"No way!" Jamie nudged Ally with an elbow. "Ally, that's great."

Ally held a hand up, indicating she wasn't finished just yet. "It's still early days, and the Argyles have only asked for samples, but it's a start, right?"

"Holy shit! The Argyles?" Jamie grabbed Ally's raised hand and closed her fingers around it in an excited grasp. "My mom shops there all the time. Argyles is her go-to place for housewarming gifts. You should see my apartment. It's full of their groovy pots. I'm pretty sure Mom would set up a tent and live at an Argyles if she could."

"Really?" Ally did a little dance where she sat and turned her joy-filled beam to him. "I knew they were big, but I had no idea."

The muscles in his throat became suddenly too thick, and he struggled to pull his gaze from hers. Not that he wanted to. Only, his news and her news combined to bring his heart to a slow and reluctant beat. "I'm happy for you. I'm really happy for you."

And really, he was. Even as he reached out and stroked the pad of his thumb over her cheek. His way of holding on to her when he knew he couldn't. Even as her smile dimmed, and her attention homed on him like he was the only person in the room, a reminder of just how much it would hurt when they'd have to let go. *Again.*

Caught in the moment, he let himself forget about the others. She had a chance at her artistic dreams. To have money and, therefore, independence. Perhaps one day, she'd travel the world. Just as she wanted.

As much as all those things would lengthen their divide, she didn't pull away from him like she had before, and so he dared to lean in and drop a quick kiss to her lips.

"Wow!"

He turned to Sarah standing across the table with a tray of plates in one hand, her mouth agape. "Onto public displays of affection already? You move fast."

Dean barked out an uncharacteristic, hearty laugh and slapped his knee. "That's what I said."

"I just…" Ally directed a wide expression to Sarah, her ivory skin somehow markedly paler, her jaw wavering like she didn't know how to finish her sentence. A plodding silence held before she shook her head as if to awaken from a nightmare. "This is way more than I planned on for tonight. I'm just going to go."

"No." She winced at his insistence, like just the chance of being convinced to stay brought real physical pain, but he didn't want this rift between Ally and his sister to linger without an attempt to reconcile. "You're both going to talk."

She stood, chair scraping against the floor, her strained attempt at a reassuring smile looking more like a grimace. "No, really, it's fine. I'll see you tomorrow or something."

She took a step away, but he stood and grabbed her hand. "Stay and talk, please."

The skin under her eyes bunched, and her burrowing stare fixed on him before flicking over to Sarah. To his surprise, she gave a rigid nod and so did Sarah.

Ally's hand found his, albeit in a tight hold. Meanwhile, Sarah turned to the neighboring table, serving out the meals on her tray and then twisting back with a tilt of her head for Chip and Ally to follow her.

On the brisk walk to the kitchen, Ally lagged behind, hand still in his even as they crashed through the swinging doors leading to the kitchen.

A mild wave of heat engulfed him. Gordon, Maynard's chef, spun away from the stove. "Hey, what's this about? My kitchen isn't a meeting roo—" A slow smile overtook his face, and he pulled at the tea towel tucked in his apron belt, wiping his hands. "Chip, buddy. I haven't seen you since high school."

If he'd planned to shake Chip's hand, that didn't happen. Though Sarah kept her back to everyone, whatever look she shot Gordon, had him returning to his stove, shaking his head while muttering something inaudible under his breath.

Sarah changed direction, stalking for the narrow passage leading to the backdoor. But rather than continue, she spun around and paused right there, as though she intended to lead this exchange. Only it was Ally who cut in and spoke first.

Nineteen

"You humiliated me." Ally ground the statement out through gritted teeth. In part, so Gordon wouldn't hear from his position by Maynard's stove. But also because of the leashed anger eating her up from the inside.

Now second-guessing her direct approach, she slammed her mouth shut, the kitchen's heat adding to the sharp prickle over her skin because Chip stood right beside her.

For months, she'd held on to her feelings over what Sarah had done. So now she wanted no regrets and swallowed back her unusual shyness, trying again. "You and Dean shared a connection from the very beginning. You could have told me, Sarah. I would have been happy for you. But instead, you let me act on something that didn't exist."

Sarah startled at Ally's words, as though they were a literal slap, her lips wavering in contrast to her usual stoic air before she found her voice. "It's not like Dean and I entered a committed relationship on day one, and to be fair, I spent weeks in denial over how I felt about him. So yes, we had a short prior history, but nothing that justified me fighting off other interested women. Besides, you didn't do anything more than invite yourself to his place with breakfast. You did the exact same for Emilia when she first arrived in town, remember?"

"Hey!" Chip sent her a frown, one that twisted at the corners and denoted humor. "You didn't bring *me* any breakfast."

Ally cringed and shook her head, now not being the time for *that* conversation or humor, though she could always argue she'd cooked him breakfast the morning he'd slept at her parents' house.

"You lived in Harlow once before, so technically, you're not eligible for one of my welcome breakfasts." She gave him a mock scowl and then refocused on Sarah. "Besides, Dean and I knew the intention of *his* breakfast was something more than me saying hello, which is why that morning led to a damn awkward conversation about how his feelings for me weren't mutual. But yah know, my problem here isn't even about Dean. Up until the day Blaine uncovered who Dean really was— his criminal past and his reasons for being in Harlow, as well as your secret relationship with him—you let me, and everyone else in this town, believe layer upon layer of lies. Only for the truth to hit us harder than if you'd just tried to be upfront. You acted like an outsider. Like you had no obligation to the people who looked out for you when you needed it most. And on a personal front, what hurts me most, is that you treated me like a child who couldn't handle the truth. I thought we were closer than that."

A prolonged silence settled over her, Sarah, and Chip. Sarah's attention shifted about Ally's face, the woman failing to blink while a small muscle at the corner of her jaw rose from clear strain. Even Chip appeared floored, his gaze darting between her and Sarah, his cheeks looking sort of hollow, like he hadn't thought Ally capable of cutting to the core of an issue quite like she had.

Now, Sarah's head moved in a slow and seemingly unintended nod before she finally blinked and then shook her head, as though emerging from a dream. "Yah know…you're right. Which means, I *was* wrong. At the time, I was reeling from my breakup with Blaine, his injuries, and the Syndicate. Then Dean came along, and I was drowning under the pressure to figure out what all these changes meant for me. It was an onslaught, Ally, a literal onslaught of shocks. I was overwhelmed and frightened and too busy protecting myself to tend to my other relationships. I know none of that excuses the selfish approach that I chose, but I'm sorry. I really am sorry."

Ally's lips parted, and she took her turn offering frozen silence—her mind racing, while the rest of her held numb. Long seconds passed until she pried her attention from Sarah and onto Chip, his wide gaze extending a similar bewildered sheen.

Sarah Overton wasn't the sort to say sorry—not without great reluctance anyway—and she showed no reluctance here. Then again, no matter how genuine or out of character an apology, feelings of betrayal and bitterness didn't just disappear the moment she, the perpetrating party, uttered, "I'm sorry."

Ally didn't want to forgive Sarah out of pure and simple pressure or because her convoluted relationship with Chip made the quarrel feel somehow bigger. Did he think less of her for fighting with his sister? And what about her past crush on Dean?

As always, Chip's face gave nothing away, nor did his general upbeat personality. Especially not the small shrug he gave her now, as though he had no answers on how she should receive Sarah's apology.

So Ally turned back to Sarah and sought some open answers. "You put so much effort into deceiving everyone, especially me. Why?"

Sarah's gaze dropped to the tile floor, her delay the same perpetual caution that always scrubbed Ally's nerves the wrong way. Perhaps another frustration that had added to Ally ditching Sarah as a friend.

"Apart from not wanting a whole lot of gossip over who I spend my time with?" Sarah gave a dry laugh and peered back up. "I don't know. Maybe I'm overprotective of you because of how our friendship started."

In search of a clearer explanation, Ally narrowed her eyes only for Sarah to raise her brows and nod to her brother, her stare refusing to let him go.

"What?" Chip wore a pinched look, and he raised both hands in a gesture of innocence. "What do I have to do with any of this?"

"Remember that promise you forced me to keep before you left for Boston all those years ago?" She dipped her chin low and peered up at him, waiting.

Meanwhile, the tension across Chip's face dropped, and he shook his head slowly, a silent plea for her not to elaborate.

But Sarah being Sarah, she would say her piece no matter what, and no amount of pleading could stop her. "You made me promise to look out for Ally. You said to make sure no one troubled her, and that she wasn't alone."

This time, she paired her raised brow with the crossing of her arms, her stance daring Chip to refute her claim. But much to Ally's sorrow, he didn't. He merely turned to her, his face slacker and paler than before.

"Don't get me wrong"—Sarah's softened tone called for new attention, that softening a sign she sought to ease Ally's sudden disenchantment—"I want your friendship back, Ally. I always valued you irrespective of any promise to Chip. That promise only meant that I started with a need to protect you. Maybe I should have been up front about that, and I took a great deal longer than normal to let go, but I can see how my not doing so made you feel patronized."

Though Sarah's honest appeal for friendship brought some relief, an icy sensation washed down Ally's body—over Chip's childhood meddling with her life—that neither of these two had ever stopped the charade long enough to inform her of their little sibling protection pack.

Damn right I feel patronized.

Muscles loose, she turned to Chip, her heart drumming a rebellious beat. "You too?"

His gaze darted about her face, as though he searched for the right answer to supply.

How disappointing.

A hot prickle formed behind her eyes, and she shook her head, no longer wanting to hear what either of these people had to say. And sure, maybe they'd *meant* well, but their good intentions still hurt, and she wanted to leave.

So, while she'd lost the heart to double back through the bar and face the confused stares and questions of her fellow townsfolk, she found the will to push past Sarah and Chip and shove the nearby back door open.

Balmy night air hit her, and she stormed out across the small paddock leading to the parking lot, Chip's voice following suit.

"Ally!"

Twenty

"ALLY, STOP AND LISTEN TO ME!"

Though Chip still called for her, Ally increased her already fast steps away, her pace now just short of a jog while the paddock's long and uncut greenery whipped at her bare legs.

Pissed as she was that she'd had to endure a fumbled apology from his sister, followed by this ridiculous chase to her car, she shot him a glare over her shoulder, warning him to back off. "Doesn't anyone in this town think I'm capable of surviving without a parade of secret help?"

The grass's rushing sounds half-swallowed her words, and she tugged at her knee-length dress, the hem repeatedly catching on the long blades.

"Jesus, Ally, I was fourteen." His harder tone had her slamming her eyes shut, although her desire not to fall had her once more glaring ahead. "An immature goofball who thought all women needed protecting."

Maybe that much was true, maybe she *did* overreact here, but she also deserved a little solitude to process the gut-churning news that so many looked down on her. In particular, two people she'd known and loved for as far back as her memory reached.

Her feet hit the packed parking lot's gravel, and she weaved through cars to get to hers, Chip's louder footsteps crunching just behind her. His pace did not sound as hurried, as though he gifted her a minor lead. "Ally, please."

Her heart clenched at his sinking tone, but she focused on digging out keys from her purple purse, the cheerful violet hue taunting her.

Did she like to stand out? Or did standing out serve as a defense?

A defense against what?

She peered up at Chip and found her answer before peering back down and pressing the OPEN button on her key, all while allowing her chin-length hair to fall about her face and curtain any show of emotion.

Chip already meant something to her. In all honesty, he always had. Only now, the stakes were raised, and she had a whole lot more to lose. And he had things to lose too. Way more than her and her broken heart. The career and opportunities he'd worked toward for years. She wouldn't be the reason for him losing any of that.

"It hurts, okay?" She sniffed, dropped her keys into her purse, and then wrenched the door open. So close to an escape. "It hurts, and I'm leaving."

Only she merely stared at her open car door and failed to take another step.

If I run, I prove them right.

I might be sensitive, but I'm not fragile. I'm not weak.

So, she spun around, set to give Chip her unvarnished thoughts and full attention. "It hurts to put the effort in, yah know? To wake up every day vowing to be positive, to put forth my best show, and be honest about my feelings. I know that's not how you, and especially Sarah, operate, but I don't know how else to be. I don't know what you all want from me, okay?"

Even as the pain of that admission still scraped against the inside of her throat, he said nothing, his hands curling and uncurling at his sides, the unblinking tension of his face suggesting he held back to allow her space to elaborate.

And so she did.

"I know I'm not as smart as you, Chip. I know that." She dropped her hand from the top of her car door, shoulders sagging along with the cooling of angry heat in her belly. "My prospects aren't so glittering or refined. I make rash decisions, this relationship with you included. I'm overly bubbly and a complete scatterbrain—and trust me—nobody 'round here lets me forget it. So, you can stop thinking I need you or Sarah to save me. I know who I am, and I'll survive just fine."

His white shirt fluttered in the breeze as did the longer wisps of toffee brown hair along his hairline, all while he held his silence.

She'd poured her heart out only for him to leave her hanging. Did he really have *nothing*? Her throat constricted with a burgeoning cry, but she nodded her acceptance and turned away.

"It hurts me too."

She paused at his statement, which echoed through the open space, the gravity in his tone forcing her to twist back and catch the hard press of his jaw, a muscle ticking under his light stubble there.

His skin paled to match the silver moonlight, a hint that maybe, for the first time in his life, he grappled with the difficulties of not knowing. Like he questioned every aspect of what he did. Whether he'd said too much. Or should say more.

"It hurts me to see you and Sarah fighting." His brow drew down, as did his lips, into another reluctantly lost look. "And even though it seems irrational, it hurts to hear about your past feelings for Dean. Ally, do you know that I spent years in Boston just wanting to jump on the first plane back to Harlow? Back home? And yes, back to you?"

A dull pain spread through her chest, her heart being the epicenter of all that hurt.

She swallowed at the thickness in her throat, those tight muscles refusing to remain silent while warning that her ensuing raspy voice would hold her raw emotions out for him to hear. "But you moved on eventually, didn't you? And look at you now."

She thrust a hand out to him. Out to his inordinately handsome exterior. Out to this man with a world of shiny promises clambering at his feet.

But the man, with all his promises, only deepened his frown, those overly astute eyes narrowing at her. "I wasn't finished."

He strode two paces closer, his larger torso caging her in between him and her car. "I never wanted to leave. That promise I asked Sarah to keep, it was an act of desperation, not a desire to hold you back, Ally. For a time there, whether you knew it or not, you and your friendship were my entire world. Now that I'm in Harlow again, do you know what I see every time I look at you?"

The question brought her inner world to a stunned stand-still, capturing her ability to move, much less offer an answer. What *did* he see when he looked at her? What did she see when she looked at *him?*

Don't answer that. It's a trick. Don't answer him.

Both questions were loaded with pitfalls, two forbidden doors best left locked, so she compromised with a numb shake of her head.

He pressed his lips into a thin line, a sign of disappointment directed at her lack of effort. "It's impossible not to look at you and wonder how different our lives would be if I'd never left."

Cold shock returned, and she stumbled back, the frame of her car hitting her shoulder blades. *Oh, that's right, he had her trapped.* But she didn't want to imagine the alternative. All those lost years, found. Years where he stayed, and they…

They…

They… *what?*

"You really think we would have been together?" Her raspy tone remained, and she fought with her conscience.

Truth was, had she not met him again—years later and as a near stranger—the fickle part of her might have still wasted years dismissing him as just a friend.

He gave a small shrug, and a gentle smile tugged the corners of his lips upward, forever endearing, a clue he enjoyed knocking her off-center.

"Maybe, we would have been together." He reached out and brushed her chin with his knuckle. "Though you probably would have dumped me the moment Dean came to town."

A broken chuckle detached from deep within her, and an unexpected tear rolled down her cheek. Meanwhile, his smile grew wider, like he knew her.

He'd only just met the "grown-up" Ally, and still… *he knew her.*

She moved to swipe the heel of her palm over her wet cheek, but

Chip got there first, shifting in closer and proving again that he would *always* be at least one step ahead of her.

Why does he like me? Jesus, Mary, and Joseph, why does this man even like me?

All she wanted now was for him to kiss her. To drown out the dull ache in her heart and the questions swirling in her head.

Maybe she wasn't quite up to his standards. Maybe she *was* a complete flake. But she'd never been called dishonest, so perhaps the truth would compensate for some of her flaws.

She lifted her arms and draped them around his neck. "I have to admit, all those years ago, I *did* begin to suspect you had a thing for me. I just… I didn't know how I felt. More precisely, I was *scared* of how I felt."

He lifted one brow in a wordless question.

She gave a weak shrug, face heating at her admittedly understandable immaturity at the time. "I don't know, *maybe* because I'd begun to feel at least a little the same."

He gave a rueful grimace, his gaze fluttering about her face before he replied, "Now, that doesn't make me feel any better."

His hands made contact with her waist, and she allowed her eyes to drop momentarily shut at the warm strength of his touch. "All I'm saying is, maybe there was just a smidgen more to me asking you to kiss me before you left."

"Ally." He growled her name in a soft warning.

But that warning, and the clear affect her admission had on him, had the power once more shifting in her favor. She didn't even try to hold on to her next easy smile. "And another thing, I'm kinda glad you didn't kiss me. Can you imagine two awkward teens, with way too many cringe-worthy years ahead of us, before we landed in the place we are now? Maybe we needed those years apart just to figure ourselves out."

The low set of his brow lifted and genuine light entered his eyes, like he joined in her humor now, happy to let her lead. "And where *are* we now?"

As much as she pulled her grin wider, the attempt at being care-free faded, and the muscles in her throat crushed her voice to a soft whisper. "At a place where I can genuinely appreciate you."

The sting returned to the back of her eyes. This time, for an entirely different reason. "You and I, we were so close, yah know? Sure, I got on okay when you left, but I never did find someone to click with like I did with you. I don't think Harlow ever felt more like home than these last few days with you back—"

Chip's mouth crashed over hers, stealing her words, stealing her desire to care how this all looked to anyone passing by.

All she felt was his hungry need for her, an apt reply to the heat that still simmered within her since their reunion at the ball game. Now, his body pushed her hard against her car, her own desire embracing the pressure.

If she'd feared her persistent ache for him might swallow her whole, that fear now stepped aside to allow her to pull him closer, to grasp at the seemingly never-ending struggle to get her fill.

What with all the hot and heavy clawing, she must have crushed her keys in her purse and pressed the alarm button because just then, her car's siren screeched to life.

The close horn-and-whoop combination struck like a drill to her brain, her heart jolting to an impossible clip and fit to pop. Chip laughed and untangled himself, giving her space for a frenzied search for her keys. He cupped his hands to his ears while she lacked the same luxury.

Just as she disabled the alarm, she peered up at him, the gold in his eyes a true glitter, his lips twisted in a poor attempt to hold back more laughter. But being the sympathetic sort—or maybe just experiencing the relief of escaping that sound—her own laugh broke free on a loud howl, and she pushed her hands to his chest in a jest for him to get away from her.

Every time she tried to gather her senses, her gaze met his, and she fell apart again. That he now joined her only meant that a solid minute passed before they won the struggle to regain control.

Her tummy ached, and she pressed her fingers to the inner corners of her eyes, stemming more tears. He reached out and put his hands on her hips, pulling her in for a kiss. A kiss that brought a sudden hush to her otherwise frantic soul.

"Get in the car and drive." His voice hit her on a molten whisper, and he turned her to her still-open car door, dropping another scintillating kiss to the side of her neck. "It's safe to say we never finished what we started yesterday."

Twenty-One

Long before Mark's chauffeur-driven car rolled to a stop in front of his new building, a group of eager-to-please suck-ups gathered at the curb ready to meet him. He shook his head behind the tinted glass and pulled his sunglasses from the beige console beside him in the backseat, quick to obscure his eyes.

Only a small handful of people knew his true identity or his plans here. Everyone else was meaningless. The quicker these blow-hards learned not to bother with groveling, the easier life would be for all.

He steeled his focus forward and away from the horde until his driver stepped out and held his door open, the man quick to push people back and leave room for him to cross the pavement.

What he did now was an act of pure theater, one where he set the tone for how others should treat him. As was customary, he'd already paid-off and fired this company's board. And given the excess money he'd blown, they'd provided Mark early sway on certain projects and allowed him to place a few, choice calls.

The official change of power complete, the building's giant tinted sliding doors welcomed him. His Italian leather shoes made first contact with the cavernous foyer's glossy dark tile. Black and blue fixtures stared back at him. The classic colors of a tech company. A palette he'd always very much enjoyed.

Inside, more people stopped to stare, but he powered on toward the glass lifts, one of which designated for his use only. Yet another thing he'd negotiated in his plan to set the scene here.

And make no mistake. This *was* all part of a greater plan. A masterclass in revenge, so far beyond anything anyone at the Syndicate could hope to execute. No, they would have merely sought to kill Sarah and Dean, but Mark had more talent and brains than all of them.

He'd done his research. He'd found Chip Overton. Found Stonewall. Then set the wheels in motion to capture both. Now the clock ticked on what would be his magnum opus.

Nothing here would resemble the actions of a low-level street thug. He'd move beyond basic theft and violence. He'd co-ordinate the same perfect dance he'd performed time and time again, albeit on a smaller scale.

A dance called, *Shared Liability*.

He paused before the lift's doors and ventured to turn his head. To lower his glasses and eye the bold and glowing sign above the entry's big sliding doors. A sign that merely said *Encode*.

Chip Overton *would* return to Boston. He'd give his presentation and hand over access to his code, no threats or theft from Mark required, and he'd even go so far as to ensure all Mr. Overton's dreams came true.

He'd win his coveted Graduate's grant…

Then sign the rights to Stonewall away.

So easy. So above board. Overton would simply hand over Stonewall *and* his entire life. Because *liability* bought obedience.

Whatever Mark's deplorable plans for Stonewall, Chip would be implicated. He'd incriminate himself in speaking out. He'd also die just trying. So being a quintessential spineless geek, he'd have no choice but to dedicate his life's work to making Mark richer.

Twenty-Two

A WEEK LATER, Ally sat amongst fifty other guests in her parent's back garden. Her mom and sister sat on wooden deck chairs beside her, a fragrant barbecue sizzling clear across the yard, where Chip stood chatting to a few others.

What had started out as a small family party for him had turned into something much bigger since word of the event had gotten out, and Harlowans liked to take on the personal mission of inviting themselves and everyone they knew to these kinds of things.

It wasn't all bad though. No one in Harlow ever showed up without a tray of food or a cooler of drinks to share, and the extra people added life and community to this party.

Aggie, the sheriff, Gordon, Blaine and Emilia, even Dean and Sarah had swung by. Though Sarah held a tense and reluctant air about her, she wasn't to know that Ally understood her a little more now and intended to make nice later on in the day.

Ally caught Chip's stare and offered a wave, the other guys—Dean, Blaine, and Gordon—predictably smart-ass enough to wave back at her along with Chip.

Ally's mom laughed, although her light brown eyes held a slight sheen. "I'm so happy for you. Your art business is coming along, and you have Chip back."

"Thanks." Despite the lighthearted response, Ally frowned at the iced tea nestled between her palms in her lap. Her mom best not to pin her happiness on Chip being any kind of permanent fixture or Ally's ceramics turning any real profit.

"I'm still waiting on my thank-you, by the way." Laila smiled over at Ally while she bounced a giggling Whitney on her knee. "Wasn't I the one who angled for you two the day Chip first came over?"

Ally pitched a flat stare. "That's *not* when things happened for us."

Her sister dipped her chin in a disbelieving manner, her stare boring into Ally in a way that only older siblings could do, the sort of stare that always melted her resolve.

"Okay, fine." Ally swept a hand upward and released a groan. "We kissed."

Laila flopped back into her seat and let loose a loud laugh, instant shame forcing Ally to elaborate. "But we regretted it instantly."

Laila's laugh only intensified, and she doubled forward, shifting Whitney off her knee and lowering the tall glass in her hand to the nearby slatted table. "Chip that bad a kisser, huh?"

Ally tried so hard to press her lips together and hold back any amusement, only to abandon her defenses and join in on her sister's goof balling. "None of your business."

"Oh, no." Laila chuckled some more, only pausing to wipe tears from her eyes. "That must mean *you're* the bad kisser!"

Though still giggling, Ally twisted and grabbed an outdoor cushion from behind her and then tossed it at her sister. "Stop it, you—"

She caught a glimpse of her mom, her lips curled in a small smile, and her far-off gaze stuck on her boisterous daughters. Laila glanced to their mom too and released a sigh, a short hush descending between the women.

"Seriously though, I'm glad you and Chip are having fun." Laila's lips pressed into a heartfelt grin in Ally's direction. "Those early days of being in love are something special."

Ally's heart swelled at the chink in her sister's support, Laila's ordeal from young love to single-motherhood a cautionary tale that sent Ally's attention back to Chip.

The experience of sitting here amongst all her family and friends—the cozy sense of belonging—narrowed her feelings for Chip into sobering focus.

Yeah, sure, she wanted adventure and time away from this little town, but wanting that and wanting *him* felt selfish.

Her mom's smile dropped, and deep shadows overtook the space below her eyes. That worry-filled expression confirmed Ally's fears and made her heart slow to a fast and thudding beat.

Chip's imminent return to Boston already lit a constant wish in her to drop everything and follow him, which only left her in an increasingly difficult position.

Lose these people. Or lose him.

No matter what happens, I lose.

She took a deep swallow against the lump forming in her throat and blinked up to find Laila peering over the rim of her tea glass, her analytical stare seeming to catch Ally's reticence. "How's things with the Argyle deal? Any news?"

Ally set to peering across the yard again and shrugged, her attempt to appear casual likely failing. Laila had been a know-it-all since the day she was born, intuitive about everything but her own personal life, that is.

Laila *did* know because Ally's insides did a little flip every time she thought about the whole Argyle thing. Her art had a chance of becoming more than something she alone enjoyed. More than a side project or the occasional bit of loose change in her pocket.

"No word yet." She braved looking at her sister again, offering a carefree smile. "They might not even tell Emilia if the answer is no."

Laila made a breathy *pfft* sound with her lips and swatted her hand as if to dismiss the idea. "Emilia won't let them slip away quietly. The woman's stubborn in the best sorta way."

Ally glanced back to her uncharacteristically silent mother, her fallen gaze rising from the lush lawn, along with another weak smile that scrubbed away all pretense of happiness.

Though Ally opened her mouth to ask if her mom was okay, her mom shook her head and rejected any show of concern.

"Big things are coming your way, Ally Bear." She paused while her chin gave a perceptible wobble. "I can just feel it."

Ally moved to stand, to get closer to her mom and extend some comfort, but her mom shot a hand out, once more shutting down an offer of help.

Instead, her mother pushed out of her seat, a wet tear rolling down her cheek and over the light makeup she'd bothered to wear that day while she choked out a broken, "Excuse me."

Twenty-Three

CHIP RAISED the beer in his hand high in the air and stumbled back just as a child from the party crashed through the huddle he had going with Blaine, Dean, and Gordon at the barbecue.

"So much for a quiet family thing." Dean fixed his attention on Chip with a shrug. "You should start worrying this event is less about welcoming you back and more about convincing you to stay."

Dean's suggestion had Chip slipping his gaze to Ally seated with her mother and sister, his heart shifting as she waved. He waved back and forced an easy smile, the other guys figuring it would be funny to do the same.

Their chuckles surrounded him, as his thoughts clung to how less complicated life was around here. These people, his first home and community, so quick to welcome him back like a much-loved family member. The pace was slower with less pressure to tie himself into knots trying to impress.

"If that's the plan, I'm sure to sorely disappoint everyone." He snapped his focus back to Dean and took a quick swig of his beer. "I have too much to return to in Boston."

That much was true. He *did* have things to achieve and a skillset and career that needed exploring. He would never be happy without seeing that part of his life through. But then Ally—the woman he fast envisioned his future with—well, she lived here in Harlow and perhaps always would.

"You mean, like that grant everyone keeps talking about?" Blaine pointed his bottle at Chip before retracting it. "I hear you'll be outta here in about nine days, ready to collect your prize."

Chip's quick chuckle faded to a silent frown. *Everyone's talking about this grant.* Maybe the pressure to impress wasn't so removed from Harlow after all, although the people here would likely give him less flack if he failed to win.

His father's voice whispered in his ear, "*Mediocrity is not an option. You have to be flawless.*" Physically. Intellectually. Professionally. But right now, Stonewall had flaws. The security components weren't fully stable yet, and being a security program, that was a huge deal.

But Encode doesn't expect a finished product.

But if Stonewall was imperfect, then so was Chip, and imperfection opened him to failure and scrutiny soon after.

He took another sip of his beer, his focus pinned to the meat sizzling on the grill ahead. As much as he rebelled against his dad's thinking, his fear of failure was so ingrained that incessant doubts left Chip something to prove. To himself. To his father. As though proving himself would heal him or set him free.

Perhaps financially, but not in the ways I'd like.

"It's nice not to be the one cooking for a change." Gordon nodded to the grill Chip stared at, as if the man assumed Chip's line of sight meant he'd been thinking about food.

"Here's hoping Ally's dad can level up to a Gordon O'Dwyer steak." Blaine gave Gordon a friendly slap on the back. "Otherwise, you and the rest of us might be heading back to Maynard's for a meal after all."

"I think I'm morally obliged to stay." Chip shrugged and gave a mock sigh. "But Sarah tells me Gordon's pies net Maynard's a healthy stream of positive online reviews, so save one for me if things don't work out here."

"Uff-dah." Gordon gave a light-hearted chuckle and nudged Chip with an elbow, his pale cheeks sporting a distinct flush. "Thanks for giving me a reason to hit Sarah up for a pay raise, but I'm sure Mr. Egan is more than passable on the grill. I'm also sure he, like the rest of us, is just glad to see Ally Egan happy for a change."

Chip took a few moments to stare down at his beer bottle, pretending the red and white label held far more interest than it actually did. "For now, anyway."

"I don't know, Chip." This time Blaine spoke, the jovial spark in his green eyes expressing hopefulness. "You've brought a new spark to her eye. Maybe you'll both figure out a way to make things work."

Though Chip opened his mouth to express his doubts, Gordon cut in first. "Not as though we haven't seen more unlikely couples end up together."

He, Blaine, and then Dean gave a unified and knowing nod.

"Oh, yeah?" Never one to admit defeat, Chip jutted his chin in Gordon's direction. "And what about you? Have you ended up with anyone lately?"

"Ha!" Dean threw his head back before returning his focus to the group. "The man's caught in a perpetual loop of hiding in Maynard's kitchen or sleeping off a late shift. I'd be surprised if any woman here even remembers what he looks like."

"Hey!" Gordon sent Dean a mock glare. "I'm here now, aren't I?"

A flurry of activity exploded from Ally's general direction, and Dean's chance to reply died.

Chip twisted around to see Ally's mother hurrying toward the back porch, her hand pressed over her cheek in a gesture of despair. Laila ran close behind, her daughter Whitney, joining the train of Egan women disappearing into the house.

All but Ally. She sat alone on her outdoor chair, her fingers clawing into the wooden armrests, her wide and baffled gaze flicking over the crowd of visitors before stopping dead on him.

His first instinct was to race over there, but in his momentary shock, Aggie, Maureen, Emilia, and Sheriff Marlin got to her first. All those people.

All far more reliable than he could be. Maybe he had no place in that huddle. Maybe it was unfair to establish himself as a source of comfort in her life. Aggie turned to him, her gaze sage in color and in character, a slight tilt of her head commanding him to gather some courage and come on over.

So, he did. He excused himself from the guys. He crossed the lawn. And the gathering around Ally parted through some unspoken pact to have him be the one to soothe her.

She lifted her watery gaze to him, and a silent beat passed before she rose. Instinct took over, and he wrapped her in his arms, dropping a kiss to her forehead and only disconnecting enough to ask, "Are you okay?"

She slid back and nodded, her throat bobbing in denial of whatever ease her nod conveyed. "I only half-know what just happened."

She peered over her shoulder to the house, to where her mother had disappeared, the space between Ally's brow now indented with shallow wrinkles.

His pulse climbed, and his mouth dried at the unspoken things she half-knew about her mother's sudden exit, and the pure anguish of not knowing had him capturing Ally's chin and turning her back to him. "Are *we* okay?"

Her expanding pupils paired with a non-reply, his question seeming to hit a pertinent dilemma while her unsteady nod once more failed to convince.

All signs of chatter and joy left the people around him, and the burn of their stares seared into his skin. He didn't want to ask her to follow him wherever his career took him. Harlow was her home. She'd said that herself. She'd said that she couldn't leave the people she loved. This gathering alone attested to the value they added to her life. A value he'd experienced for himself, where his own family fell short. A value he could never hope to replace. Besides, just asking would be too close to a commitment—a commitment he wasn't sure either one was ready to make. Still, anguish surged into desperation and his once-reliable logic fled.

"Come to Boston with me."

He clenched his jaw shut, and his insides shifted at his impulsive and completely selfish invitation. Probably the last thing she needed right now. Probably the last thing he needed, too. What about his plans to establish his career ahead of anything personal? And what if she wouldn't follow him? Would he ever stay here?

That he even posed that question meant that something had just changed, but he didn't want to analyze what. So, he scrambled to put things right, by adding, "Not to stay. Just a visit to decide what you think of the place. You know, a chance to see somewhere outside of Minnesota?"

Crapola. Her mouth wavered open and closed, but she said nothing, his reasoning not much stronger than his initial invite. Not that he could retract anything now. Heck, did he even want to?

A few creaks escaped her lips all while a new rush of thoughts conspired to convince him that having her accept his offer was suddenly critical.

But the background screech of hinges left Ally's attention pinned to the house, where her mom and sister soon came strolling out the backdoor. Laila's hand rested on her mother's shoulder, and Velma's chin tilted down, half-obscuring a sheepish smile.

Her cheeks held a red glow, but she extended a small wave to her guests. "Don't mind me, everyone. Just having a moment."

Her trudging steps took her across the lawn to her seat, and she gave a wobbly laugh, winking at Ally, which drew a few, relieved chuckles from the engrossed crowd.

Renewed conversations broke around, but the lighter shift in mood couldn't be applied to him and Ally.

He reached out and pulled her into him, admitting through embrace that their problems had no clear solution. That maybe he'd been wrong to ask for anything more than what they currently shared.

And still, he couldn't keep from asking because asking was, by far, less excruciating than having to leave her behind.

Twenty~Four

THE NEXT DAY, Chip stood amongst the bustle of children and parents gathered at Aggie's nursery, a place he hadn't visited since *he'd* been a kid. New shade cloths stretched overhead, sun rays piercing the in-between spaces while nearby fountains burbled a soothing and watery song.

The woman of his affection hadn't yet noticed him and sat at a table surrounded by children, wincing at the green paint Whitney dabbed at the center of her forehead.

An overly enthused beam tugged at his face, and he drew closer. From her fitted pink t-shirt to her short and fluttery green skirt—plus, the fact she didn't mind Whitney's form of artistic expression—Ally looked a vision in what was a very *Ally* moment.

He tracked his gaze down to the skirt again, a scintillating portion of her thigh exposed, though he was quick to wipe his grin away, his current thoughts not right in a family setting.

"How did you know to find me here?" Ally's bright lilt jolted him from his daydream, and he snapped his attention to her upturned stare.

"The flyers around town tipped me off." He shrugged, and she squeezed her eyes shut in an *I should have figured as much* expression.

He jutted his chin to the tables teaming with children, paint, clay, wayward soil, and potted plants. "The flyers also said you'll be finished soon. So…"

"So you're staging an ambush?" She smiled, then winced again, another spot of paint hitting her right cheek. "There's a lot to clean up before I can go anywhere."

"All good." He pulled out a chair and sat beside her, waving away Whitney's slow approach to paint his face too. "I'll help you."

Her eyes shone their brilliant blue, causing his heart to do a hard thump beneath his ribcage. "Well, thank you."

Seeing her here, absorbed in her self-created world of color and fun, a world that contradicted her claims of being a woman incapable of pulling her act together. She had her act together just fine. Only her act looked a million ways different to his, and he couldn't help but be transfixed.

The mess. The squeals of laughter. Seedlings in pots and splashes of paint. Her presence sat at the core of all this joy, a joy only marred because he'd asked her to come with him to Boston, and she hadn't yet given him an answer.

Then again, how can I take her away from all this?

"Nice to see you again, Chip." This time, it was Aggie's voice that interrupted his thoughts, and she strolled toward him from between a line of tall shelves. "I'm gonna guess your presence means I don't have to help tidy up?"

He stood and confirmed her theory with a laugh, giving her an obligatory kiss on the cheek when she reached him.

Meanwhile, Ally clapped her hands, her outward gaze vying for the children's attention. "Judging by the state of this nursery, it's safe to say you all had an awesome time. Unfortunately, today's session is over, so anyone with work left in the potting or painting station can take their art home now. Everyone with clay pots waiting to be fired in the kiln, you can come back and collect those in two days."

The noise level lifted, and children jumped from their seats, scattering in all directions, many to Ally for a goodbye hug before returning to their parents.

"She's great"—Aggie nudged him in the side with an elbow—"isn't she?"

He stared at Ally, his heart thudding again because the moment held a hard to define magic, and his time with her seemed to tick faster and faster away.

"She is."

He suppressed a frown. Maybe because he'd been wrong to ask her to come away with him. Maybe because she had more working for her here than he ever did on his side of the country, forever tripping over himself to make the right choices, all the while not knowing what they were.

He shook the thought off and focused on Ally strolling over while the last child skipped away. "Ready to get to work?"

He nodded, and Aggie gave Ally a farewell pat on the arm. "I'm off to shoot the breeze with whoever I can find at Maynard's. I'll set the lock on the nursery gate, just be sure to pull it all the way shut when you leave."

While Aggie strolled away, Ally turned to a table and began collecting paint palettes, leaving him to figure out the mess strewn across the potting station.

"Ahh…" He stared at the multiple piles of dirt about the tempered glass surface. "Any chance you got a pan and brush stashed around here somewhere?"

She pointed to one of three metal carts, a stack of cleaning equipment nestled on the second shelf. "Over there. But first, let's load the other carts with whatever's on the tables. There'll be less stuff to clean around, and then we can wheel what's left to the kiln room."

"Great idea."

He collected what he could, shifting spades, unused pots, paint palettes, and brushes to a cart. Fifteen minutes of comfortable silence passed before everything was loaded and the tables wiped down.

Soon, he pushed the heaviest cart toward the pottery shed, Ally leading the way to a small, white building with two windows and a tiny wedge of wood holding the solitary door open.

He wrangled his cart inside, the room's bright airiness catching him off guard. Despite the limited space, the muddy scent of clay added an uncomplicated mood—like memories of childhood—mixed with his ability to just see Ally spending all her spare time here. In her place of retreat.

"We'll leave the wet clay pots on the cart to dry, and I'll come in tomorrow to fire them." Ally parked her cart against a wall and turned to him with a smile. "They'll explode in the kiln if I do it earlier."

"Exploding pots?" He left his cart next to Ally's and peered about the room, taking in more details—the set of wall-to-ceiling shelves that supported her creations in various stages of completion, a two-person, magenta couch tucked along a side wall, the contrasting marigold and lapis blue cushions scattered on top.

He strode deeper into the room and eyed an octagonal machine he assumed was the kiln, the thing tucked into a corner not far from a small kitchenette, complete with kettle and sink.

"I'm sure exploding pots will bring about more than a few tears." She pulled her purse from atop the kitchenette bench. "And that's just the children."

She let out a quick laugh and produced a hand mirror from her bag, her expression dropping the moment she brought the mirror to face level.

"Why didn't you tell me?" She flicked her wide-eyed gaze to him, and he tried not to laugh.

"What?" He shrugged, raising his hands and professing innocence. "I thought you looked cute."

"Cute?" Her voice shouted out in an aghast tone, and she twisted the kitchenette's tap to a heavy flow. "Half my face is painted green!"

"I guess beauty is in the eye of the beholder." He jammed his hands into his pockets and bit back another laugh. "And just to be clear, I have no issues with your Princess Fiona look."

"Shrek references, really?" She growled and hunched over the sink, splashing water over her face and scrubbing away before straightening and tugging a hand towel from a nearby hook. "Chip Overton, you think yourself too clever."

He chuckled and strolled closer, reaching for the hand towel. "I have the papers to prove I *am* clever. Here, you've missed a spot."

She dropped her shoulders and handed him the towel, her eyes closing as he drew in to remove green from around her nose creases.

"Still think you could have warned me." Her voice was a sulky mumble, but the slight upward curve of her lips hinted at no real offense. "There I was, just merrily chatting to people, and the whole time my head looked like a cabbage."

Her words brought another smile to his face, and he drew the towel away to press a soft and prolonged kiss to her lips. "And miss this? I don't think so."

Her tense shoulders eased lower, and her eyelids fluttered open, her gentle stare on him seeming to muddle through some unspoken problem in her head. "Is the paint all gone?"

Her new husky tone wrapped around him like a wool blanket, just as the light dimmed and a pronounced click came from behind him. She jolted back and then shoved past, her quick steps taking her to the suddenly closed door.

"Oh, no." She wrestled with the silver handle and a repeated *clack-clack-clack* filled the air, but her efforts were to no avail. "No, no, no, no, no!"

He strode over to her, now slapping both palms to the door's glass window. "Someone must have bumped the door stopper on the way in."

A low growl rolled up her throat and released on a loud and frustrated "Arghhh" before she took out her mood on the ineffectual door stopper, kicking it across the lead-gray polished concrete until it bounced against the nearest wall and then rolled to a stop.

She sent him a taut and silent stare, then stormed across the room and back to her purse. Soon, the contents lay strewn over a small table, tubes of lip gloss, loose tissues, her phone… she sifted through it all in fevered sweeping motions, only to turn to him with shadows under her now glistening eyes. "They're not here. My keys, they must be in my cardigan pocket, and that's draped over my chair at the outside tables… I'll… I'll have to call Aggie."

A small silence lingered, and she wandered over to the couch, plonking herself down onto the bright, velvety cushions, her cell phone clasped in her hand. "She'll have to double back all the way from Maynard's. I'm such an idiot."

But she was so much more than she gave herself credit for, and he hated hearing her speak that way. "What about the windows? One of us could climb out and—"

She pressed her lips together and shook her head. "They only open a few inches. Aggie's idea to stop anyone breaking in."

She pushed out a heavy sigh and began pressing buttons on her phone, the forward roll of her shoulders and the deflated tilt of her head sparking a fire low in his gut.

He fought a sharp ache to reach out and touch her, to make her forget this misery, only he didn't need to fight that ache at all. "Don't."

His tight command had her crystal blue stare pinned to him, her brow pressed into a quizzical straight line. Meanwhile, his gaze slipped to the silky white texture of her forearm and her phone in her hand, a new rise of desperation spurring him on. "Don't call Aggie."

Twenty~Five

ALLY FROWNED up at Chip's unwavering stare and long strides toward her, making her sink deeper into her work shed's couch. His hand was quick to clasp hers and halt her ability to call Aggie.

"Just don't call her yet, okay?" He pulled the phone from her hand and laid it gently on the table beside the sofa, her heart rate spiking at what his interjection meant. "Let her enjoy Maynard's for a bit longer."

He knelt on the fluffy mint rug before her, leaving her few places to look but the rich hazel of his eyes.

"What are you doing?"

He leaned in closer, hands pressing into the cushions either side of her. "Do you need to ask?"

She ran her tongue over her upper lip and recalled the kiss he'd given her moments before she'd discovered they were trapped in this room *together*.

Oh, but I'm trapped in more ways than one.

Her heart confirmed her theory of entrapment with one solid beat inside her ribcage, her pulse racing because she *did* know why he knelt so close. Especially now his gaze did a small dance about her face, hinting his knowledge on her realization.

"Ally, kiss me."

He paired his vulnerable whisper with tugging her to the couch's edge, one hand pushing at her knee, her body instinctively doing as asked and parting to make room for him.

Heat rose up her neck and into her cheeks, and as much as she wanted to say, "Someone might find us," even she heard the weakness in that excuse.

"Ally."

There came that whisper again. The one that burrowed deep into her heart and brought a solid thump to her chest, his fingertips tilting her chin up so that her lips aligned better to his. "Please."

And even as his forehead met hers, she slammed her eyes shut and surrendered, hooking her arms around his neck—every breathtaking second bringing an awareness that she became evermore reliant on him.

She would have to let him go. And one day soon. Oh, but he was here *now*. Temporarily *hers*.

She would take what she could get, and what she got was the hard crush of his lips while she drank him in hungrily and cursed her lack of control.

His kiss drank her in too. His arms holding her to his impossibly firm body, the jut of his excitement pressed against her inner thigh and obliterating any doubt that he dominated the moment. Just as he had last time.

He can't be the only one leaving scars.

No, she would claim her piece of him too.

She bunched his pale blue shirt and pushed the fabric higher over rigid contours and the heat of his skin.

He obliged her exploration, helping with the task of lifting the shirt past his head, only to return to his habit of matching her every effort, his fingertips brushing her exposed waist and sending sharp pangs of need throughout her entire body.

He pulled at her shirt, tossing it to the couch's armrest, his frantic gaze darting over her short skirt and sheer pink bra—like he didn't know where to focus, only that he worked off pure instinct—even as he caught her again and unleashed another onslaught of kisses.

Never having felt so wanted, she moaned at his unbridled desire for her and slipped her head back, making room on her neck for his mouth, her nerves bursting to life the moment he yielded to her request.

In return, she offered the surrender that he wanted, melting at the sweep of his open palm over the bare skin between her breasts, enclosing her legs around him.

But then she remembered her vow. That he couldn't be the only one here leaving scars. So she straightened and quit melting, setting about staking her claim of him too. Starting with the front of his jeans, where she ignored the burn of his gaze in her periphery, and worked his button open.

"Ally?"

She pushed the heavy denim down his hips until she had him free and heavy in her hand, only then did she allow him contact with her direct gaze.

His eyes slammed shut, and she rewarded his compliance with one firm, long tug at his length, his head tilting back and his shoulders dropping, as though a measure of his strength left.

She hooked a hand around the back of his neck and pulled him in, her lips finding home at the center of his Adam's apple. While he sighed at her touch, she sighed at the scent of him, all masculine heat and musk, paired with the salty, crispness of his cologne.

In time, her breaths turned ragged, and she sought control with a push at his shoulders, directing him to take a seat on the couch where she climbed atop him.

There, she allowed her kiss to wander from the edge of his jaw to the edge of his collarbone, all while his hands slid in rough movements up her thighs, under her skirt until his fingers curled at the waist of her underwear, signifying for her to stand so he could strip her.

She let him have that small win, and the wisp of soft lace brushed her legs before hitting the floor, though he left her skirt on—his victory only lasting as long as she took to kneel before him.

She caught the sharp surge of his excitement in her hand, hot and hard, her every nerve humming from the power trip of having him so completely caught and at her command. She drew closer, intending to have him in her mouth, only for his grip to hit her shoulders.

"Stop." He lifted her up, and the wide look in his eyes conveyed the same concern she'd held earlier.

Too much. And in a partnership, dripping with uncertainty. As though he worked to avoid the absolute truth that, once experienced, certain things could not be taken back.

A distinct ache wrapped around her heart, and she nodded, easing back. Agreeing to help him dampen the pain they would both have to deal with later.

He caught his pants from the floor and rummaged through the pocket, soon producing a condom and slipping the pack into her hand. His quiet stare acknowledged her disappointment, before he pulled her in for a heart-wrenchingly tender kiss. His compensation for playing safe.

Even as he kissed her, his fingers curled in a desperate hold at the nape of her neck, but she inched back and held his gaze, taking a moment to bring his beauty and perfection into focus.

In that instant, the space beneath her ribcage swelled, as did the muscles in her throat. She was trapped in this tiny room with her childhood friend, his light touch to her bare tummy sending an overwhelming thrill through her entire body, another reminder of exactly who she shared this moment with.

She slammed her eyes shut, the first to kiss him this time while tearing at the silver packet in her hand. He helped her blind attempt to roll the condom down his length, his other hand shifting her onto his lap and above him. Soon, his lips caressed the base of her throat, and his hands pressed her hips down, the breath of his whisper stroking her skin. "Ride me."

She groaned at what was both an order and an expression of desire, savored the lead of his touch on her hips, his hot girth slowly filling and stretching her, her fingertips curling into his chest in mutual punishment.

His relentless kisses stole her every moan while his hands guided her movements, and she moved over him, slow and testing. The unhurried pace spoke of how he would return to his life in Boston. And she would do her best not to drop everything in Harlow just to chase him there.

A man is not a plan.

A man is not a plan.

She wouldn't let go of her own dreams.

What if he was fast becoming one of her dreams?

A light snap at her back brought her mind to the bone-melting awareness of him unhooking her bra. His gaze claimed her now, and his fingers dug harder into her hips, his grip pushing her to a faster pace.

An avalanche of desire swept her over, and she indulged the all-consuming compulsion to move. They didn't have forever, but they had *now*. And she had his unrepentant kiss and the hard lap of his tongue over hers.

There was more.

The soul-nourishing sense of belonging to someone. Not once doubting this man wanted her.

That he'd wanted her *first*.

"You're killing me here." Though he kept his eyes shut and tilted his chin back in clear pleasure, his strained tone pulled a sudden light chuckle from her that only lasted until he bucked against her.

"Oh"—she clenched at the renewed pressure, her voice weak, his move perhaps spurred by vengeance for what she did to him—"now you're killing me."

"I hope not." His soft laugh washed over her, and his lips hit her shoulder. "This isn't how anyone should find our bodies."

Even as he released an effort-filled groan, she laughed back. "Or maybe it is?"

"I guess that's one way to stay together." His brow flexed as though he'd said too much. About what he wanted, what she wanted, but was too afraid to admit out loud.

As if to distract her, he flipped her under him, her previous laughter turning to a surprised squeal. Now, she lay on the couch, him knelt before her, the tables once again turned.

His hands grasped her waist and he plunged into her, movements demanding and desperate, each firm thrust forcing her arms to wrap around his back for purchase.

His exploding breaths matched hers, and her heart charged like a fierce bull, Chip being everything red and inciting. All that remained was her keening cry tearing from deep within, one that spelled out the rise of her peak.

His mouth found hers and swallowed the sound, claiming each wild and satisfied moan as his, not once stopping to grant her reprieve from the rush of light building behind her shuttered eyes.

Her heart nearly ripped in two, and her world turned all glittery-white and starry. She arched into him and found blissful release, his lips on hers as he did the same.

In time, she turned all pliable beneath him, and one by one, her senses returned. He rested his head at her neck, which offered the sumptuous soft brush of his hair on her cheek. Next came an awareness of this room's pale light and the plush cushions beneath her back, a reminder of the spontaneity of this encounter.

But more than any of that came the crushing knowledge that something here had changed. *She'd* changed. She'd grown. She found what she'd been chasing all these years.

And what exactly had she learned from all of this?

That no amount of bargaining could undo the pain of knowing that true love really did exist.

Twenty-Six

CHIP STOOD before the open kiln, his shirt still in his hand, and Ally perched on the couch's edge, her phone pressed to her ear. The kiln stood shy of waist-height, the door opening more like a lid from the top up, the empty inside insulated with a wall of white, heat-resistant bricks. He squinted at the control panel and tried, but failed, to make sense of what each button did.

"Thanks Aggie." He peered over to Ally with her lips dipped in a frown, although he tried not to smile because she wore no more than her short skirt and bra, his body thrumming at the sight of her and the knowledge of having just been inside her. "We'll see you soon."

She hung up, and he hurried to hide his staring, tugging his shirt on over his head before retrieving her shirt from the couch's armrest and handing it to her. "Sounds like that went well."

"Yah, Aggie's on her way." She took the shirt but didn't rush to put it back on. "Thanks"

She tilted her chin up to him, and a quiet pause unfolded. Though he couldn't say what went through her mind, all he could think about was the hard-to-define shift that seemed to have occurred. Like the connection here had deepened all while he braced for a greater than ever fall.

He leaned over her and caught her lips in a sumptuous kiss, a kiss he imbued with the hollow hope of making her more than a short summer fling, even though he'd come to Harlow with no desire for anything serious.

She obliged the kiss, rising to drape her arms over his shoulders and sinking into his hold, the silken skin over her bare lower back filling his palms only for her to push away from him.

"Nah, ah." A flurry of hard breaths followed her denial, and she went about jamming her shirt on. "We're *not* going to let poor Aggie walk in on round two."

He let out a laugh and turned for the bright red kettle in the pottery's tiny kitchenette. "Okay, fine. What about coffee? Is coffee safe?"

An easy chuckle wafted from her general direction. "Sure, but there's no fridge so no milk."

He caught her strolling over as if to help, but he shook his head and pointed to a chair tucked under the small, nearby table. "You sit. I'll make coffee. Straight black still gets a pass from me."

She frowned but did as told, folding her legs beneath her on her designated chair. Even at school, she'd struggled to sit in chairs the traditional way, contorting her legs into weird shapes that seemed comfortable only to her.

The memory brought a smile to his face, and he ruffled his hair with one hand while depressing the kettle button with the other. More silence passed as he searched the bench's lower cupboards for cups and processed this room's distinct earthy scent of potter's paint.

That smell brought about an unexpected reminder that a world outside his computers and bug-fixing existed. A world of handcrafted art and the woman who made it. The woman he fast fell for and would lose within a week, unless…

He pulled two cups out and placed them on the bench, the thick ceramic walls and mottled mauve and turquoise glaze a blatant Ally Egan creation.

This train of thought prodded him to learn more about something clearly important to her, so he nodded to the kiln and set about making her talk. "How hot do those things get?"

She narrowed her gaze at the kiln in a pensive look. "Well, that one is from Germany, and her name is Brunhilda, so I like to say she's 1300 degrees Celsius. But if we must stick with local figures, I guess you could say about 2370 Fahrenheit."

She shot him a smile that produced another chuckle from him. "Your kiln has a name?"

She tilted her head to one side in a way that said, *Do you even know me?* before adding, "Sure, the name Brunhilda means armed for battle, and trust me, that girl likes to put up a fight. Between bisque and glaze firing, a lot can go wrong."

"Let me guess"—the kettle dinged, and he went about pouring water into a nearby plunger—"explosions?"

"If I'm not careful, lots of explosions."

He lifted a glazed cup from the bench and inspected the swirling colors anew. "And how did you get this one to be so glossy and colorful?"

"Hmm…" She rose from her seat and wandered over, a thoughtful indent forming between her brows. "It's the way the oxides react when heated—cobalt, manganese, potassium—most go on one color and come out something completely different when fired. The turquoise in this cup is made from copper, and the top glaze is essentially powdered glass mixed with water. The glass melts in the kiln and fuses into a high gloss when cooled. Over fire, and you get pinholes all over your work. Under fire and your piece looks like it's coated in opaque glue."

"And this one has neither." He smiled at her, her attention still fixed on the cup in his hand. "Also, the way you describe the interaction between chemicals and heat. Ally, I wasn't joking when I said you know how to science."

She blinked up at him, her frown slowly easing. "I never thought of my work like that. Thanks."

A small laugh escaped her, and her gaze continued to search his face, the bend in her brow and that thought-burdened look returning. "Was it hard leaving Harlow?"

He reeled a little at her question, not sure where the thought came from, though maybe his reference to her work got her thinking about leaving.

As much as he wanted to sweeten the truth, to make leaving seem simple so that she'd love Harlow a little less and him a whole lot more, his conscience got the best of him, and he vowed to share the truth.

"Harder than you'd think." A lump took up space in his throat, and he spun around to the coffee plunger, hoping the subject would pass once he had coffee to serve.

But then, his next confession slipped out. "People around here seem to think leaving was the admirable thing to do. You know, like I instantly embarked on a bigger and better life, in a bigger and better city. But everything happened so fast, and I wasn't ready, Ally. Everyone forgets that I watched my mother's mental state disintegrate before my eyes. That I came home from school one day to find all our possessions strewn across the front lawn, and her bleeding from the countless wounds she'd inflicted on her arms. What if I hadn't returned when I did? What if I'd done the usual that day and went out with you after school?"

Though he couldn't see her, he imagined Ally's stare hitting his back, his attention hooked to the unserved cup waiting on the bench before him.

No matter how much he told himself to move on from that day, the sense of being that same overwhelmed fourteen-year-old never seemed all that far away.

"Chip?" She called to him.

Though he turned, he failed to actually look at her and, instead, stared at the black speckles of rock amongst the floor's polished concrete. "I had no control over any of it. Not how Mom reacted. Not about dropping everything I knew to move to Boston. Much less, I didn't *want* to move to Boston. Especially not to live with Dad and his new woman."

He swiped up a cup and ferried it over to her, his shoulders easing a little at having something to do.

"I always thought things were better for you there." Her husky whisper had him meeting her gaze, although the softened sympathy in her eyes made him regret sharing so much. "There were stories about your dad's career taking a sharp upward turn after leaving our dinky nearest hospital. How he'd bought a huge house in a well-to-do area. That he'd finally met his potential. I'm sorry, Chip, I always just believed the rosier version I'd heard."

"Well, that version isn't all wrong." He leaned a hip to the table and stood before her, his fingers hooked around the robust handle of his coffee cup. "I eventually made new friends and did well in school, but that home in Boston was never *my* home. Dad was too busy social climbing and working. Even when he was around, I got the distinct impression he only cared about my presence so long as I had some story of success to share."

"I mean, look at you." She gestured up and down his body, although the gesture seemed to incorporate more than just a reference to his physical appearance. "It's not like you fall short."

"For a man hellbent on sticking his fathering skills to Mom, I did. Dad wanted to raise his ideal version of a man, someone who could do and be it all, an intellectual athlete. Someone less inquisitive, more enterprising. Someone engaging, but aloof. You know, someone like him."

She gave a scoffing sort of laugh over the rim of her cup. "He doesn't ask for much, does he?"

Chip laughed at her soothing sarcasm. "Right? Most people think 'heart surgeon' and assume he's a saint by default, but even brainy people in care industries can be wannabe corporate highflyers. Heck, he had me enrolled in baseball classes and private golf tutoring within weeks of landing in Boston. You know, all the things that were meant to help my future impression on the world at large."

She reached out and clasped the hand he pressed to the table close to her, her uncharacteristic silence seeming to make space for him to process his thoughts.

Ally saw him in ways that his own father never could. She accepted and comforted, two qualities missing most around him in all his years away from Harlow, his more selfish side wishing to hold on to her for that reason alone. To have her help him in ways no career or overbearing father could. Even though he had many other reasons to persuade her to come away with him.

"I never quite fit in his world."

And Ally will fit in even less. She'll have to run Dad's gauntlet, all while I pray she likes Boston enough to want to give up Harlow.

What was I thinking, asking her to come?

"I just wanted to stay home and learn everything I could about the topics that interested me." He lowered his cup to the table and then pressed his palm to the softness of her cheek. "Which is why your crush on Dean kind of threw me. He has the same tough air my dad always wanted for me. That, and you only ever seemed to like athletes and outdoorsy guys."

She gave a small chuckle, her eyes glinting their brilliant blue. "I can see how you've kind of developed a sore spot."

He laughed. "Well, thanks."

"But it's safe to say you don't need to worry about any jocks, rugged men, or social climbers." She started off with another wide smile that slowly softened into something else entirely, her voice turning husky in the end. "I like you a lot more than I've ever liked any of them."

For a long while, he grappled for something to say, ultimately settling on turning her earlier question back to her. "What was Harlow like after I left?"

She gave a small scoff and ticked one corner of her lip upward. "Nowhere near as fun, that's for sure. You and I were always together, and even when I did find a new rhythm without you, I envied you."

His brow squished together, and a strain gripped his chest. What did Ally Egan have to be envious of?

"Time and time again, I watched our peers pack up and move. As much as I wanted to do the same, I forfeited any idea that I *could* do the same. Harlow was just too safe, and my dreams of being an artist, way too risky. " She gave a tight shrug, the hard bob of her throat denoting anything but ease. "I get that your home life was a mess and mine wasn't. So, I'm sure it sounds like I'm complaining about nothing, that things were just so comfortable and stable. But most days, it feels like I'm still waiting for my life to start."

He took his hand back and toyed with the white laminate on the table's edge for a while. Contemplating her concerns. Weighing up the contrast with his own life.

"First of all"—he set his focus back to her wide and expectant stare—"if it means something to you, then you're not complaining about nothing. Also, Ally, you *have* done things. You completed an art course. You have a job at Oak Tree, your potential deal with the Argyles, and a full life here in Harlow. All of those things bring value into the world. Even without all that, you still have decades ahead to start anything you want."

"Except for being an Olympic level gymnast." She pointed a finger at him and smiled, her expression seeming to say, *I got you on that one.*

He laughed and gave her a jovial shake of his head. "Yeah, you've probably already aged out of that."

The serious edge returned to her face, and she puffed out a heavy sigh. "I haven't travelled, Chip. I haven't taken any real risks. I used to dream of living in a different city, maybe many different cities. I've never felt smart or ready enough to try my hand at something big, and even if I did, Mom and Dad have given Laila and me their entire world. So, there's this background pressure of feeling that, if I did leave, I better do something amazing, otherwise, any empty-handed return home would be soul crushing and pointless for everyone involved."

"You mean, kinda like when I left Harlow? Or even what I'm trying to achieve with Stonewall?" He paused and clenched his jaw for a beat, his next words something he'd only now come to admit. "Like everyone is looking at you with a sense that whatever risk you took better have been worth it?'

Her gaze held on him a while, her downturned mouth sending forth sympathy. "Exactly like that. And the time you lose playing those chances, you never get back. I don't know where to start. I don't even know if I *should.*"

Those same thoughts had plagued him about her, the rising risk coupled with the fear that he'd be taking her away. But she deserved more credit than he'd given her thus far. She deserved to see what the world had to offer. To make the choice of where her life would go.

"Let me help you." Once again, his words surprised him, but if he'd learned anything from this woman, it was that sometimes impulsive moves turned out for the best.

"How are you gonna do that?" She raised a brow and held a mischievous grin.

"I'll make you a promise. If you ever do get around to busting out of Harlow, no matter what happens between us—if you're ever lost, scared, or confused—this experienced city slicker will always be just a phone call away." He pulled her hand from around her coffee cup and pressed a kiss to the center of her palm.

"That's a big promise, Chip. Not all endings—"

"And you shouldn't worry about not being able to figure your way around. You're smart, Ally." He smiled, fully aware that she'd been about to remind him that many couples parted ways and never spoke again. He didn't want to think about that right now. Didn't want to believe anything like that could ever happen to them. "You're keeping up with me just fine, and that's got to mean something."

She reached out and poked him in the ribs. "And what about you, Mr. Brave and Worldly? How do you feel about the looming Encode pitch?"

He worked to keep his shoulders from slumping and watched the cheeriness in her expression fade as she grasped his change in mood. "Terrified, Ally. I'm terrified, but I'm going to try anyway. You know why?"

She gave a small shake of her head.

"Because facing the fear is better than being left questioning who I might have been." He gave a shrug, as though the choice really could be that simple, but the slow churning in his belly warned that he and Ally faced huge, life-altering decisions, and there was nothing simple about the gambit of change coming their way.

A heavy silence drew, with nothing but the bunching of muscles around her eyes, though she shook her head again, the action more decisive this time as her loud intake of breath hinted at renewed focus.

"So then, ask me to come to Boston with you again." She blinked up at him, her unbroken gaze boring into him, like she was deathly serious.

He gave her a sideways stare, not quite sure of her motivations or whether he should do as told. Then again, he'd been the one to preach on taking risks, so he'd be a hypocrite not to lead by example. "Ahh… want to come to Boston with me?"

Her lips split into a toothy grin, and she offered a quick and repeated nod. "Yes. Yes, I would."

She tore her hand from his and gave a light *Ally* squeal, clapping her palms together while he wrestled with his stunned silence.

"Really?" The question half-stuck on its way out, and he cleared his throat against his previous rough delivery. "You mean, you want me to show you around the big smoke? Maybe even come as my date to the Encode dinner?"

Her mouth hung limp for a beat before she snapped it shut and seemed to recover. "That does sound awfully intimidating, but… yes to it all."

Twenty-Seven

BOSTON WAS everything Ally expected and more. More buildings. More noise. *More people.* All on the tail of a week filled with a mountain of things to do before she could even get here, the plan being that she would stay for three days and return to Harlow the day after Chip's presentation, their status as a couple murky thereafter.

Now, having already left her luggage at Chip's dad's house, she strolled through the Back Bay district for some quick sightseeing with Chip before dinner. Her brain hurt from the overwhelm of endless lines of upmarket galleries, boutiques, and mega-chain stores she could never hope to see in Harlow.

"Is that Hancock Tower?" She stabbed a finger at a tower covered in reflective glass up ahead, one that dwarfed all other nearby historical stone and red brick buildings.

He squeezed her hand, a seeming gesture of pride that she recognized the building from her research on Boston. "That it is."

She tugged back on his hand, making him stop so she could marvel at yet another giddy sight, her eyes not used to the dizzying shift of clouds above high rooftops. "How do you ever get used to all this?"

A smile pulled at her lips, and she went with the mood, releasing her hold on him to do a full-circle turn, the sudden honk of a nearby car the only thing to pull her from her spinning.

Chip laughed and grabbed her hand again, probably scared she'd fall onto the busy road or that her current break in the flow of foot-traffic might cause a passerby to trip.

"Trust me." He pulled her back into a stroll and around a corner. "Give this place enough time, and you'll be rushing around like the rest of us, too busy trying to get from one place to the other to notice the sights."

The space around her opened up, and she recognized the red roof of Trinity Church on the edge of Copley Square, where people sat on patches of grass as well as benches.

Where Harlow all but shut down on Sundays, tourists and locals alike jostled around here, her heart soaring because she was just like them, but at the same time, panging because her sensory overload pointed at how sheltered her life had been.

With the Argyle deal still unsettled, every day without word led her to think the answer would be *no*. Without that deal, unlike Chip, she ran the real risk of not knowing where she would go next or what she would do.

Chip squeezed her hand lightly, and she redirected her attention onto him. "So what do you think? Could you get used to a place like this?"

"Without being lost?" She bumped him in a joking manner. "I think I'll need more than five minutes here to know for sure, but this is a beautiful city. I'm glad you're the one to help me take my first steps out of Minnesota. Even if I am only here for three days."

He turned the green and gold mottle of his eyes to her, leaning in to kiss the bridge of her nose. "Well, my next days ahead don't seem as scary with you here. So *thank you* for joining me."

Her attention caught on the public library, a rectangular 1800s-looking building about a thousand times bigger than any library she'd ever encountered.

"Then, let me provide you with more distraction." While Boston's cold North Atlantic breeze brushed her cheeks, she peered up at the mostly clear sky, the wind's watery smell another stark difference to landlocked Harlow. "Entertain me with what's next on Chip Overton's great tour of this city on the hill."

"Sure thing." He increased his pace, and she sped up to follow. "Next up, a short walk around the Jay River, and while we're at it, a detour past my old college stomping grounds. It's a long walk, so I don't know if we'll have time for much more after that."

His reference to time forced her to recall her impending meeting with his dad. Even as a child, she'd avoided Bill Overton, his terse personality well-known in town, and something she'd witnessed first-hand, like he always had something more to do and somewhere better to be.

"Ooo… fancy." She offered a somewhat fake giggle at her own joke on Chip's sightseeing tour, although the idea of getting a closer look at his life in the years she hadn't known him did appeal.

They took a quiet turn down Commonwealth Avenue with yet more old-timey looking buildings and then down Harvard Bridge where the Jay River lapped against the bridge's stone pillars.

The bridge alone was a walk and a half, so he hadn't exaggerated the distance, but the city skyline cut an impressive figure, and all she could do was take it all in.

The world as she knew it grew by the second. Harlow would always be Harlow. A place slow to change, where one could coast through life easy enough. A place she knew about as well as her own reflection. *But Boston.* Boston was a city on the move. A place that changed and challenged whilst expecting the same from its inhabitants.

Few could merely "coast" in this city. Survival required real effort. Real success. And maybe, despite his problems with his move from Harlow, the challenge and change of this big city gave reason for Chip's motivated personality.

The bridge came to an end, and Chip guided her right, where an expansive lawn opened out to a light gray building with long stone columns and a giant domed roof.

"Whoa. *That's* MIT?" She'd seen pictures but had never really fathomed the sheer scale.

"That's MIT." He paused and allowed her time to absorb the sight before adding, "In fact, every building you see for a number of blocks is MIT."

She turned to him now, but her lips merely parted without producing any sound. How had a boy come all the way from her small town and succeeded not only to fit in this place, but excel above his peers?

One sure thing, this *boy*—now a man, but not *her* man—made her braver. He helped her leave Harlow. He helped her to consider possibilities she would have laughed off before. Including being with him to begin with. Even though a voice within her questioned her chances of ever keeping up with someone as brilliant as him.

Chip, extraordinary, compared to her *extremely* ordinary. Unflappable stability to her chaos. His success practically guaranteed from his first ever breath…

And still, she took his hand and forced the reminder that he'd *chosen* her. His choice meant something. As did her reasons for being in Boston, a place he'd *chosen* to invite her to, by the way.

She wanted to have *fun* here. To see the sights. To live in this moment with her hand in Chip Overton's, a man she cared so very much about, and who she could at least support through his next nerve-racking days.

Being realistic though, the next days would likely be their last, and as much as she fell short, she could give him this. She could give him moral support until his long-held dreams sped closer to reality.

Twenty-Eight

ALLY SAT at the large dining room table opposite William Overton, his stern blue stare a few shades more intense than hers, stirring childhood memories of how much more time she and Chip had spent *not* at his house. That choice in location suddenly seeming not at all unintended.

She peered at Chip beside her and gave him a light smile designed to reassure, even though she wasn't clear which of them she sought to soothe.

This large room sat in proportion with the rest of the house, the deep, moss green walls offset with stark white furnishings. Meanwhile, the table before her sparkled with faceted crystal and silver while a white table runner cut over its rich, dark wood. Everything here was a classically bold statement on the elegance Chip lived amongst.

"So." William Overton Senior narrowed his gaze, like a lion deciding whether to maim or outright devour its prey. "Maybe you could fill me in on what life in Harlow entails these days?"

Once again, she turned to Chip, his jaw now set in a firm position Ally had never witnessed on him before, the fire in his stare combating the ice in his dad's.

"Well"—she clenched her hands into fists in her lap, fighting an urge to fidget with her woefully empty wine glass—"I'm sure Harlow hasn't changed all that much since you left, Mr. Overton. Small towns and all…"

Just then, Chip's stepmother, Kelly, powered in, all tall and slender with the flared hem of her navy dress swishing at her knees. She set a bowl of green salad on the table, along with some roast potatoes, before releasing a *tsk* and hurrying over to fill Ally's wine glass. Just as quickly, she disappeared back into the kitchen.

In all honesty, like Chip, Ally wanted to glare at Mr. Overton too, if for no other reason than he could have gotten up to help his clearly stressed wife.

But then, she was a guest in this house and a temporary figure in Chip's life.

So she held off berating the man and pushed a loose lock of hair from her eyes, clearing her throat in another attempt at polite conversation. "You might remember Blaine Callaghan, he's a carpenter now, and I'm a sales assistant at his store, Oak Tree furniture, where he sells his handmade furniture. Aside from that, I attended art school over in Marston and have a pottery studio at Aggie's nursery, where I make and sell plant pots and home decor to the tourists passing through."

William raised both brows and turned back to his son, a mocking sort of silence dragged out before he offered, "Plant pots?"

Once again, Kelly raced through the room, this time with a pile of plates. While the men continued their quiet stand-off, Ally rolled her eyes and stood, grabbing half the plates from Kelly's arms, distributing them to her and Chip, but not before catching Kelly's momentary stunned pause.

"Ally's underselling herself." Chip's voice punched through the air, commanding attention. Now, she was the one holding a stunned gape. "She's in talks to distribute her pottery through a major retailer. Argyles. You know, the place Kelly shops at when she's looking to update the balcony gardens or re-pot an indoor plant"

"No way." Kelly's face lit up, and she nudged out an elbow in a you-go-girl show of support.

Meanwhile, a distinct lightness spread through Ally's chest. At Kelly's reaction and the pride in which Chip had defended her.

William pressed his lips together, as though still considering Chip's words, the man's face a harsher version of his son's, his hair a similar length, albeit styled back and about eighty-percent gray these days.

"Not bad." His attention landed on Ally. "What are your plans if the deal falls through?"

Her mind drew a blank, and she plodded back to her seat, where she swiped up her wine glass and took a long swig. Frankly, the whole Argyle thing had been Emilia's idea. Ally had just assumed a scrapped deal would mean her prospects simply ended there.

"She has a business consultant." Chip's hand slipped over hers under the table. "A ruthless one who won't stop until another deal is found."

She startled at his artful description of Emilia. Strong minded, sure. But *ruthless?* Anyone who'd met the diminutive woman would not agree.

His defense had started to slip into dishonesty, and his ongoing insistence on her potential made her skin prickle.

Why was he trying so hard? And what if the Argyle deal *did* fold?

Would he be less proud of her?

Needing a moment to sift through her thoughts, she frowned at her empty plate, only for Senior Overton to hit her with another question. "So, let's say this or another deal goes ahead. It sounds to me you're a one-woman production line. How will you keep up with demand?"

She forced the muscles on her face to remain loose, the desire to shoot William a pinched scowl all-too strong while a hot, swelling sensation pushed against her lower ribcage. "I haven't thought that through just yet."

The glacial edge to Senior Overton's eyes defrosted slightly, a hint he saw her lacking plans as a win for him. "One perk of being in private practice, I have a number of wealthy and grateful former patients. I'm sure I could pull some strings to help you expand. Someone who can organize other artists to increase production, maybe even an investor, or—"

"Dad, no." Chip's stern glare held firm on his father's, two men wearing the same expression but for different reasons.

She sat silent, her face cold, and a sharp tension clawing at her heart.

"And what if another opportunity knocks tomorrow?" His dad leaned over the table, his tone harsh and his fingers curled tight around his scotch glass, as though he rebuked one of his cardiac patients for picking up smoking again. "She won't be prepared."

"It's still early days." Chip's statement was delivered in a taut staccato, the clench of his jaw further hindering the sound.

His dad scoffed. "She still needs a plan."

"Ally will wait and see what happens next."

A short pause ensued, and she opened her mouth to say something, but Kelly got in first. "Bill. Please."

Do I get a say in any of this?

He flicked a hand through the air, dismissing his wife, and she settled into her seat beside him, sending Ally a shrug.

"Businesses rise and fall." Bill stilled a beat before pressing on. "People go bankrupt far quicker and easier than you think, William."

That was the first time, outside their school days, Ally had ever heard anyone refer to Chip as William, his father's formal approach strengthening the divide between them.

But Chip plastered on a derisive smile, not even flinching at the address, as though icy exchanges were the usual price of entry into this house. "Nice of you to acknowledge that I even think."

Not yet ready to look at the two bickering men, she shook her head at her plate, an uncontainable heat pushing to burst out from within her.

Bill Overton's attitude, the pressure he laid on Chip, much less on her—a woman he'd met for the first time in a decade. No wonder Chip believed he wasn't enough.

And still, as much as he disliked his upbringing, the speed in which he spoke for her, lumping her with the same burden to excel. Well, she couldn't deal with that either.

"I've been in this room all of half an hour." She spoke in a low, frustrated tone. "And you're both already planning my life."

She lifted her attention to Chip but refused to look at his dad, mostly because of what she might do if she did.

Chip's lips parted in a sign he meant to say something, then abandoned that idea to look at his father, the two men silent now and picking up their cutlery.

"Well, that was fun." Kelly spoke in an overly bright and sarcastic tone, then pressed her lips together and gave Ally a smile, her brown eyes wide in approval. "Believe it or not, the man beside me is, at times, capable of fair play. The man beside you, even more so. And I, for one, am sorry for their brutish behavior. I'd like to say it's rare, but I also don't like lying. See my dilemma?"

Ally laughed and nodded.

Kelly spoke again, "Anyway, *I'm* glad you're here, and it's nice to have another woman within these walls for a change."

Ally's heart thudded with gratitude, but also because she still didn't quite know what to think of this woman since she'd been part of Bill's dramatic exit from Harlow.

Though Chip never spoke much of her, some people in town did.

Never anything nice.

What with Kelly's earlier nervous fussing and her kind support now, Ally suspected she'd been misled.

"So, can I say you two are officially dating?" Kelly's focus bounced between Ally and Chip before finally stopping at Ally. "Chip's never brought a girlfriend home. It's nice that you both share some history."

That last statement brought genuine warmth to Ally's face. Kelly's well-meaning curiosity and desire to keep the conversation flowing, marked her relationship with Bill as a case of opposites attract.

Maybe this woman was everything he'd needed all along. The sweetness to his sour. Maybe Ally would ease up and react in kind. Less on the historically nasty gossip, and more on what she witnessed with her very own ears and eyes.

"Weren't you dating that law major we met at your graduation?" Though Bill spoke to Chip, the way he sawed at the chicken on his plate seemed extra disturbing, given his work as a surgeon and all. "Dionne something-or-other. Great conversationalist, bright, from an esteemed family. Yes, I liked her."

The air disappeared from Ally's lungs, and Chip pressed his eyes shut. She'd never heard of any woman named Dionne, much less someone he'd dated so soon to returning to Harlow. And what with his dad listing Dionne's achievements, did the man *ever* let up?

"Bill!" Kelly shook her head at her husband, brows squished together in a clear sign she too was done with his barbs, her compassion-filled gaze soon connecting to Ally. "Don't listen to him. Dionne was *not* Chip's girlfriend."

"No, she wasn't." Despite Chip's confirmation, his stabbing words seemed aimed at his dad. "We went on one date. She spent the whole time listing her social connections or grilling me on which law firm she should aim for partner in ten years' time, like I would know or care. I can understand why *you* liked her, but I hadn't spoken to her since that date or when she insisted on introducing herself to you at graduation."

Bill eyeballed Chip and chewed in silence, soon returning to his meat, like he hadn't been at all offended. "Well, she seemed nice."

An incredulous laugh broke from Chip, and because Ally sensed his rising anger, she lay her hand over his arm on the table in a gesture for him to calm down.

"Kelly?" Though her voice caught a little, she smiled across the table at Chip's stepmother, the only person to offer solidarity. "Could you pass me more wine?"

Kelly gave a choked laugh, although something in her smile hooked in Ally's mind. The slight waver. That her brown eyes dimmed even as she joked, "Sure. I think I need more too."

The heavy silence as she slid the tall, green bottle closer spoke volumes. Like she saw a common thread in Ally. Maybe the one reason they couldn't be friends.

That Ally would be another woman to divide this family. A family already thoroughly shattered.

Twenty-Nine

THE NEXT DAY, Ally rested her head on the grass within Boston's Common gardens. Chip laid out beside her in the hot, early afternoon sun. Having strolled past the Southwest end's softball fields, the Soldiers and Sailors monument on Flagstaff hill, and then a spray-pool-turned-skating-rink in the winter called the Frog Pond, she rubbed her feet, ruing the heels she'd have to wear at tonight's Encode dinner.

She turned to Chip, where the frown he directed at the clear sky prevented him from noticing her, so she ran a hand over his wrinkled brow and vied for his attention. "You look worried."

He shuffled on his side and nestled his head in her lap, his small act obscuring her sense of impending doom with belonging. "I *am* worried."

She nodded. They both had so much happening, each complication like a loose kite string blowing in the wind and getting caught with other kites. The whole, giant tangle destined to hit the ground soon enough.

"Because of tonight?"

He peered up at her question before adding his reply, "Tonight. Tomorrow's presentation. Other things."

Wanting to make him feel better, wanting to maintain this loose connection, she ran her fingertips through his soft hair, her heart shifting at this losing battle.

His eyes drifted shut, and his scowl eased. As much as she resigned herself to an end here, wobbly uncertainty still wrenched at her tone. "Other things as in, me? Or your dad?"

His head shifted in her lap from a nod, his eyes still shut, as though he preferred not to meet her gaze. "Both, but he was rude to you last night, and I regret you had to deal with that."

She scoffed, and that wobbliness turned to an incredulous laugh. "You were rude too."

His eyes flicked open. "He was worse."

A frozen tension passed between them, but he eventually reached up and stroked her cheek. "I'm sorry. That's a weak excuse. I don't regret making him feel bad, but you're right, I could have handled things better."

She stayed silent for a while, just stroking his hair and allowing her frustration to dissipate a bit, though the pangs of doubt that dogged her since Chip's return didn't budge.

"Chip. what if this is all there is?" She caught his jaw's mild slackening and his face turning hollow just below his cheekbones. "For me? For *us*?"

A harder set took over his brow, like he read her reference to his dad's pestering her about her future, then Chip's exaggerating her potential if his dad could only wait a little longer.

"Ally"—he launched to a seated position and cupped her face— "don't let last night get to you, okay? Don't let it affect how you feel about yourself. Or me. Please."

She huffed out a sharp breath. "I wish controlling my feelings were that easy. I don't know if there are things about me that need fixing or if I'm just the way I'm supposed to be, but when you and your dad push—"

"Oh, God. Ally. No." His voice turned brittle, and his hands tensed at her face. "Whatever I said last night had everything to do with me and nothing to do with you. *I'm* the one who's never been enough. Not in his eyes, anyway. I thought talking you up would get him to lay off. That I'd spare you feeling inadequate, and maybe he'd play happy family for just one night. Heck, I was so busy trying to salvage that illusion, I should have just told him to back off from the start."

She held a quiet pause thinking over what he'd said, and although she'd already forgiven him, her mind stuck on the other details. "Why is he so hellbent on giving you a hard time?"

He gave a harsh laugh and let his hands fall away from her, his attention slipping to the grass between them. "Want to know what his real problem with you is?"

Her heartbeat caught, and her ability to speak dried with the sense that a truth bomb was about to explode. Still, she did want to know. "Tell me."

"He sees history repeating, Ally." His voice weak and raspy, his gaze lifted to her again, his pupils wide, and expression slack in a way that said the admission hurt him too. "He sees me as an extension of him, and right now, in his eyes, you're my mom 2.0. The one who will bring it all down. The small-town girl forcing me to waste my potential in Harlow."

She flinched at the comparison. A comparison she'd never really considered, but one that somehow rang true. *Too true.* And that truth bore deeper with each passing thought, a chasm seeming to open within her, painful enough to bring a sting to her eyes.

"Wow." She tore her gaze from him and gave a rapid series of blinks, the open, sunny space around them suddenly not big or private enough. "Way to pour cold water on things."

"Ally—" He reached for her, his forehead crinkled in a way that said he was only half-done, that he was about to get to the part where he would make her feel better about ruining his life, but then her phone rang on the grass beside her, and she held a hand up gesturing for him to stop.

"It's Emilia, I have to answer." She took a drawn-out and steadying breath, but the trembling sound wasn't all that convincing. So she pressed the heel of her palm to her right eye to stem any possible tears.

On the phone, Emilia kept a bright and fast tone, all while Ally offered the excited laughs and engaged responses expected of her. Before long, her insistent tears flowed, and she hung up, squeezing her eyes shut against the confusing mix of sorrow and glee.

"I got the Argyle deal." The words shuddered from her, and her heart beat faster.

Momentarily still, Chip stared back at her before his smile finally broke, and he pulled her into a full embrace. Even as he held her, her mind caught on that split second where he'd done nothing. His moment of doubt mirroring hers.

Things weren't right here.

More and more, she couldn't keep up, and everything she knew slipped unwillingly from her grasp. Chip. Harlow. Her burgeoning career. She couldn't do it all. Couldn't *have* them all.

He pulled back and swept his gaze over her face, his continued grasp on her arms denoting a yearning to hold on. "What happens next?"

She leaned out of his hold and frowned down at her lap. "I guess there'll be contracts to sign once I get back to Harlow. Emilia will help me figure out how to honor the Argyle's order. After that, I get straight to work making pottery."

She wanted to peer up and feel the sense of release that she got from looking at him, but something had changed there too. No matter how much Chip meant to her, she wasn't like him, and there was more that worked against this relationship than just living in different states.

She didn't thrive on problem-solving. She was outgoing, but not adventurous. Like so many artists, she lived in her own head and moved at her own pace.

"Now who's the overachiever?" He lifted her chin and forced her attention to his lighthearted grin. "I guess that means I really can't mess up with Encode now."

She laughed, acknowledging his point. For this super brief moment, she was ahead of him.

He shook his head, brows pinching together, as though he'd witnessed her earlier doubts playing across her face. "About before, I'm not him. Ally, you *are* more than enough. You are everything."

A heavy weight pressed on her chest, and she tried to offer a reassuring smile. "Things are so new, Chip, let's not—"

"No. Let's." He clasped her hands between his, his firm hold pleading that she listen. "Your business is picking up. Encode's interest will at least shine a light on my work. We have more than enough potential that's worth exploring. Move to Boston with me. We'll get an apartment. You'll be closer to the city action and all that means for your art. If you really want to stay in Harlow, then we'll make something work there too."

"You mean, a long-distance relationship?" She raised a brow, ensuring he knew she didn't love the idea.

"It's not ideal, but—"

"It's also not what I want."

No. She'd spent her entire life dreaming of love, and having a relationship unfold via video calls and text messages wasn't what she envisioned.

As for his offer to leave Boston, well, Harlow had no tech industry and his moving there wouldn't be fair. So, the question remained, could she move away from Harlow?

"Ally, we work." He paused to swallow and gave a hesitant nod, as though he second guessed what he planned to say. "And the truth is I—"

"Don't say it." Her heart clenched, his pause between phrases only making her demand more valid.

Whatever he felt, she felt too. The glowing hazel of his eyes said enough that words weren't needed. And putting words to a thing made that thing real.

"Real" meant upending their lives. So, she didn't want real.

Even if her heart already treaded deep waters, she didn't want to hear that he loved her. And just *thinking* that he might, caused her pain.

Her attention dropped to the grass beneath her, the cheerful green and prickly blades under her fingers an insufficient distraction from her darker thoughts.

"Ally." He said nothing more until she focused back to him. "If the Encode funding doesn't happen, I'll find a tech job somewhere else. It might not be as grand as having my own invention, but I'll get us an apartment here or work remote from Harlow if I have to. We can—"

She shook her head, the act alone enough to make him stop.

"This is too much." She shrugged, her throat tight and having reduced her voice to a twisting whisper.

His face tightened, his frustration now undeniable. "Too much what? Reality?"

Exactly that. Even though his question hit her like a literal blow to the gut, she gave him a side glare, warning him not to point out her problem with reality, major change being something she'd waited her whole life for, only to pike out now that it was here.

He rubbed a hand over his face, the strain there easing into something softer and more imploring. "This is what people do when they're in—"

She held up a finger, another sudden warning for him not to say the thing she wasn't ready to hear. "I know."

He loves me. He loves me.

How long have I been waiting for someone to say that?

Only now, I don't want any part of love.

Love meant leaving her family. Not seeing her parents, sister, or niece for long periods of time. Dealing with his dad, alone, because no one she knew would be around to help. Her small taste of this big intimidating world grew increasingly frightful, and what had Chip said about settling down and getting married? That he was a *long* way off wanting that. So what changed? And where did that leave her?

Too chicken to ask. That's what!

Her eyes pulled wide, and her cheeks felt overly cold, once more she fought like hell to never again appear desperate and clingy. His lips spread into a small and knowing smile, perhaps seeing the humor in her evasion. So many had described her as "sunny," but this guy shone in his own way, like he only ever let things bother him to a manageable degree. Meanwhile, she fought against scenarios that often didn't even exist… to the point of complete and inescapable confusion.

He took hold of her hand and kissed the fingertip she'd tried to silence him with, the slow, intentional gesture speaking volumes. That he was everything she hadn't known she'd wanted. Or needed. And while she twisted through each thought and worry, he merely accepted each one as a simple fact of life.

As if to catch her concern, he scooped her into his lap and

unleashed a torrent of playful kisses all over her face, shifting the weight off this moment. She laughed and wriggled in his hold, all while his father's sentiments seeped into her body and mind.

Here in Boston, she and Chip had painted a near-perfect picture of what life together would look like, the biggest downside being that Chip would give up everything to be with her. So a pretty damning flaw, really.

And yes, he did share more with his father than he wished to acknowledge. She could see Chip one day regretting her chaotic, overly idyllic, sometimes immature, nature. That these early moments of joy hadn't been worth his professional and intellectual sacrifices.

So for all her wishes of love, maybe love wasn't meant to be so complicated. So full of sacrifices. And as much as she'd come here thinking she'd gain enough insight to make a choice, she had no real choice at all.

Thirty

ALLY'S FINGERS tightened around Chip's hand, and she allowed him to guide her through the cavernous hotel ballroom where the Encode gala took place. Her breath caught at the monochrome interior, all the ultra-modern black and mirrored surfaces in striking contrast to the white tables and chairs, and the chandeliers supporting linear-shaped crystals that hung like icicles from the roof.

This ballroom looked closer to an upscale nightclub. Not that Ally had been to one of those either, but she'd seen interpretations in TV shows and movies, and *this* was pretty close to *those*.

All around, people gathered into close groups, the dark and bold theme repeated in the clean lines of tailored suits and perfectly fitted dresses. A hint that even the lowest paid person here likely earned more than most anyone in Harlow.

Chip's hand suddenly seemed no longer enough. So she clung to his arm instead, which prompted him to turn and tip her chin upward so she looked at him.

"You'll be fine, Kid." He smiled and landed a kiss to her forehead, the action soothing the churning in her tummy.

Even though she was supposed to be supporting him, he pulled away and slid his attention down her sapphire blue silk dress's low neckline. "I know I've already told you you're beautiful tonight—"

"About ten times, at least." She matched his smile, hoping her joke would help him relax too.

"Then, make it eleven." He touched his nose to hers but didn't go so far as to kiss her. "And add to that, the blue of your dress doesn't even come close to surpassing your eyes."

He ran a finger where her dress met her shoulder, and although she opened her mouth to point out that she'd picked her dress specifically *because* it brought out her eyes, her chance to say anything never came.

"Hey!" Greg bound toward her and Chip, Chip's expression shifting to a quick frown.

"Hi, Ally." Greg gave her a quick wave and then focused on Chip. "You have to come meet my friends from work. They want to hear about Stonewall and what you'll be pitching to the execs tomorrow."

Chip directed a pained look to Ally, indicating that he'd be pulled into a conversation she'd not enjoy, much less understand.

"Can we have a minute?" He spoke to Greg. "We've only just arrived."

As much as she breathed an internal sigh of relief, her stronger desire remained on not holding him back, which meant not getting in the way of him making new connections.

"No. Go." She gave a short giggle, like being left alone in a strange room with strange people was all fine by her even as she backed away and pushed him toward Greg. "Go talk shop. I'll grab a drink and find something else to do."

Though his brows drew heavily, she smiled wider and nodded for him to walk on, not to make her the reason he shied away from the new life awaiting him.

Her smile began to wobble, and she spun away, pretending she knew just where to go in this huge room. A server stood ahead with a tray of champagne flutes, and she strode straight over, swiping up a glass, the delicate stem fittingly cold in her hand, the effervescent, golden bubbles inside, offering a somewhat unwanted cheerier vibe.

The crowd surrounded her, and the occasional person bumped into her, as though standing alone made her invisible. Or maybe because she tucked herself away so that Chip wouldn't see her sipping and staring at the empty stage with two big, pull-up Encode banners on either side.

If he did see her, he'd drop whatever he was doing to save her, and she wanted his saving less than she wanted the awkward solitude.

"Now, here's a new face!"

Ally startled and snapped her attention to a woman to her left, the woman wearing a loose white shirt tucked into her tight pencil skirt, the sharp line of her ice-blonde hair at her jawline, and her stark red lips, intimidatingly meticulous.

The woman lifted her hand and hooked a finger in a gesture for Ally to join the three other women gathered near her. Like a stupefied puppy, Ally did as commanded.

"Angeline." The woman raised her champagne flute in welcome. "And you are?"

"Ally." She stared ahead, not sure what else to say.

The woman looked her over, as though she hadn't been the one to see Ally first, the muscles over her face slightly stiff. "You don't work at Encode, do you?"

The question sent icy shivers through Ally's veins, but she shook her head and answered anyway. "I'm here with a Graduate grant candidate. Chip Overton."

Angeline raised her chin in a *that figures* sort of way. "My firm has been sifting through the legalities of his Stonewall idea. Impressive. And what is it *you* do?"

Stalling for time, Ally took a long sip of her drink, the years having taught her that most people didn't know how to react when she talked about her art, Chip's dad's reaction being case in point. "I'm a potter."

Four silent and blank stares pointed her way before a shorter woman with red curls swept into a high up-do spoke. "As in, clay?"

Relieved to at least have something to respond to, Ally shrugged. "Vases and plant pots, mostly."

"Oh, how delightful." Angeline squeaked with an overly bright tone, her gaze darting between her friends, like she shared a secret Ally wasn't in on. "I thought they had machines for that stuff these days, but good for you!"

"You're right. Pottery has been *very* good for me." Ally lifted her posture because, unlike in the past, she finally had a weapon to defend her life choices. "In fact, I'm in the process of signing a distribution deal with Argyles. Have you heard of them?"

A tall brunette to the redhead's right gasped and pressed a hand to her chest. "*Heard of them? I love* Argyles. Congratulations."

Maybe it was the show of enthusiasm, but right then, Ally decided the brunette's face was much kinder than Angeline's.

Ally took another sip of her champagne, her body far more relaxed now that she'd stood up for herself—for once in her life—finding a place in what was an otherwise ill-fitted situation. Enough to address the group at large. "And what is it that you all do?"

"Corporate law." Angeline spoke and tilted her head to the redhead. "And Sandy here does tax law."

The tall brunette gave a sheepish wave. "I'm in final year med school, hoping to specialize in cardiology. The name's Andy, by the way."

"And I'm Janice." The fourth woman, one of Asian appearance and brave enough to wear color in her magenta pants suit, smiled and added, "Biochemist. I work in cancer research."

Each woman's life seemed so different from hers, each profession not something she would have ever considered an option. Not growing up in Harlow, where there were no lawyers, much less biochemists. The women here appeared to serve loftier purposes, their paths clearer-cut than her own.

Janice—in all her brilliant magenta glory—seemed to see Ally's doubt and reached out, patting Ally's elbow. "You know, I wish I had at least one creative bone in my body, and I *do* adore handmade art. Do you have a business card? I'd love to see your work."

Ally bit the inside of her cheek. *Why had she never thought to make business cards?*

"Heck." She gave an apologetic cringe. "Not yet, but I probably should."

Janice giggled and swatted a hand. "Never mind, I'm sure I can find you on social—"

"Must be nice"—Angeline's flat tone cut straight through Janice's lighter delivery, obliterating Ally's last doubt that this woman might like her—"spending your days quite literally pottering around."

Angeline directed a little chuckle to her friends, all of whom now stared at the ground, their wide eyes saying, *Here we go again.* As though they encountered each other at these events at times, and this backhanded comment was Angeline just being Angeline.

Ally, unwilling to sink beneath the intended shame, rolled her shoulders back and made no effort to hide her frown. "Well, no, *it* is really hard."

Janice shook her head. "Ally, don't worry about her, she's—"

But weeks, maybe years of frustration overflowed, and Ally had no desire to hold back now. "It's hard working other jobs while living for the next chance to do what I actually *want* to do. It's hard sacrificing what little money I earn for materials and equipment, all so people who don't care to know any better can belittle me. So, they can bargain down the price of art that uses techniques that took me years to perfect. Oh, and it's hard fronting up to conversation after conversation with people who imply I'm a few braincells short of a tomato and too damn ignorant to even notice their condescension. Or worse, those who compare my work to the mass-produced, unethically made items they probably saw on some iffy-looking website for less than the money they'd impulse spend on a takeout coffee."

Though her eyes pricked, and her cheeks burned, she raised her chin and stared Angeline down, daring her to talk back now.

Thirty-One

If Ally's weekend with Chip hadn't already left her feeling like an inadequate burden, this woman, Angeline, with her crisp accent and legitimate livelihood, drove home the fact that Ally would never truly fit in. Not in this place. Not with *these* people.

Though some did accept her, others discarded her in harsh and dismissive ways. An enemy for choosing a life they hadn't. As if she'd *had* a choice on where she lived and the personality she'd developed.

To them, she would always be unrefined country folk. A flakey-brained artist. A person with a path too meandering and vague.

And maybe she could ignore all the subtle criticism and learn to be content to never fully belong in Boston and this particular social circle. But Chip's future lay with these people. So maybe, yet again, his future couldn't be with her.

Her eyelids took on an uncontrolled flutter, and she felt her cheeks go slack, an automatic reaction to holding back tears.

"Ally." Janice's voice broke through on a soft whisper, awakening Ally to the whole group still staring. "Don't mind Angeline."

Angeline's eyes flew wide before she pressed her lips into a hard line at Janice, as though she'd expected the woman to back her up.

Ally scarfed the last of her champagne in a sharp and hurried movement. "I'm fine, Janice, but I *am* leaving."

She turned from the group, although one woman muttered a quick, "No. Please, stay," and another, "I like her."

As much as Ally could have laughed at that and fulfilled their wishes to stay and stare down Angeline some more, Ally's wild heart told her to run, that she shouldn't *have* to constantly defend herself.

That said, her short dress and heels made running look like an undignified trot, so she settled on powerwalking across the room to another server, where she deposited her empty glass onto their tray and collected two new full ones.

The bass-thumping music faded, and she glanced over her shoulder to the stage lit with a projected announcement about the Graduate grant. Chip, along with two others—presumably the other finalists—ascended up the stage stairs where another group of senior level-looking people stood.

A heavy ball of emotion filled her chest and obscured her pride for him behind a strong urge to ugly cry right here amongst his peers.

Keep moving.

Just keep moving.

So she barreled on, brushing past people listening to the stage stuff, as well as those maintaining conversations despite the noise up ahead. Before long, she shouldered her way through the black bathroom door.

A couple of women stood before a wide vanity washing hands and fixing hair. Meanwhile, the first stall on her left lay open and slightly bigger than the others. She hurried on in and, since she still balanced a champagne glass in each hand, used an elbow to twist the latch shut, a small amount of bubbly liquid splattering over her fingers and onto the white tiles below.

She swore under her breath and oh-so-ungracefully reached a foot out, kicking the toilet seat closed and then plonking her weight down on her makeshift chair. Gross? *Sure.* But maybe she was where she belonged. Away from the action. In the most basic of rooms. Which still managed to be the most glamorous bathroom she'd used, outside the one in Chip's home.

She scoffed, her jaw aching from unknowingly crushing her teeth together, but not enough to keep her from gulping down another drink. Drops of champagne spilled down her chin and landed on the front of her dress.

"Nice." She wiped at the dark patch blooming against the blue silk, sniffling at the sudden moisture gathered in her nose. "Real nice."

A fat tear rolled down her cheek and landed in her lap, creating another mark on her dress, producing a low growl from her and more frustrated tears.

She was trapped in an endless spiral. Ruined dress. Ruined makeup. Which only caused more tears through the painful hitching of her breath.

She attempted to drown her sobs with more champagne, but her last remaining glass didn't go far. If only she'd had more hands. If only she'd thought to take the server's whole tray with her.

How would she get out of this mess? There'd be no leaving unnoticed, not in her current state.

The stall door shook as though someone wanted to get in, but she shut her eyes, already a little woozy since she wasn't much of a drinker. Still, whoever tried to enter would soon figure this stall was taken and move on.

"Ally."

A sudden coldness hit her, and she flung her eyes open, a pair of pointy, magenta heels peeking from beneath the door.

"Ally. It's Janice. Are you okay?"

Ally bowed her head and swore under her breath.

"Yep. I'm fine. Just needed a moment to myself." Even she heard the tight hesitation in her voice. "Go back to the party, okay?"

As much as Janice highlighted the kinder side of Boston's intellectual crowd, Ally's short jaunt here only made her love her small world in Harlow more. The open spaces and grassy hills, her little pottery shed, the slower pace.

Now that she thought about it, maybe even the Argyle deal was too much.

"Ally, you're *not* fine."

Her spine stiffened, and the chill in her veins turned to hardened ice. "Chip? Is that you?"

"Ally, open the door."

Three solid thuds hit the stall, and she couldn't tell if he was pissed or worried. Or even what the heck he was doing breaking into the women's room.

"You know"—her voice echoed through the space, her reedy tone regrettably unmissable, although she carried on—"harassing women in the ladies room won't do you any favors."

"Neither will leaving my girlfriend to cry alone while I party it up out there." He paused, this time shaking the door handle. "Ally, come out. Please."

She sagged forward, shoulders rounded while she took a minute to catch her breath. To summon the courage to face him.

Could she face him?

She had to. He deserved better than her running and hiding.

So, she planted her feet on the ground and stood. Though her balance wobbled and her hands shook, she turned the door handle, releasing the latch.

All too soon, Chip's heart wrenching hazel stare caught her, and she wanted to stumble away. Back into her stall. Back to hiding. Janice retreated from behind his left shoulder, her downturned gaze a sign she sought to give them space.

Chip's focus shifted all over her, from her face—with no doubt puffy, red eyes and smeared makeup—down to her crumpled dress with distinguishable marks of spilled champagne and tears.

Though her throat turned raw, she choked out a pitiful, "I'm sorry."

She couldn't tell if she apologized for fleeing to the bathrooms, for being somewhat tipsy, or for looking a complete mess.

So she offered a weak explanation to patch over the pain she'd caused and would *still* cause in due time, her next words paired with a deceptive shrug.

"I'm not much fun tonight." Her lip trembled, but she managed to hold back any more tears and add, "Go back to the party, okay?"

His gaze moved about her face before he grabbed her hands and pulled her into him, his forehead finding hers.

"You're overwhelmed." His voice was low and intimate enough

that only she could hear. "And we're leaving this party, right now. Together."

"Chip." Her voice shook, husky and hollow. She was doing it again. Hurting his chances, when he really needed to stick around and mingle some more. "I'll be fine. Just go back and make more friends"

His brow pulled lower with an expression that said she was absurd to think he'd ditch her for people he barely knew. Maybe he was right. Maybe his loyalty was just another reason she needed to let him go.

He pressed a firm kiss to her forehead, as though he saw her pulling away and refused to let her go. "I've talked to everyone I need to talk to. We're leaving."

He stepped back and caught her elbow, nodding a silent thanks to Janice before guiding Ally out the bathroom door.

The pounding of loud music, the rush of unfamiliar faces, and the numerous glances up and down of people noticing her disheveled state. As much as she loved Chip, she'd made him look bad.

And another thing, I love him too much.

Even if he didn't feel embarrassed, his inability to save himself from her only made things worse.

He deserved so much more than she could give.

He deserved someone more intellectual and worldly. Someone with the stamina to counter the moments when his self-sacrificing failed him.

Perhaps a kinder version of Angeline.

Definitely not some Harlow blow-in named Ally Egan.

Thirty-Two

C HIP PEERED across the cab's backseat to Ally, now turned to her window to conceal the doubt he'd already witnessed dragging at her face. And even then, her frazzled inner state flowed through the stiffness in her drawn shoulders and her arms wrapped tight around her waist.

The outside streetlights flickered blue and gold on her skin, skin that puffed under her eyes while stray makeup ran down her cheeks. She was a mess, but none of that had anything to do with how she looked.

He'd asked too much.

Bringing her to Boston had been a mistake. His fault lay in telling her what he'd give up to have her in his life. Then again, all those weeks ago, she'd voiced a wish for love and escape. And yet, he'd never seen anyone so bereft at getting what they wanted.

A frown pulled at his brow, and he reached out to tug her hand into his. Her gaze momentarily hit his before she squeezed her eyes shut in a pained grimace, as though his touch hurt her more than her solo window gazing did.

What a fragile and rare moment. Rare because Ally Egan seemed to want silence. Fragile because, well, he could feel her pulling away and didn't know exactly why.

He worked through the possibilities. That she was less concerned about change, more restless about what she'd seen so far. That she outright hated Boston. Or worse, she figured he was selfish to ask her to stay when she was so new to this wider world.

Not much had ever confused him, but now he couldn't get a single thought of his in order.

Not so worldly or smart after all, huh?

The cab pulled up to his dad's house, a house that now, more than ever, didn't feel like home. His connection with his dad yet another relationship not working.

And even as he paid the driver, Ally pushed her door open, her steps too quick to take her up the stairs to the townhouse's large and glossy burgundy door. But without a key, she had to wait for him.

He rushed after her, her hands still around her waist in a seeming quest for self-comfort, when all he wanted was to be the one giving her that.

A push of the front door revealed little more than darkness inside, Kelly already asleep and his dad working late, though a muted blue light filled the stairwell.

Ally's rigid steps led the way, and he lifted a hand to touch her shoulder, only for second thoughts to pull him short. Despite his desire to have her speak, he got the distinct feeling there wasn't much to say. That or anything said would not be productive.

Not now. Not tonight.

Not when emotions ran so high.

He'd gleaned a little on what had happened at the party from Janice. That someone had spoken unkindly to Ally. That she'd run away to the bathroom ladened with drinks.

But he'd witnessed the hurtful comments directed at her from his dad too. Witnessed her wounded expression and confidence crumble in the wake.

Why do they care so much about what she does?
Why does she?

She paused at the stair's landing and merely stared at the white-painted door belonging to his bedroom. A bedroom they'd shared up until now.

But she doesn't what to share tonight.

That alarming thought had him pausing mid-stride, his fingers curling into the banister.

Though he wanted to move on from the landing, he battled the ache of admitting his dreams of loving this woman quickly unraveled.

"Don't run." His plea cut sharp against the silence. "Please."

That last word came as a rough whisper that had her face turning to him in a pale and frozen expression. He abandoned all pride and strode toward her, only for her to jolt away again.

Inspecting her some more, he shook his head and once again drew nothing but blanks. "What did I do?"

She blinked at his question, and the tension over her face slowly collapsed, her chin the next to move on a small tremble. "You were too perfect."

Her husky delivery, the way her glossy focus stayed on him, her cheeks hollow and the skin around her eyes still red. What should have been a compliment, landed as a heavy blow square in his gut, his entire life refocused as one monumental failure.

He'd been taught to maintain an air of perfection, to do and *be* his utmost best. But here he stood, that perfection turned against him.

The reason the woman he loved would not love him back.

And still, he didn't understand.

She shifted toward him, and the tremble of her lip increased until the whole dam broke, and tears rushed down her cheeks, harder than ever. Even as she cried, she stepped forward until she held her palms to his face. "You were too perfect, Chip."

The pain low in his ribcage morphed into a shuddering sickness. One he sought to quell with something far more tangible. *Someone* who could put things right. *Her.*

So he pulled her in, and as if they drew to the same conclusion, her lips simultaneously crashed into his.

If a kiss could make everything right, then this one would.

She raised against him, and he picked her up, following the rush to have her in his bedroom. Though this wasn't how he'd expected the night to end, his heart thundered a hopeful beat, her muffled moans lingering long after they collapsed to the bed.

She pulled at his shirt, and he slid her underwear free from beneath her dress, her nails digging into his back as he found relief in burying himself deep within her again.

Emotional and confused. With each desperate thrust, he sought to reassure her. To demand she stay and allow him to overshadow any doubts.

She *was* his. All his.

And he would not let her go.

Maintaining this relationship wouldn't be easy. At least, not at first. But they were made to be together and would be each other's strength. They would get through this. They would be okay.

Hours later, Ally awoke to the early dawn's pale light slipping through the blue-gray curtains, the bisque ceiling illuminated at the top. The soothing weight of Chip's arm draped over her from behind, pressing her bare waist while she closed her eyes and drew a slow breath, savoring the feel. Not just his touch, but the soft lap of his sleep-laden breath on her neck, his warmth and support.

No matter how long she stayed here, the moment would pass too quickly, so she forced herself to slip from his hold and collect last night's discarded dress, now a puddle of blue silk on the floor.

She ferried the dress to her suitcase tucked inside a closet, then pulled out one of her signature floral sundresses to wear now. Next, she went to the ensuite, her heart racing as she brushed her hair and teeth before gathering her few belongings and taking those also to her suitcase.

Not wanting to wake Chip, she took her time snapping the two locks shut, continuing to move quietly and quickly on her short walk to the bedroom door. Only then did she stop and glance at him one last time and only for a second—where he slept with the soft lines of his back to her, his arm outstretched, as though she still lay within his hold.

The heat behind her eyes forced her to turn away. She didn't want to cry. Didn't want him to wake and stop this. Even without all that, her journey down the stairs wasn't easy. Not with her heavy suitcase reluctant to descend each damn step. Not with each step taking her farther away from everything she'd ever wanted.

But everything I've ever wanted isn't for me.

It took maturity to admit that. And she'd wanted maturity too.

She followed the light breaking from the windows bracketing the front door up ahead, a beacon to her future, whatever that would be. The hour's devastating stillness only added to the roiling in her tummy, as though even this city slept through her escape.

"So, you're leaving."

She startled at William Overton's weighty statement.

If the city slept, he certainly didn't!

Chip's dad sat to her right, within the living room's archway and on one of two brown leather armchairs. He nursed a round-bottomed glass of high-priced whiskey, something she'd learned he preferred, as well as his tendency to grip her in his unyielding stare. As he did now, halting her next steps away from the stairs.

Still, she womaned-up and nodded all the same.

He drew a sharp breath, and his expression relaxed some before he moved his glass to a small wooden table beside him. "Whatever you think of me, I only ever wanted my son to do well."

Still lost for words, she blinked, *his* words dispersing through her mind like water to dry soil. And again, his stare held while he added, "My job isn't to be nice to him, Ally. I'm not his friend. I'm his father."

She thought about where she'd been just hours ago. At the Encode gala. All because of Chip's success so far. Top grades. Top college degree. Top opportunities. All because his father's we're-not-friends approach had succeeded in its own right.

Her lips pressed into a frown, and she dared to step away from the stairs only stopping when she had Bill right before her. "Chip's not a kid anymore. Maybe it's time to try being nice to him?"

Chip's dad gave no reply. He barely acknowledged she'd spoken, save for the slight softening of tension around his eyes. That softening was enough to prove that he *had* heard her, and enough for her to resume her original plan.

"Just do me a favor"—she turned and grabbed her waiting suitcase and then marched for the front door—"when Chip wakes, tell him I've gone for some solo sightseeing and won't be back for hours."

Hand poised on the door handle and ready to pull, she glanced over to his dad's uncharacteristically slack expression. He saw where she went with this, and yet, he hadn't expected she'd sacrifice what she wanted in order to help Chip succeed.

Just to make sure her plan wouldn't fail, she added one last instruction. "Don't tell him I've left until after his presentation."

Thirty-Three

Chip's morning was an endless list of hurried tasks, complete with a panicked journey downstairs to find Ally, only for his dad to let loose that she'd left to do some early sightseeing so Chip would have space to focus on his presentation.

Though he would have preferred to have her presence, he'd had no time to dwell, his early hours filled with checking presentation notes and slides, then choking down some toast for breakfast while racing out the door.

Encode presentation now over, he pushed through his front door and plonked his leather laptop bag to the nearby ornate upholstered chair, quick to make his way to the kitchen in search of more food. Even if his thoughts did run full speed over each minor detail of this morning's meeting.

The Encode board would see the other candidates today, then set about critiquing and searching for any reason the code he'd provided wouldn't work. A lot of money rode on this decision, so he couldn't blame them. Still, he'd got a feeling from the board members that something wasn't right this morning, and his nerves wouldn't settle until he knew the result.

He rubbed the strain at the back of his neck and stepped into the kitchen, the room's familiar brightness a small relief until he spotted Kelly and his dad staring back at him from their seats at the large, white marble island.

Their faces tight and wary, his dad's arm wrapped around Kelly's shoulder in an unusual show of support. They looked as though they'd been waiting in this room a long time.

"What's happened?" He darted his gaze between the two, his heartbeat thudding loud in his ears.

Kelly peered at his dad again, seeming to seek support before her focus landed on Chip with a pained sort of grimace. "Ally's gone."

His world stilled, and he fought to decipher her full meaning, although the twisting sensation in his gut offered instant understanding. "As in, back to Harlow?"

A long silence hung in the air before Kelly's grimace deepened and she nodded. "We're sorry, Chip."

His limbs turned instantly cold and numb, and he looked to his father, expecting to see a happy smirk there since Ally had done exactly as he'd wanted. But his dad's lips held a firm line, the deepened wrinkles around his mouth denoting a man not at all pleased.

Never the sort to withhold a stare, his dad's gaze fell to the counter, the action corroborating Kelly's claim. "She left this morning. She asked me to lie to you about going sightseeing, although I didn't lie about her not wanting to distract from your opportunity today."

Despite the angry heat rushing his body, plus his desire to lay into his dad, Chip spun away and raced up the stairs. He needed proof. Needed to see his empty bedroom without the hurried eyes of a man hurtling toward his once-in-a-lifetime chance.

Screw opportunity.

Grief and panic swallowed him, and he swung his bedroom door open and stormed across the cream carpet to his wardrobe, indeed emptier than last night. Her suitcase, missing. The shelves he'd cleared for her, once again bare. He dug his phone out of his pocket. No messages there. No missed calls. She'd left. *Just left.*

As though she'd never been here to begin with.

The skin over his cheekbones turned impossibly taut, and he ran his hand over his mouth, sifting through his racing thoughts. He wanted to yell. He wanted to hate her. But yelling and hate were a cheap cover for pain. So he'd find something more useful, something to deal with the tidal wave of emotion crushing him now.

Ally rarely left Harlow and would be traveling alone. The phone still sat in his hand, so he'd focus on making sure she was okay.

His stomach churned as he pressed CALL on her number. Her silent exit hinted at not wanting to hear from him, but they'd known each other in ways that ran far deeper than being just lovers. They had history. Had grown up together. He couldn't end their relationship on silence.

But she didn't answer.

Spots flashed in his eyes over what that could mean, but he told himself that she was on her flight home already and had simply put her phone on airplane mode. She couldn't take calls. Not that she *wouldn't* take *his* call.

How did we get to this?

He paced the area beside his bed and refused to answer that question. He'd make another call. His sister. Maybe Sarah would know if Ally had arrived back in town.

Only, he got no answer there, either, so he tried calling Dean next.

"Hey, what's up?" Dean's distinct and always-easy baritone didn't give Chip much hope he knew anything.

"Is Ally there?"

"What?" A few rustling sounds, like he had Dean's full attention now. "Shouldn't she be with you?"

"She left and isn't answering her phone."

Silence. Dean didn't seem like the type to muse on emotions, so maybe Chip couldn't be surprised at the man's prolonged pause and lack of condolences. "Do you know when she left?"

Bless Dean for not asking for details on *why* she'd left, only for the practical facts to find her now.

"At least six hours." Since she'd slipped out before he'd even woken that morning. "Enough time to board a plane, I guess. Maybe even catch the bus from the airport back to town."

"Hmmm..." Dean paused, seeming to take a moment to think. "All right. Leave this with me. I'll chat with the Egans, see if she's there. If not, I'll check if she's just blocking your calls and may be willing to speak with her parents. Hey, wasn't your big presentation today? Hell of a time for a lover's tiff."

Chip gave a derisive laugh. "Tell me about it. I'm living through an avalanche of bad right now."

"Bad? What else isn't working?"

"Okay, not *bad* exactly. Just, I got weird vibes at the presentation this morning"—trying to sort through his thoughts, he pinched the bridge of his nose, his unease predating learning about Ally's exit—"their past and recent questions about my work seem out of sync with what I'm actually pitching, and when I asked the receptionist if Jay Evans, the guy who first called me about the presentation, would be in the meeting, she had no idea who I meant. I put that down to the new CEO owner doing some standard corporate reshuffling, but even then, I've never heard of the guy, which is unusual for this industry. He apparently owns a bigger non-tech company in New York called Laset Enterprises, so maybe I'm just imaging th—"

"Hang on. Laset Enterprises?"

"Yeah, why?"

"That name sounds familiar. Give me a minute."

Chip's ears filled with Dean's muffled footsteps and then typing, like Chip must have caught Dean at home. "Was this CEO at your meeting?"

"Yeah, but he didn't say m—."

"Holy shit."

"What?" An icy tingle swept down his spine. Dean wasn't a guy all that easy to surprise, and he sounded truly shaken now. "What is it?"

"You're right. Laset did buy out Encode, and Laset is Mark Farro's company."

"Mark? Mark Who?"

"Did your CEO today have blue eyes and brown wavy hair?"

"Yeah, why?"

"This is bad news. Really bad news. If there's any chance they sought you out specifically." Dean let out a low growl, followed by a frustrated sigh. "I need to get off the phone and find Ally. Shit, I need to break the news to Sarah too."

"What? Ally? Sarah? Why?" Chip's heart thundered, and sweat prickled along his hairline. A prospect far more frightening than Ally solo-traveling cross-country taking over. "This doesn't have something to do with the Syndicate, does it?"

"Afraid so." Dean paused, as though a couple of seconds of silence might be enough to quell the overwhelming buzz filling Chip's ears, his nerves well and truly fried. "Mark Farro is Luciano Conti's cousin."

"Oh, shit." Chip wasn't one to swear, but he did now, pieces from the last few weeks falling into place.

"Mark's worse than Luciano. Smarter. More covert. I'm going to need some heavy evidence to believe him buying Encode is just a coincidence."

Dean and Chip both. Though Chip now regretted not looking deeper into Laset Enterprises, a task he'd skipped over in favor of working on Stonewall, relegating any research as something to do only if he was offered a contract.

He'd been too busy chasing success. On proving himself to his dad. On convincing Ally that a life together could work. Not only had he allowed her to pass him by this morning, he'd inadvertently put her in danger.

"I only know basic details on your Stonewall program, but my guess is"—Dean's voice broke through Chip's panic—"he's done his homework on me. On Sarah. And when he found out about you and what you were working on, he saw his golden ticket to gain revenge and a profit."

Another moment passed, and Chip's mind hooked on the questions Encode had lobbed at him over these weeks—the implications of reverse engineering Stonewall, and how his code could be misused. Then his thoughts jumped to the fact that Mark Farro might hurt anyone Chip loved. Maybe even Ally.

"As of this morning, he has access to my code. This *is* bad." He shot to his feet and headed out of his room. "I need to fix this."

In seconds, he raced down the stairs, collecting his laptop bag on his way out the front door. "Dean, find Ally for me. I'm on my way."

Mark's focus faded from the woman speaking ahead of him in the long boardroom. Despite the potential in this candidate's idea and his love of making money, his mind clung to nothing but closing his deal with Chip Overton.

Even if he already had access to Chip's partly finished code, he wanted Stonewall in its entirety—he wanted Chip's signature in a watertight contract—and thus, control of his work as well as the man himself.

Every bit of research he'd done on Chip, on his idea, on his future potential, said this investment *would* pay out. And so far, everything was going to plan.

Mark sat taller and listened a little closer to the woman's ideas on tracking customer's online behavior, although she had zero chance of winning the Graduate grant over Chip. Maybe in time, Mark would find the headspace to approach this lady with some other offer.

"Boss." The man beside Mark, his new lead tech, cleared his throat and leaned in closer. "Something's not right."

His rough and low voice added weight to his words, and his attention didn't shift from the laptop in front of him. "Overton's work. It's disappearing."

The man shot his gaze to Mark, his eyes wide and his jaw slack as he spun the laptop to face Mark. Line after line of code vanished, white space taking over where reams of precious information once lived.

"Fuck!" Mark shot out of his chair, his voice ricocheting within the room's wide, glass walls. "Overton knows."

The five others around him stood. His most trusted associates. Each one in on the plan to seize Chip and Stonewall. Meanwhile, the candidate fell silent, her gaze sweeping over the group of suddenly animated people.

He stabbed a finger at his tech lead. "Save what you can."

The man's blank stare confirmed what Mark already knew. There wasn't much to save. And still, he barked out a final order. "Now!" As if demanding the impossible would salvage his fast-sinking dreams. No, he'd sought to avoid Luciano's more brutish methods. Tried civilized over barbaric. But this world was not a civil place, and Rudolph Manzinni would not forgive repeated failure.

That disappearing code took away Mark's chances of breaking even with the Syndicate, much less the money he'd already sunk into buying Encode. And then there was protecting his family and redeeming everyone's broken dignity.

But now, dignity only sank deeper into the gutter, and that was all Chip Overton's fault. Mark would have no choice but to set new rules.

Cruel incentives to force Chip on board.

"Find out where Chip Overton is and find the woman who accompanied him to last night's gala. She's our leverage." He addressed his head of security while storming out the boardroom, his team of five already sticking close, and leaving the gawping female candidate behind. "Take no shortcuts. Spare nothing and nobody. Just find them. You hear me? He'll do what I say or lose everyone he cares about. His woman dies first."

Thirty-Four

Just once, I want to know what it's like to fall in love. Even better, to have someone love me back. Is that too much to ask?

Ally's past words to Chip haunted her into closing her eyes, the way-too-happy Harlow sun beating down on her through the bus window. Her elbow dug into the ledge, and she pressed her forehead to the warm glass, dejected because she *had* asked too much. She'd fallen in love, been loved, and would now do anything to hand those feelings back.

Those feelings hurt like a knife twisting in her chest, not even the act of breathing came as easily as it once had. So no, she didn't want love. Love cost too much. She just wanted her old naivety and ignorance back.

By now, Chip's presentation would be over, and he'd know she'd left. Her next breath shuddered into her, and she flung her eyes open, hoping the golden fields flicking by could distract from her pain and shame. No matter how well-intended, she'd betrayed him.

She wouldn't be there to congratulate him. To comfort him. Heck, she wouldn't even be there to know how things had unfolded at Encode.

She simply wouldn't *be there.*

The bus rounded into the small parking lot behind Main Street, the brakes hissing at the stop next to the post office. Soon, the driver launched from his seat and down the few stairs leading out the side door.

As he'd done for other disembarking passengers, he'd pull her suitcase out from the undercarriage, and she'd be forced to call her parents to come and pick her up.

But maybe she'd dawdle for a while first.

Kinda as she'd done since leaving Boston airport.

Not once had she picked up her phone to let anyone in Harlow know of her return. The thought of having to explain, of having to admit her failure. Her throat clogged up, and new tears sprung to her eyes every time she tried to use her phone.

What a weird twist in events. She—Ally Egan—succeeding in business, while deficient at love. How had that happened? Her return to Harlow would be a return to square one. Alone. This time, far more damaged.

She pushed to standing and ambled down the bus's aisle, her slowed journey an attempt to delay the moment her feet hit Harlow soil. But all too quickly, she was outside in the mostly empty parking lot, hugging her purse and squinting against the sun. The driver returned to the bus and the vehicle rumbled away.

Only one thing to do now. Call home.

She rummaged through her purse in search of her phone, and in her peripheral vision, a white car drove up the parking lot ramp and snaked through the wide-open space, only to stop before her.

She lowered her purse and stepped back. Whoever drove had their pick of spots, so why park in front of her? The passenger window slid open to reveal her answer, Sarah leaning across a beige middle console to address her. "Get in."

Ally frowned at the short demand. She'd seen Chip's missed calls. Did her silence not speak loud enough? One thing was certain, she wouldn't let his sister guilt her into changing her mind.

"No." She went about stabbing at the icons on her phone's screen. "I'm fine right here, thanks."

"Ally, I don't care what's happening between you and Chip. Just get in." Sarah reached across and tugged the inner door handle before pushing the whole thing open, an action designed to prod Ally into doing Sarah's bidding.

Not shy to convey suspicion, Ally narrowed her eyes. "Why are you here if you don't care?"

The hot sun blanketed her along with the overly still and stifling air, that thick oppression, coupled with Sarah's presence, leaving Ally to regret not calling her parents earlier.

Abandoning Chip was bad enough without having to spend time with Sarah. Despite the recent truce, his headstrong sister would have questions Ally didn't want to answer.

Sarah's peeved stare bounced away from Ally to a point past her left shoulder, the woman's expression turning instantly slack.

"Ally!" The alarm in Sarah's voice had Ally turning to find two men racing toward her from a laneway running between the stores at her back.

One solid and short, another tall and wiry, their scrunched glares and fast approach enough to shatter her daze and pull a scream from her lips.

She wasted half a second grasping for her luggage, but her scrambled movements sent the suitcase crashing to the ground. The men's speed had her ditching her belongings altogether and launching into Sarah's open car door.

"Go. Go. Go!" Her unintended screech proceeded the vehicle shooting forward before she even had a chance to close her door.

She had no idea what happened. Or why. Only that everything happened far too fast.

"Wh...who are they?" She wrenched the door closed and then placed her trembling hands around the latch of her still-unbuckled seatbelt, failing at each attempt to fit the metal plate into the lock. "Sarah, who are they, and where are we going?"

"It's the Syndicate, Ally." The roaring engine muffled Sarah's roughened voice. "They got to Chip, and now they want you."

Sarah's energy turned erratic, and a reel of expletives burst from her lips while she pounded the heel of her palm to the steering wheel's edge.

"The Syndicate?" Ally's question felt weak and breathy. "The Syndicate has Chip?"

She wanted to jump out of this car just to escape the news, to run and never, ever stop. *What had she done?* A broken heart paled to the sheering panic dizzying her thoughts with all the things that could have already gone wrong.

"No, Ally." Sarah called over the revving engine and the rumble of rugged road below, the noise increasing as she planted her foot to the accelerator and sped up. "Chip's on his way back to Harlow. He insisted on returning for you. The Syndicate bought out Encode. They had Stonewall. Dean thinks they'll use Chip's invention to siphon money from bank accounts and other holding institutions, that they'll bankrupt millions, and everyday people will be the collateral damage here. Only Chip deleted Stonewall from the file he shared with Encode, and I figure from what you just escaped, they've already noticed."

Ally's head hurt from the onslaught of information, that the Syndicate's pure cruelty had no limits. However, the only words she could choke out was a weak, "But I don't want Chip to come back for me."

That much was true. She wanted him to hide. To forget she existed. She wanted the two men who'd tried to kidnap her to leave and never return.

One thing was certain. The Syndicate had a habit of latching on to Harlow, and right now, those men would be out there looking for her. And if the Syndicate sent more, well then, no one in this town was safe.

Two men just tried to kidnap Ally, but Sarah got her first. Sheriff to meet them soon.

Chip blew out a hard breath at Dean's message. Great that Sarah had found Ally, but his stomach turned rock hard over the attempted kidnapping. A concrete sign that Mark Farro's involvement with Stonewall was *not* a coincidence.

If only Chip could do more. If only he wasn't stuck at the airport with nothing more to do than wait for his flight back to Minnesota with his laptop, phone, wallet, and keys his only company.

He'd deleted his code little more than an hour ago, and already Mark Farro had men on the ground in Harlow. Meanwhile, Chip wouldn't return to his hometown for hours.

What else will happen between now and then?

His head pounded at the enormity of his situation, an endless downward spiral since the Syndicate would never simply give up. They'd come for Emilia and Blaine. Come for Dean and Sarah. Now, him and Ally. Would anyone in Harlow ever be safe?

The echoey ding of the airport speakers caught his attention, boarding for his flight finally open. He stood and exchanged his phone in his jeans pocket for his boarding pass.

Just a few steps took him to within yards of the steward already checking passes, but a heavy hand landed on Chip's left shoulder, halting his progress.

A robust man with a round and stubbly face stood behind him, shaking his head. A clear warning for Chip to remain still.

Another man rounded the first and stood before Chip. A man he recognized from his presentation. Encode's new owner. *Mark Farro.* "Make a scene and you die."

His blue eyes stayed stone cold, his cheeks hard and unsmiling; a pointed object jabbed Chip in the back.

A gun? The man behind him had a gun? In an airport, of all places.

Though Chip figured his assailant did his best to obscure the weapon, Chip skittered his attention around the expansive space around him. To the people bustling by. Some on phones. Some wrangling small children. Some struggling to drag cumbersome luggage. All too busy with their own lives to notice the risk to his.

As if to confirm the threat, the man holding him leaned in, allowing his low drone to spell out Chip's only option. "We have a different flight for you to catch."

Thirty-Five

ALLY PINNED her attention ahead to the long and dusty road, the loud roar of Sarah's speeding car adding to the sense of devastating alarm. Sarah had only just hung up from updating Dean that she and Ally were on their way. As usual, Ally remained a few steps behind on everyone's plans. "So… umm… where next?"

The driver's side window sat half-open, and a prickly breeze whipped through the car's cabin. Sarah flicked a lock of hair from her forehead and spoke. "The sheriff has a safehouse for us. Your family will be informed to leave town for the moment. Just in case, you know."

Silence filled Sarah's unfinished sentence. But Ally *did* know.

She knew all about the Syndicate hunting down Emilia and for nothing more than a shot at a big payday. How they'd hounded Dean for no reason other than an unwillingness to let him have a new life away from their sordid dealings. How they'd kidnapped Sarah to get to him. How they now targeted Chip, a flimsy secondhand connection to begin with. Even then, they weren't below hurting Ally just to eke a little more revenge.

So now, not even her family was safe. Not her parents. Not Laila.

Oh God, what about Whitney? She was just a child. But nothing and no one seemed sacred to the Syndicate. Only money and vengeance.

Even as the open road shaded over, and the car drew near the woods surrounding Mirabelle River, her mind stayed on what her family would be doing right now. The panic of their rushed escape. The terror she could barely endure for herself, much less imagine in her parents, in poor Whitney. They, of all people, didn't deserve this.

Giant oaks, elms, and spruces loomed on either side of the car in blurs of brown and green. Occasionally, an intersection would open, allowing a quick burst of sunlight before the thick forest swallowed them again.

Sarah barely slowed at each crossing, seeming to trust the rarity of another Harlow resident passing through, or that they'd at least do the predictable thing and let the speeding car pass first.

Throat too tight for words, Ally stayed silent, her mind too overwhelmed to hold on to a single clear thought.

"Ally." Sarah's hand landed on her shoulder, the woman glancing over with an unconvincing smile. "We'll get through this."

Ally wanted to cry at the reassurance. Wanted to cling to those words until she actually believed them. After all, Sarah had come for her. She'd overcome their differences and offered comfort now. So, Ally held back on voicing her doubt and opted for nothing more than a shaky, tight nod.

"Dean and the sheriff make a good team." Sarah's expression hardened on the road, and she took her hand back, as though she saw through Ally's weak attempt at bravery. "They'll have outside reinforcements coming in."

Sarah's flat delivery belied doubt. Like her encouraging words were, in part, also intended to keep her motivated too.

Even if we survive, then what? Do we live out the rest of our days in hiding?

A lifetime void of any real life?

The car shot toward another intersection, and wanting to acknowledge Sarah's efforts, Ally turned back to her friend and prepared to offer a weak thank-you. Only the driver's side window behind Sarah filled with an ever-growing white blur.

Ally's mind pieced the image of a van moments before her entire world exploded, and a sharp scream tore through her throat.

The unstoppable impact. The *BOOM*.

The wrench of her body. Head hitting her window before inertia swung her loose the other way. Sarah's car screeched and spun from one side of the road, all the way to the other, then slammed to a sudden stop into a tree.

The unforgiving violence dropped to an eerie kind of quiet, the engine no longer running, though the soft ticking from within joined the smell of wet earth, burned rubber, and oil.

Ally groaned and focused on Sarah. The tree's thick trunk filled her crumpled window and blood wept from the top of her forehead where she'd likely made contact with the steering wheel.

Though pain crept into Ally's lower back, she was thankful to see Sarah dab a hand to her new wound. As if by instinct, Ally followed the same gesture, ignoring the multiple aches along her spine and shoulders where whiplash already set in, her fingertips touching the side of her head.

Just like Sarah, Ally's fingers came back slick with blood, and she twisted to find her window a glistening spiderweb of cracks, the center-most point level with her head and splattered with red.

The engine made a reluctant choking noise, and she peered over to Sarah stabbing at the start button, her breaths bursting in and out as she slammed her foot to the accelerator and yelled for the damn thing to start.

But nothing happened. Before Ally could form any bright ideas, her door swung open, and she peered up to find the solid-set man from the bus stop glaring at her.

Disallowing any room for escape, he filled her door and wrestled with her seatbelt, seemingly unaffected by her screams in his ear, or the scratches she soon inflicted on his forearms.

The seatbelt released with a jolt, and he wrapped his meaty hand to the front of her sundress, yanking her from the car in one long sweeping movement, her legs collapsing beneath her so that she skidded onto the rough forest floor.

Her attacker pulled her from the ground and shoved her back into a tree, his fingers wrapped around her throat, as though every rough gesture reprimanded any defiance.

"Hurry up and get the other one." He spoke in a rough yell to his lanky friend behind him, this man's dark stare not leaving hers.

She wanted to yell too. Wanted to warn Sarah. But the pressure at her throat made air hard to come by. Helpless, all she could do was glance around wildly. Her attacker's attention didn't budge, his lip curling in a sign he took pleasure from her pain.

The wild beat of her heart filled her ears and pounded at her ribcage. His focus slipped to his hand at her neck, and his tongue darted out to lick at his cracked lips, bringing focus to his unkempt, dark facial hair speckled with gray—only for his mean scowl to move lower still. To her chest. "Not often we get two ladies."

Sarah's screams filled the air, along with the frantic thuds of a scuffle, and Ally took that chance to avert her gaze to Sarah.

The other guy had his hand hooked under her armpits and dragged her backward through the open passenger door. She twisted in his hold, forcing him to lose grip and fall back to the ground. Ever the fighter, she tried to crawl over and past him but stumbled while doing so, and he wrapped his arms around her ankles, slowing her escape.

Breaking one leg free, she kicked him in the eye.

"Fuckin' bitch!" Blood poured from his upper cheekbone, and he lashed a hand out, catching the front of her orange t-shirt and tugging her face closer. "You're not the one we came for. I should put you down right now."

He wrestled a gun from his back pocket and pressed it into Sarah's temple.

"No!" The command escaped Ally on a shrill scream, shrill because of the hand compressing her throat. "The Syndicate. They'll want her too."

The man holding Sarah kept his gun in place, along with his focus, only moving to flick the safety on the gun. "Wanna bet?"

"You came for me because of Chip Overton, right?" The pounding in her head mingled with the growing sickness in her tummy, but she nodded as best she could to Sarah. "That's his sister."

There'd be hell to pay for outing Sarah, but that would come later. Right now, Ally set her mind to surviving one moment at a time.

The man with the gun shuffled to standing, leaving Sarah on the ground, her hands supporting her from behind while she stared up at him. He pulled the trigger, hand veering at the same time.

Sarah winced, the bullet skimming mere inches from her head and hitting the earth behind her, silent tears quick to streak her earth-smeared cheeks.

"Now, you get one thing straight"—he used the gun's muzzle to tap her chin up, ensuring she had nowhere else to look but at him—"I don't know who the Syndicate are. I don't care either. Only that they're paying good money to bring you in. So maybe I won't kill you. *Maybe.* But I sure as hell *will* shoot. And that's without saying all the other things I could do to you without leaving you dead, got it?"

He paused for a moment, and the man holding Ally rubbed a thumb down the side of her throat, as though sending a message on the other things he would personally do besides killing her.

The man before Sarah rose and peered about. "Are we all done here?"

Though Sarah's complexion turned sheet-white and her throat bobbed in restrained fear, she gave a slow and silent nod.

"Good." Once again, the man yelled, swatting the gun through the air in a *move-along* gesture. "Then, get up and get in the fucking van."

The van in question sat yards away, idling in its mangled state, the front passenger side smashed in, and the windshield cracked. Sarah stood, walking on despite her likely pain and fatigue, her stare connecting with Ally's in a soulless and resigned gaze.

The man holding Ally pulled her into a walk ahead of him, his hands gripping tight at her upper arms and crushing her against him from behind. "You might be able to get me not to hurt you."

His beer-scented breath struck her neck, and he gave a soft chuckle, his thick fingers sliding under her bare arm and grabbing at her breast. His touch nothing like the soft and considerate man she'd loved and left behind in Boston.

The ache in her head intensified, and a wave of dizziness rocked her, her ears ringing with a thin and tinny sound. Her focus fell to her shuffling feet, to the blurring earth and leaves below.

A need to vomit rose in her gut and burned her throat. Not just because of the man touching her. But because something wasn't right here. As though her injuries from the crash ran deeper than the merely visible surface wounds.

"You really gonna risk your life for a piece of ass?" She lifted her attention to the other guy glaring from outside the open van door, gun still pointed at Sarah as she disappeared inside.

The man holding her shoved her the last few steps to the van. "Two of them. Two of us. You know what I'm sayin'?"

The other man caught her and chuckled, looking her dead in the eyes before adding, "Yeah, maybe you got a point."

As much as she tried to hold back, those words and this man's new smirk stirred the sickness rocking her body, and she doubled forward, puking on the ground at his feet.

His friend hollered a menacing, mocking sort of laugh, but she peered up at the man before her, his smirk fallen to a cold and disgusted grimace. One that left her fearing he'd abandon his deal with the Syndicate and kill her now.

"I'm sorry." Her apology came as a pleading cry. For the first time in her life, she wanted pity, but all he did was push her onto a seat and slam the van door shut before her very eyes.

In an odd moment of stillness, her mind latched to all the action movies she'd ever watched that had left her hugely misinformed.

Neither man bothered to tie her or Sarah up. They didn't even restrain her with a buckled seatbelt. Only the low *thunk* of the van's central locking alerted her to her narrowed chance for escape. That, and the threat of being shot.

The man who'd held her to the tree now sat in the front passenger seat, his torso turned as he pointed a gun at her and Sarah. A perpetual sleaze ball, his leering returned. Not wanting to vomit or cause any more trouble, she focused on the gray fabric seat in front of her, absorbing the first jolt of the van rolling forward.

Her incessant nausea rose again, and she pressed her eyes shut, scrambling for composure. She was being taken farther from freedom

—perhaps closer to her last moments alive—the pain and fog in her head offering a louder warning.

As though her fate had already been sealed before she'd even stepped into this van.

As much as she wanted to, she couldn't look at Sarah, a woman who'd escaped the Syndicate once before, only to gamble that escape on trying to save Ally today.

Tears trickled down Ally's face.

Nothing about this situation was fair, and maybe she couldn't *look* at Sarah, but she could reach out and offer the only thing left to give. *Solidarity.*

She did just that, wrapping her fingers around Sarah's hand on the seat and imparting what would perhaps be her final words. "I'm sorry."

Sorry that she had anything to do with Sarah being in this situation.

Sorry for the stupid fight.

Sorry for every hasty misunderstanding. That she'd deemed a decade of friendship tainted because of some panicked promise Chip had convinced Sarah to make.

Ally *was* sorry.

Sarah wouldn't have come for her today if, at some point, this friendship hadn't turned true.

Ally feared Sarah hadn't heard her, and long moments passed before a gentle squeeze on her hand confirmed her concern unfounded. Sarah accepted the apology. For better or worse, they were in this together.

Ally's tears fell thicker and faster, and she closed her eyes to slow the dizziness gripping her brain. She'd been so childish. So insecure and too quick to react, every perceived slight heightened because of a squabble over a man.

The van shifted and mingled her shame with fear, forcing her eyes to open to witness the road change to a long driveway leading to an abandoned farm. *The Dalton farm.* Empty for three years now, the Daltons long ago moved to the city. The farm so vast and far from town that it still failed to sell.

Ally's hope fizzled to nothing, and a sob squeaked up her throat, this place one of the most isolated in an already remote town. So isolated the no one would find her and Sarah. Not for a long time. Not until it was far too late.

Thirty-Six

CHIP'S HANDS remained cuffed behind his back, even within the lavish interior of Mark Farro's private jet, the man's hired goon seated across the aisle and pointing a gun Chip's way.

Another guy sat on a tan leather seat up ahead, Chip's confiscated laptop open on the tray holder while the man's nimble fingers tapped at the keys.

Close to three hours passed, and this man hadn't paused for a break, his flustered pace indicative of fear. Like his life depended on finding Stonewall's now deleted code.

Chip could predict what went through the guy's head. Hope that the code was in the OS temp file store. Or if that didn't work, try to recover it from the hard drive cache. All the typical places deleted data might hide. But now, the plane's weight shifted, and Chip's attention fell to a stretch of field appearing below a dipping wing, Harlow's distinctive landscape prodding the heavy feeling already pulling at his stomach.

Now, all he wanted to do was jump up and down, to cause any sort of distraction to turn this flight around, but then his focus left the trees dotting the Mirabelle River and hit the goon with the gun. The man's lips were curled in a "try me" expression, and the promise of death wilted Chip's will to fight.

So he slumped back in his seat, as much as he could without his hands jabbing him in the back.

Of course, Mark would take me here.

Chip thought back to his initial phone call from Mark, back when he'd pretended to be Jay Evans, Encode's slightly too enthusiastic senior manager. He'd mentioned Stonewall's unique capabilities and the idea of reverse engineering Chip's program.

Now, Chip couldn't stop thinking about all the evil things reverse engineering might achieve. Stolen identities. Broken bank networks. Untold damage…

The Syndicate wasn't above indiscriminately ruining lives. He'd seen that through his sister's ordeal. And people who already struggled would lose even more. Maybe *everything*.

For some inexplicable reason, his mother came to mind. The day of her breakdown. All the rubble. All the blood. All the lows one hit when hope seemed lost. And this time, Chip would play a grand scale part in that outpouring of grief.

I have to find a way to stop this.

He would cling to Dean's news about Ally and Sarah being safe. That Mark would arrive in Harlow minus the people he sought to target. Only Chip's life would hang in the balance, the Syndicate likely to keep him alive to get to Stonewall.

He had no illusions. He'd ultimately die. But maybe those close to him would survive.

The uneven field below was not fit for landings, and the plane took on a series of rough bounces, but soon, the plane came to a complete stop, and the gun-wielding goon waved his weapon at Chip to start walking.

He took his reluctant stroll to the exit and passed the guy working on his laptop. The guy stopped to give Chip a glassy stare, his brow holding a light sheen of sweat despite the cabin's cool interior.

Mark already stood at the exit but hung back, allowing Chip and the goon to leave first. Maybe because he feared any bullets fired would go through Chip and into him… *What a chilling thought.*

"Welcome home, Mr. Overton." Mark's optimistic tone followed Chip down the ramp.

Though tension pulled at his chest, he focused ahead and said nothing. An old barn he didn't recognize lay on the field's edge and close to a road; the guy with the gun prodded him to walk faster. Off the stairs, his cuffed hands impeded his balance through the obstacle of unkempt and dry grass.

A white van with North Dakota license plates sat before the open barn doors, the tires caked in semi-dry mud—as though the van had passed through the wetter woods by Mirabelle River—the vehicle's front radiator area crushed in and the windshield cracked.

The van's presence signaled more people had come to partake in his demise, and his side-on approach meant he couldn't yet see inside the barn. The mere inability to know what awaited him sent bile rising through his chest while his forced pace crushed his habitual need to stop and think.

"Chip!"

His name exploded on Sarah's ragged and torn cry, his eyes slow to adjust to the barn's darkness before he formed a clear visual.

When he did find her, she knelt amongst a scatter of rotting straw in the barn's echoey center, hands bound behind her, a man hovering near with a gun pointed at her blood-smeared forehead.

Chip shuffled back a step, only for a different gun to jab him in the ribcage, that jab lurching him forward while his limbs lost sensation and turned cold.

Ally.

They had Ally too. She knelt beside Sarah, her shoulders rounded and strings of her ice-blonde hair—matted in blood—hung over her eyes. He drew near and found her lower lip trembling, her usually loud presence now inordinately silent.

"Surprise." The goon behind him offered that sarcastic mumble while the men standing over Ally and Sarah displayed wonky-toothed grins.

Mark strode ahead, completely at home amongst the chaos and pointing at Ally.

"Tie Mr. Overton to the sniveling one." Mark flicked his gaze to

Chip, steel-blue eyes uncharacteristically bright, like this scenario was his happy place, and his corporate persona an ill-fitting suit he begrudgingly wore to support this part of his life. "That's your woman, isn't she? It's only right that you feel it when I put a bullet in her brain."

Thirty-Seven

ALLY WINCED at the press of Chip's back to hers, his familiar hard warmth only making this hostage situation evermore painful. As one of Mark's men lifted her hands and tethered Chip's cuffs to hers, her already raw wrists hurt even more, while Chip's fingers were quick to wrap around hers, the intimate gesture breaking her heart anew.

The barn's musty smell of hot, rotting wood mingled with the stench of stale, damp hay. Senses distorted from her head injury, her face burned and sweat trickled over her collarbone, the discomfort of summer's high heat making her world seem on literal fire.

"Ally." Chip's voice broke through her deepening weakness, and she winced again, her name delivered on a heartsick tone. "Just hold on, okay? I'll get you out of here. I'll give him what he wants."

She squeezed her eyes shut, not wanting to hear about what he'd give up for her, all while she failed to block out the man standing near with a gun pointed to her head.

Didn't they know she'd ended things?

Why bring her here to hurt him some more?

She hated having him so close. Hated him because he didn't hate her.

And he really should have.

Though she'd never been all that brave. Though she wanted to live. She didn't want Chip to give the Syndicate more power than they already had. So even if the effort of speaking agitated the already minimal contents of her tummy, she found her voice all the same. "Please. Don't. He won't let us survive anyway."

Yes, they *would* die, but this evil man would leave empty handed.

When had she become so gutsy? Maybe because, regardless of whether Mark killed her, she could already feel herself detaching from everything around her. She was getting so drowsy. So lightheaded. So confused.

Mark chuckled, making it clear he'd heard what she'd said, his crisp and clean powder-blue shirt and black pants a harsh contrast to her bloodied and muddied white summer dress.

"No, honey, *you'll* die. And your friend here too, of course." Not bothering to hold a weapon, he shifted his smug stare to Sarah, his reference to her acknowledging her part in Luciano Conti's arrest. Meanwhile, Sarah's eyes turned wide and glossy, and new tears slid down her cheeks.

Mark's smile grew, and he crouched closer to Chip. "You might still be useful, but only if you're willing to play along. What do you say, *Chip*?"

His over-pronunciation of Chip's name dripped with disdain, but Chip was still quick to reply, his voice a soft rumble against her back. "Their life for mine and Stonewall. Let them live. Once I know they're safe, you'll get everything."

"Now, let's make one thing clear"—though Mark's tone grew rougher, she couldn't completely see him, like he put his face way too close to Chip's—"you and this god-awful town have already caused me irreparable damage. I might respect the art of negotiation, but you're not going to get everything you want, so it's best you come to terms with that."

"What do you want?"

Seeming mildly appeased with Chip's question, Mark eased back, giving her a view of his slow shaking head. "Your sister was a bonus, and I have a moral debt to pay to my cousin. I'm not letting her go. No. She dies. And since I'm here now, so does Dean Holloway. Once we comb through the town and find him, of course. Now, your girlfriend?" He scoffed. "I'll kill her just because I can, but there might be room for you to change my mind."

The scorn in Mark's plans turned her muscles lax while her heart found the energy to thunder in her chest. Sarah's survival was off the table. The Syndicate would tear Harlow apart looking for Dean. And Chip's only hope was bartering for her life.

His hands gripped tighter, his breaths a burst of sound and movement against her, like he grappled with grief and fading hope. "You know I have the code."

His hollow tone held less confidence than before.

"It's not enough anymore."

Mark's matter-of-fact delivery rang through the air, stealing all attention, stealing all will to debate, and so a laugh broke from her, manic and irrational.

Her shoulders shook from that unabashed and deep-down sound while more tears fell, and her head lolled forward. "Chip, the question isn't whether you can change his mind."

More laughter. More tears. Was the damage to her body and spirit so bad she'd lost her mind too? "The question is, can you trust him?"

She grimaced at having to crane her neck to eyeball Mark, the implicit answer to her question being no.

She meant to seem stoic, as though she didn't care what befell her and that he'd lost this sordid game already. But she lacked the physical strength to maintain the façade for too long, and her eyelids began to flutter in an uncoordinated way.

Meanwhile, Mark's gray stare gave nothing away. Literally, nothing. As though he regarded her with little more affection than he would a common moth trapped between two competing flames, his focus switching back to Chip.

"Like I was saying, Stonewall alone isn't enough anymore, Mr. Overton. Your program is in its early stages and not designed for the purposes I need it for. So, the girl goes, and you stay to finish the job. Do you understand?"

"No, Chip," she whispered, her eyes set on staying closed. She shook her head against the back of his so he could feel her. "Please. No."

But once again, Mark spoke as though she wasn't there. "You fly back to Boston with me now, and we let her go, Chip. You get Stonewall running, and she continues to live as if we were never here. And since you're smarter than the average programmer, you continue to work for me, only me, and maybe, you'll do well out of this whole ordeal too."

Chip didn't reply right away, but she felt the oh-so-slight sag of his posture, as though he mourned the use of his hard-earned talents for nothing more than aiding the Syndicate—his future reduced to a lifetime of engineering misery for people who really didn't deserve to succeed.

She could imagine a world without her, but not without Chip, and she couldn't see him remaining the same under Mark's conditions. If this bargain did secure her survival, if they found a way to stay together, Chip's sacrifices now would leave him even more soulless than her earlier fears of what a life in Harlow would do to him.

As for her fears back when they'd been in Boston—that he'd give up too much just to be with her—they were a heavenly dream compared to what unfolded now. Now, no matter how this played out, they would never be the same. Sarah and Dean would be dead. The people of Harlow would be traumatized. And he *would* most certainly come to regret choosing her.

"Chip, listen to me." Her voice was a still whisper, and she squeezed his hand in a grab for his attention, for him to feel her unspoken love, and that maybe choosing the greater good was the only real choice he had. "This is so much bigger than us. Don't give him what he wants."

The little world she'd clung to. Harlow. Her art. Her family. Him. She'd never had to pull her head from the clouds long enough to fully embrace reality, but something changed here in this cold savagery of armed men and crushing ultimatums. *She knew what she wanted.*

She, too, could make hard sacrifices. Perhaps the ultimate sacrifice.

And so she let go of his hand. A metaphorical step away since she was bound to him and lacked the freedom to leave as she wished. To give him the space to decide without her shadowing him.

Even as she fought her instinct to survive, she knew she could release that too. For the sake of a world that she wouldn't get to enjoy.

But her parents would. And her sister. And Whitney. *Yes, Whitney.* So many good reasons to run head-first into the inevitable. To force her eyes open now and stare into Mark's cold glare.

"Chip won't do it." She gave Mark a small nod, even though she didn't have the strength for any satisfying, smug smirks. To press the point that she'd come to terms with the truth of this situation and figured he could rot in hell for all she cared. "You won't do it, will you, Chip?"

Mark's frown dropped, providing the satisfaction she'd sought. He saw just how much she wasn't bluffing. And even as she stared him down, she directed all her words to Chip. "I know you want to save us both but say you won't. Say you'll let me go."

Though their hands no longer touched, Chip leaned his head back into hers, the action and his next words a plea for her to give him some other choice. "Ally."

But as far as she was concerned, there was no other choice. As much as she wanted to demand his compliance, the best she could muster was an imploring whisper. "Promise me."

"Chip, she's right." Sarah's hushed tone cut through the tension, as ever, a voice of reason. "Either option is bad, but what this asshole is offering is worse."

Sarah scowled at Mark, a glare that seemed to say, *Fuck you* before her gaze softened and fell to Ally. Ally closed her eyes and nodded. Her silent way of saying, "Thank you."

Seconds passed under the weight of Chip's implied thought, like he battled against what he wanted. To save her. And what she asked of him. To let her go.

Meanwhile, Mark's gaze bore into her, as though he sought to gouge holes through her resolve with his voiceless promise of hell to pay should Chip choose against his wishes.

"I promise."

Chip's hands found hers again, his tight but reassuring squeeze a seeming goodbye. A goodbye she hadn't given him in Boston, but one she wanted all the same.

Sarah's eyes slammed shut, and her face crumpled to a grief-filled grimace. Next came the smoothing out of wrinkles over Mark's cheekbones, his soulless stare assessing Ally one last time, like he too had something to come to terms with.

But then, his gaze flicked to the man with the gun pointed at her head. That man removed the safety while looking at Mark. "Boss?"

Mark nodded, and she squeezed her eyes shut, ready to die.

A series of echoey bangs shook the air. A hard thud hit the ground beside her. Where was the pain? The oblivion? Was she dead already?

She opened her eyes. *Not dead.*

The man nearest to Sarah fell to his knees, a small round wound at his collarbone seeping a wide bloom of blood over his shirt before he toppled over completely.

Mark fell too, but not out of injury, more like him taking cover behind her. Another explosion of bullets had Chip's tormentor dropping, too, his chest quick to coat in liquid red.

Ally's entire body coiled in defense. She couldn't cover her ears, and her head rung from the deafening sounds, exacerbating her incessant need to vomit.

The man nearest her groaned, the same man who'd leered, and groped, and threatened her in the woods. As much as she should have smiled at his agony, all she felt was weak and numbness while trying to decide whether to be elated or horrified at this twist of fate.

Once again helpless, she watched as Mark lashed out a hand and stole that man's gun, quick to roll in the opposite direction until he held the weapon to Sarah's head. "I'll shoot her, Holloway."

Ally startled at Dean's surname but forced her body to twist so she could see over her shoulder to the open barn doors. Sure enough, Dean was there with the sheriff, both men's weapons trained on Mark.

"Not if I shoot you first." Dean glared through his gruff warning. "Drop the gun."

Mark shook his head, the skin over his face glistening with sweat, his once-pristine shirt torn and soiled from his interaction with the ground.

He fished a hand into his pants pocket and produced his phone, using voice-command to place a call, although his only words to the person on the other end were, "Start the jet."

He tucked the phone back into his pocket and stood, pressing the gun closer to Sarah's temple. "Just one bullet and she's gone, Holloway. How much do you trust you can kill me first?"

He narrowed his harsh stare at Dean while Sarah's forceful breaths pushed the loose flaxen strands from her ruffled ponytail, her wide stare also glued to Dean in a plea for him to do something. To save her.

"And there are two guns, to your one, Mr. Farro." The sheriff's calmer tone filled the space, perhaps a man with less skin in this race or just a man with more years and patience on his clock. Sarah was near to a daughter to him, after all. "You don't have enough time to kill us all. Step down."

Mark held impossibly still and silent, his attention bouncing between Dean and the sheriff. A man who'd made Chip weigh the value of his life, now forced to do the same for his own.

High-pitched jet engines howled from outside, the ear-splitting whir adding pressure to the moment, a pressure the sheriff seemed to capitalize on. "Last chance, Farro."

Mark's jaw tightened in a show of disdain, and he kneed Sarah in the shoulder, the gun still pointed at her head. "Get up."

She did as asked, rising as he hooked an arm around her neck and used her as a human shield. Her breaths turned to pitchy gasps, and she clawed her fingers into his arm, fighting for freedom.

Not slowing to allow her any kind of sure footing, he pulled her backward, the hiss of displaced straw following each rushed step toward the barn's rear exit. If anyone followed, he would shoot. But time was quickly running out, and there was no knowing where he would take her.

The barn door gave a loud and rusted creak that matched the lurch of Ally's tummy, and he disappeared around the corner with Sarah, Ally's world turning overly still.

Dean and the sheriff's thudding footsteps boosted the race to save Sarah, the pinpricks of light through the barn's wooden beams betraying Mark's direction via his shadow.

What would he do when he got Sarah to the plane?

Would he take her with him? Let her go?

Or kill her before takeoff?

Though muffled against the jet's engines, more loud shots broke from outside. Unable to protect herself from sounds she didn't want to hear, Ally dipped her head and buried her face in her knees, too afraid to lift her gaze long enough to see who, if anyone, would return for her through those barn doors.

Thirty-Eight

THE JET TOOK OFF, and its roar soon faded to the background, making room for Harlow's rural quiet to take over. Ally dared to lift her head and open her eyes, but nothing had changed in the barn to signify who survived the commotion outside.

There'd been gunshots. Indistinguishable words. While dead or dying men lay strewn on the nearby ground around her. Chip, he remained tied with his back to hers.

"Are we the only ones alive?" Her weak voice cut through the barn's empty stillness. "Oh God, are we going to starve here, alone?"

That's if my injuries didn't get me first.

"I'll break us out of here somehow, okay?" Chip rubbed a thumb over her hands still clasped in his. "Now, *shhh*, what's that noise?"

She did as told and even held her breath so she could hear. A female cry filtered through. Sarah? Ally had seen no other women here. It had to be her. *Sarah was alive?* Plodding steps joined the chorus. *Footsteps.* As in, plural.

More than one person survived.

The sheriff was the first to re-enter the barn, the afternoon's sun behind turning him into a glorious silhouette. He removed his hat and rubbed the back of his wrist over his brow.

Dean walked through, and she almost cried, his arm wrapped around Sarah, who half-sagged against him. Still bloodied and covered in dirt, of course. A different kind of tears welled in Ally's eyes, and her mouth dried with an inability to speak.

As this new reality settled in, a strange calm took over. Mark was gone. Everyone she knew survived.

While Dean sat Sarah on a low wall and crouched before her, inspecting her wounds, the sheriff cuffed the only surviving henchman, who groaned on the ground beside Chip.

"I've already radioed the medics, so you two just hang on." He got down and placed his hat on the ground before tinkering with her cuffs. "Pulled a bit of old wire off the front fence. I might be able to work these free."

One of her cuffs popped open, and she pulled herself loose, her hands leaving Chip to meet with the rough barn floor while she curled forward and dry heaved—her stomach already empty from her vomiting in the woods.

She lifted her gaze to the sheriff's smile, albeit with a crosshatch of wrinkles over his forehead that denoted concern. "It's a normal reaction, dear."

He hooked a hand under her arm and tried to help her stand, only her world spun, and she stumbled.

Chip, still cuffed, turned, his scrunched stare darting about her face. "That bit's not normal, is it?"

"No." The sheriff shook his head and helped her to the ground again. "Best you stay down for now."

So she stayed on the ground, legs folded before her, and tried not to look at Chip, though the sight of her red-raw wrists also made her want to cry.

The sheriff huddled in front of Chip and worked on releasing his cuffs, too, a light chuckle escaping him. "Seems my experience with these things have finally paid off. Figure I can open just about any pair."

Chip's cuffs clunked to the floor, and he shot forward, kneeling before Ally. "Your head."

Despite her attempts to avoid his gaze, he cupped her face and peered into her eyes—the soft concern in his forced her tummy to stiffen. She didn't want concern. Especially not his. Not over her. Not over the breakup. Not over this. She also didn't want to give him false hope.

Even as he took her hands, she winced at his insistence, sensing a need to unleash the talk she'd avoided in Boston. Only now, things were worse, and she didn't know how.

So of course, she went with changing the subject, turning her attention to the sheriff standing over her. "How did you and Dean find us?"

The sheriff scrubbed a hand over the back of his neck, and his lip twisted into a small grimace. "Well first, you and Sarah didn't show at our agreed meeting point, then came a report of an undeclared jet landing."

"Once we spotted the plane, we hid the patrol car down the road and legged it over here," Dean called over from next to Sarah. "We held our position on the opposite side of the barn, making it hard for anyone on the plane to see us."

"Yeah, well"—the sheriff shook his head, his attention cast to the ground—"I don't suppose that's the last we'll hear of Mark or the Syndicate."

Dean's expression firmed, and he nodded. "We'll need reinforcements around town."

"Lots of folks won't be happy about that." The sheriff jammed his hat back on. "But I'll see what I can muster."

"We'll need more than that. They have my laptop." Chip turned to the sheriff just a little behind him, his hands still holding hers. "I buried my work in an encrypted file and deleted any obvious data outside of that, but it's not impossible that Mark could still recover something."

"Still wouldn't want to be Mark Farro." The sheriff frowned at the ground. "Possession of your laptop makes him a national security risk. I'd say he's not about to show his face anytime soon. In fact, he's lost a lot coming after you, Chip. His assets may well be seized."

"For some reason, none of that makes me feel better." Chip's gaze dipped, like he worked through the implications of what he'd just heard. That he was more at risk than ever.

"Maybe I can help."

The statement came from an unfamiliar voice, and everyone quickly turned to the barn's back door. A man stood there holding Chip's laptop satchel high in one hand. His other hand rising in an act of cautious surrender.

Dean and the sheriff drew their weapons again.

"Put down the bag," Dean barked out the order.

"Whoa. Hold on." The man's voice shook and sweat beaded his dark skin, his brown gaze flicking between the two armed men as he bent his long limbs and lowered the bag. "I'm so done with guns. I'm done with deranged people. I want out of the Syndicate. I just want out."

"That guy's from the plane." Chip's forehead wrinkled and his eyes held a hardened stare. "He was the one hacking into my computer."

"No, man. You got it twisted." The guy lifted his shoulders in a stiff shrug, the move shifting his loose t-shirt above his baggy jeans. "I'm just some tech guy, like you. Mark took over Encode, and my life has been hell ever since. Arrest me if you want, but I snuck out of that plane to get away from the guy. And I brought your laptop, didn't I?"

He pointed at the satchel, and Dean and the sheriff yelled at him to keep his hands up. He did so with a quick, panicked motion, and Dean shuffled forward, collecting Ally's discarded cuffs, his gun aimed until he had the new arrival restrained.

"Can we please make up a story about my arrest?" The guy's voice took on a quick sort of rambling, and Dean marched him toward Mark's other surviving employee. "Tell everyone I got caught trying to defend him. I'll do the time, okay? Just make it sound like I was on his side, so he'll leave me alone."

Dean pressed on the guy's shoulder, forcing him to sit, the other Syndicate man scrunching his face at the geek in a look of disgust.

Ally felt for the guy. She could see a lot of Chip in him—this man only a few steps in deeper with the Syndicate—just another pawn with his skills held hostage. Meanwhile, the sheriff strolled over to the satchel, slow to open the front flap before pulling out Chip's laptop. "This yours?"

Chip nodded, the laptop cover decked out with a distinctive sticker of a cityscape Ally had also seen before.

His attention returned to her, his pupils dilated and his unwavering focus seeking the answers she still didn't want to provide. "We're still not okay, are we?"

His question referred to Boston. To her leaving. The small lines between his brows a sign of his pain over her exit, no matter how quiet the execution.

She shook her head, stirring her dizziness. She wasn't okay either. "Nothing's changed."

He pulled her hands closer and kissed her knuckles, the tender gesture filling her heart with even more excruciating guilt. "Ally—"

She squeezed her eyes shut and forced herself to recall her ordeal in Boston. His dad. That woman at the gala. How out of place she'd felt. If she didn't keep remembering, she'd cave. She'd take Chip back.

"There's a reason you hesitated on telling me about the Encode grant." She opened her eyes to find even more strain on his face, all of which begged her to change her mind.

But he pressed his hand to her cheek and wiped her tears away with his thumb, still caring for her through this difficult moment. "I didn't want to lose you, even then."

She gave him a small nod, thankful for his honesty. "And your dad."

His brow hardened. "Who cares what he—"

"I care." Despite her unsteadiness and the sickness churning her belly, her voice still held a firm insistence. "I don't want to be the thorn in your family's side."

"You're not." He tugged at her hands, color raising on his cheeks and dulling the whites of his eyes. Frustrated. Grief stricken.

She tilted her head to one side and implored him to once again be honest with himself, the tension easing on his face as he eventually nodded down at the ground between them.

Sadness sweeping over, she bit into her lower lip, wanting to believe that today's traumatic events could change things, instead of being just another reason she, Chip, and Harlow couldn't be one.

"Chip, you shouldn't have to defend me against him." She dropped her attention to his crumpled white shirt, the button-up one he'd likely worn to his presentation at Encode, only to find himself embroiled in the Syndicate's vendetta against his sister and hometown. "I don't *want* to have to justify who I am anymore. We don't fit together, Chip, and being with you forced me to accept that. To accept who I am, even if others won't. So if I'm lucky enough to survive today, I won't use my precious second chance trying to fit in where I'm not wanted."

Water pooled along the edges of his eyes, like he acknowledged the change in her and knew he couldn't ask her to compromise who she was to be with him. Still, he spoke again, "Ally, you *are* wanted."

"I know." She gave him a tight smile, the whomp of an approaching helicopter cutting through her disorientation. She'd be leaving him soon. Her reasons this time, clear and final. "I know you never meant to make me feel like anything less than the woman you loved—and believe me—I do feel loved, Chip. I love you too. I love you enough to spare us the next years pretending we can make things work in ways your parents couldn't."

Heavy tears trickled down her face, and she finally reached for him, hooking her hand desperately around his wrist and pulling him in. "For the first time in my life, I know that love isn't always about throwing myself all in. I'm giving you up because it's the right thing to do. I need you to make that decision, too, Chip. Remember your earlier promise?"

As though he recognized her reference to his negations with Mark over her life, Chip pressed his lips into a thin line, a defined stillness dominating him. "You want me to let you go."

He spoke in a statement more than a question, but his dejected tone revealed a desire to bear down on his reluctance—even as he pulled her in so their foreheads touched—he shook his head in denial of what he had to do.

The light around her dimmed, and she turned to a group of five medics rushing through the barn's front doors, their fast approach raising a sense of frantic panic. She and Chip—her childhood friend, now the love of her life—*would* be wrenched apart.

"Chip." Her voice cracked along with her heart, an unmissable fissure opening with a need to hear she wasn't alone in her decision. "Say you'll let me go too."

Thirty-Nine

Two weeks later, Ally sat at her kitchen table with a clear plastic sheet spread over the wood surface while she painted her most recent set of plant pots. Only now, she angled the thin brush away so she could press a hand over her eyes and not get paint on her face.

"Headache, again?" Her mom peered over from the sink, already filling a glass with water.

Ally gave a disingenuous laugh and squeezed her eyes shut against the dull ache in her brain. "Did they ever leave?"

"Oh, honey." Her mother's footsteps drew near. "Here."

Ally opened her eyes to her mother's outstretched palm, two white pills sitting in the center. More painkillers. Just about all she could do while she waited for her brain to heal from the concussion she'd sustained when Mark Farro's men had rammed Sarah's car.

The same day she'd lost Chip.

"Thanks." She took the pills and the glass of water and then downed both in quick order.

"You're over-exerting yourself." A series of wrinkles lined her mother's forehead, that look of concern Ally had gotten all too used to lately. "You're supposed to be taking care of yourself, but you're busier than ever. What with the Argyle job and the pieces for the wedding."

"You sound like Laila." Ally refocused on the pot before her, half-blocking out her mom, half-expecting her sister to develop some kind of telepathy and call to check on Ally for the millionth time.

Maybe her mom and sister were a little right. Ally *did* have a lot to do, but distraction served a higher purpose than lying in bed brooding. At least in this case, anyway.

Her physical injuries weren't her only wounds. She was still heartbroken. Still reeling from the psychological trauma of having her life so nearly ended. The Argyle deal and making clay hearts for Emilia's wedding offered a smidgeon of salvation.

In fact, she'd only signed the Argyle deal after negotiating to make all the pieces herself. She wouldn't mass produce her designs. Not just yet, anyway. She'd create bespoke pieces priced a little higher and use this experience to get quicker at throwing pots on her wheel. The more she made, the more she could hopefully sell.

And as for Emilia's wedding, well, that was one of the very few things Ally looked forward to. Not just the chance to celebrate, but the process of revealing her ceramic heart design—small clay ornaments on a string with Emilia and Blaine's names atop an imprint of lavender sprigs. Her nod to their first date at Aggie's lavender farm.

Even just imagining their reactions brought a smile to her face—smiling being something she didn't do a whole lot lately.

"What am I supposed to do?" She leaned back into her chair and took a steadying breath, once again abandoning her work when she really needed to keep moving. "Stay in my room and think? Bad enough Blaine replaced me with Emilia at Oak Tree."

"Now, you know he's still holding a place for you there in case the Argyle thing doesn't flourish. And it being my job to make sure you're okay, I'm one hundred percent in agreement with the man insisting on your rest."

Her mom stood at her side, as though looming might get her to pack away all the paints and do as told. Ally pitched forth a half-hearted side glare. "I love you, Momma, but I'm twenty-three now, and it's past time we transitioned to me taking full care of myself."

"Ally." Her mother's brows drew together, and she gave a warning shake of her head. "Everyone needs some help some of the time."

"I know." Ally reached out and patted her mother's hand resting on the tabletop, being sure to soften her scowl in the process. "But could you trust me on this one? I'm where I need to be and doing what I need to do. I'll be just fine."

None of that was a lie, she *was* light years closer to where she wanted to be. The real shame was that it took her experience with Chip to show her the way. To show her who she *really* was. That she loved Harlow. That there was nothing wrong with being a small-town girl. Not for her.

Maybe the Argyle deal would provide enough money to travel, but she'd always find her way back here. Even then, Emilia wanted to line up more clients for Ally's work, so making a consistent income from her art maybe wasn't as far-fetched as she'd once thought.

Maybe she'd move into her own place somewhere closer to Main Street. She'd put more pieces into the local boutiques and build toward opening Harlow's first art gallery.

Other small towns had them, so why not this one?

Dreams and direction. For the first time ever, she had both.

And still, some of her literal dreams included Chip.

Dreams where she awoke alone, feeling a piece of her missing.

Because a piece of her *was* missing.

But sometimes growth was about losing things too, right? Like how trees lost their leaves or children lost their baby teeth, all in the throes of moving from one stage of life to the next.

So she'd made the right choice, even if "right" didn't stop the persistent gnawing sensation in her tummy through every waking hour. The pain remained. As did the tears. As well as the urge to call him and beg for another chance.

Warmth touched her cheek. More precisely, her mother's hand turned Ally's face, so she looked directly into those familiar golden-brown eyes. "I never wanted to be the reason any child of mine held back."

Ally's chest muscles constricted, halting her breath while intensifying the existing pain around her heart.

"Mom...you never were—" A laugh broke from her, and she shook her head, her voice husky and her eyes prickling. "Okay, maybe you were a tiny part of why I chose Harlow, but only because you and Dad did *too* good a job creating a loving home, yah know? What woman in her right mind would abandon a life that essentially feels like one, big, long, warm hug?"

"Oh, you." Her mother's eyes brightened, and she leaned in, pulling Ally into an *actual* hug. "The big, long, warm hugs aren't going anywhere, but we're not the only ones who'll ever have them for you, my little one."

Ally chuckled against her mother's neck despite the reference to her dating life or, more pointedly, Chip.

Thankfully, her mother knew better than to push too hard when it came to love, so as much as her fondness for Chip remained, not once had she tried to push Ally his way.

Soft and predictable comfort seeped down to her bones, the release of tension working gentle tears free from her eyes. Even in the safety of this embrace, she wasn't totally safe.

Harlow hosted a larger police presence, and all residents had orders to stay vigilant and report anything suspicious. The chance of new Syndicate activity kept her on edge, and the constant thoughts of Chip doubly so.

But she'd asked for this, hadn't she? Well, not exactly *this*. Not the Syndicate. Not the heartbreak. But change.

And the universe had delivered *that* in spades.

Forty

Chip pushed another cardboard moving box into the trunk of the borrowed Hyundai Tucson parked outside his father's house. With an hour left to return the small SUV to Jamie, he didn't have much time to stop and think, and still, he did—uncharacteristic rage continuing to churn within.

His thoughts caught on the day Ally fled from Boston. More precisely, his dad's refusal to stop her. That he could have at least woken Chip so he could catch up to her. Or even just not lie about her going sightseeing. Then again, all those options would have hampered Chip's success, and his dad simply could not have that.

Get real, none of that would have stopped her from leaving.

He growled to himself and slammed the trunk closed with a firm *thunk*, then turned for the house again in pursuit of more boxes. For the first time in his life, emotion took over while daily bitterness and ruminating overrode basic sense.

Even though his dad viewed Chip's packing endeavors from his favorite armchair in the living room, Chip ignored him and strolled on by.

Whatever his dad felt, it wasn't grief over his youngest child moving. *No.* His dad wouldn't know what grief was. The man having failed to show any anguish in the wake of his divorce.

Meanwhile, Ally and I were together for mere weeks, and her absence hurts more than anything I've experienced.

He reached the stair's top landing and went straight to his room, nothing left of his belongings beside one large box and a sports bag packed with clothes. He'd be at Greg's apartment soon enough. Maybe not as glamorous or big as this house but far friendlier with more room for independence. He'd stay for a few weeks, make decisions on a few new opportunities in town, then settle on a permanent home elsewhere.

Though the sports bag weighed heavy on one shoulder, he aimed for a short and final journey downstairs, adding to his burden by hefting the last box in his hands too. Very soon, this part of his life would be over forever.

He should have left right away. Shouldn't have cared about rushing his escape. But once again, he paused. This time to take one slow and sweeping glance of his room.

Ten years of memories here. Not all bad, but not amazing either. A room that had kept him far from the girl destined to become the woman he loved. The woman others had suggested would be lucky to have him. A woman to show him he'd been the one lacking and fortunate all along.

And she'd unceremoniously dumped him. *Of course, she had.*

A deep heat filled the space under his ribs, prodding him to think over what coming to this city would have been like for her. To enter this home. To meet his father. To attend an event surrounded by his peers.

As much as he wanted to blame her for not trying hard enough, truth was, she *had* tried. She'd tried more than him. She'd pushed past her comfort zone, then pushed right back when none of it fit. Fight over. Decision made. *He* wasn't enough.

He slammed his eyes shut and bowed his head, lowering the box to press his fingers to the bridge of his nose. All those times he'd bowed to the pressure of justifying her presence in his life when his affection for her alone should have been enough.

He'd sat beside her and hadn't truly been *there* for her. For all his supposed perfection, he was the royal screw up here. So yes, he *wasn't* enough.

He let out a sigh and abandoned another self-punishing moment to open his eyes. To move on. To pick up that final box again and get the hell out of here. Down the stairs. Gaze pointed forward. Diminishing his dad's presence in the living room in favor of the front door just yards away.

"Your mother was the first to ask for a divorce."

Chip stopped, his dad's voice reverberating through the foyer, somehow breaking and adding to the existing tension all at once. All these years, Chip had been led to believe his dad was the one to end his marriage.

Even though he didn't know why, box still clutched to his chest, Chip turned to focus on his dad. "You mean, after you cheated on her with Kelly?"

"No, Son." His dad shook his head, slow and sure. "Long before then."

His dad's stare, though unwavering as always, held a weary edge— the lines around his eyes deeper, his skin somewhat gray. And still, years of animosity warned Chip not to mine for more detail. "And you're telling me right at *this* moment because?"

He offered a flat stare, suggesting his dad shouldn't answer, already turning to step away.

"I begged for more time and tried to make things work. We both tried, Chip. We tried until we couldn't anymore." Again, his dad's words held Chip captive, his direct approach often successful at maintaining calm in difficult situations. At gaining people's instant trust and attention.

But Chip didn't want to be like most people, and he flicked his gaze to the eminent front door. He'd accumulated enough regret of late and had no way of predicting if or when he'd speak to his dad again.

"If that's true"—he re-focused on his dad and narrowed his eyes, making it clear he still wasn't convinced—"why was she so torn apart after you left?"

"You think your mother's breakdown was all about me?" His dad's lips pressed into a thin line, his gaze doing an uncharacteristic dip. "Do you know what it's like to have plans for your life, and no matter how much you grasp at them, they crumble and slip through your fingers?"

Chip frowned, the tight defense in his body melting a little. "I do now."

He'd vowed to ignore his dad, to move on and out as quickly as possible, but now he lowered the box to the floor and embraced the delay while he worked to reframe a decade's worth of memories and hard feelings.

With recent experience in how a breakup could be more about circumstance than the couple involved, he strangely related to his dad's new offering. How could it be that Chip had glimpsed a future he'd wanted so badly, only to now face the impossible task of getting on with life? To never hear from the one he wanted to hear from most. To pretend his heart didn't live in another state entirely—his woman in Harlow busy painting plant pots, content with the decision she'd made.

Even though she'd also wanted some other ending.

Still, he pushed away from his present issues and returned to gathering more information on his past. "How does Kelly factor into all this?"

"Your mom and I, we wasted a lot of years making excuses for each other. Just trying to make things work." His dad's lips bent into a frown, his gaze still low, and his brows pressed into a thick and heavy line above his eyes. Chip had never seen him look so pensive. "If I ever gave you the impression I dislike Harlow, it's because I do. And I know you think I look down on the people there simply because they're small-town folk, but that's not the case. I begrudge those people because they're the reason we held on so long. That and their preoccupation with gossip and maintaining a social vacuum where no one is allowed to step out of line. Your mom's family, they had ancient history in that town, with all the expectation and scrutiny that brings. Can you imagine being the newcomer in all of that? Having to maintain the image of a perfect, happy family when you're anything but? I had no one to turn to or talk to, not without risking everyone else finding out about our troubles. Harlow was a pressure cooker for us. "

"You've never given the impression of someone who wanted to talk." Even as new understanding seeped through, Chip let out a scoff. "Hell, you made me maintain a greater air of perfection here than when I lived in Harlow."

His dad's gaze flicked back up to him, pausing a moment before he replied, "Maybe I went about building some resilience in you in the wrong way."

"You think?"

"Look, I wanted you to know a few things and a few people before I released you into the world, okay?" He stopped and clenched his jaw, his entire body seeming to tense. "Chip, I didn't want you to face the same problems I did."

"What problems?" He gave his dad a skeptical side glare. "I've never met anyone more methodical, unaffected, or enterprising."

"And you also never knew me when I was fresh out of med school, completing my residency at a rural hospital, and building my entire future around the girl I happened to meet at her family's bar in Harlow." His expression eased, and his gaze lowered again. "You and Sarah were kids, so I hid a lot, Chip. If I seem unfeeling, if I pushed you hard, it's because I wanted you to have the steady foundation I didn't. If I had my wish, it would be that you'll never know what it is to reestablish yourself later in life, all because you learned too late that being alone *is* lonely, but being in love and alone is worse."

Chip's heartbeat seemed to slow at those words, his muscles turning still and stiff. In love alone? As in, his dad had been the more invested one in his prior marriage?

"Kelly—" His dad's clear cut tone suggested he read Chip's thoughts and now sought to piece together the past, free of Chip's once juvenile interpretation of events. "We'd worked together at the hospital for years, and she'd noticed how reluctant I was to leave at the end of each shift, that hospital being one I'd only ever intended to work at for a year but then couldn't seem to leave. Not even to go home." His dad scoffed. "She never pursued me, but she was the first to say I wasn't doing anyone any favors by holding on. It was my finally moving on that blindsided your mother, all because wanting a relationship to end is a whole other beast to facing down the actual ending."

Kind of like how Ally had voiced good reasons for the breakup, but then being without her felt the complete opposite of anything good.

"I don't know what to make of having actual sympathy for you." As much as he didn't want to, a slight smile broke past his attempt at a grimace.

"Try being me." His dad gave a dry chuckle, and Chip couldn't recall the last time he'd witnessed any expression of humor from this man. "I see you reestablishing links with Harlow *and* with a local woman, at that, and I see decades of my life jumping out to haunt me."

Though the statement was said in jest, Chip couldn't find it in him to laugh. For once, he couldn't find it in him to be angry either. A sense of unexpected calm washed over him, like he could disagree with his dad, but he could see the concern behind his actions too. "Ally and I aren't like you and mom."

His dad's expression stilled, as though the accusation had him veering from his natural response to heighten any conflict. "But you are from two different worlds."

His even delivery left an unusual and unarmed space for Chip to say his piece. "We grew up together."

"Chip"—his dad scrubbed a hand over his face and released a heavy sigh—"I've never been one to give dating advice, but if I were to give any, it's to take a woman at her word. Ally told you to leave. So, save yourself the time and heartache and believe her."

Chip stood silent for a while, holding his dad's open and commiserating stare, the whoosh of traffic infiltrating from outside and calling him to tread closer to his destiny.

"We're different." The words fell from him again, a little softer and matter-of-fact, more like a self-affirmation.

And come to think of it, he knew nothing of being in love alone.

Ally *did* love him.

I just never gave her much reason to trust me.

Holy smokes! He blinked, a small frown pulling at his lips because he'd watched his dad and Kelly over the years, and they were different too. Their relationship far more stable and less dramatic than what Chip had witnessed from his parents growing up.

"We *are* different." An undeniable strain weighed on his next breaths.

As smart as he believed himself, he'd made one god-awful and bumbling mistake.

He'd believed Ally when she'd insisted he would grow to resent her differences when all he saw in her presence was the light and freedom he missed in other aspects of his life.

"You think so?" His dad eased back in his chair, for the first time in this conversation seeming in his element. "You think I'm wrong about you and your girl?"

Chip shrugged, for once not all that affected by his dad's doubt. "I know you are."

A slight, unbelieving smirk curled his dad's lips, like he knew something Chip didn't, his ensuing easy chuckle cementing whatever mystery notion ran through his brain. "If that's true, why are you here and not in Harlow?"

Forty-One

A MONTH LATER:

The old flour mill along the banks of the Mirabelle River played the perfect host to Emilia and Blaine's wedding. The mill had enough room for a small bar and modest dance floor inside its raw brick walls, as well as six long rows of tables in the open-air courtyard and a tiny army of well-dressed servers weaving through. And then there was the wisteria canopy above, where fragrant purple blooms dangled over guests from overhead beams. The soft afternoon light and the lilac display offering dream-like polarity to the mill's stripped-down appearance.

The flower's sway in the gentle spring breeze brought a smile to Ally's face, and she allowed her eyes to drift shut in this rare break from work and sad memories.

"Like a dream, isn't it?"

She snapped her eyes open to her sister in the seat beside her, although Ally's smile remained. "Just what I was thinking. Though this spot has always been nice, just… the mill… not so much."

"Right?" Laila laughed and twisted closer in her seat. "But only

Emilia could turn a pile of rubble into a classy riverside wedding venue. Can you just imagine how much work she and Blaine had to do?"

Ally giggled. "From all his complaining, I'm gonna guess Blaine did most of the dirty work. I hear the council loved the idea and are keen to hold more of these in the future to draw out-of-towners looking for a country wedding. So they helped some."

"Ahh"—Laila pointed a finger—"but Emilia would have been the visionary."

"Damn right." Ally paused, grateful for Emilia's vision. Without her, Ally wouldn't have a new channel for her pottery, and Harlow wouldn't have a new wedding venue, with all the extra money that would flow to local businesses from each event. "Hey, remember how we used to come here while Daddy would fish in the river? This place was nothing but a spot to play house and catch some shade, but five minutes in this town and Emilia envisioned opportunities none of us did."

"Sure"—Laila jutted her chin to the empty seat to Ally's right—"but I would have thought six weeks would have been enough time to 'envision' Chip not showing up."

Though Laila meant well, the mention of Chip's name made Ally drop her focus to the sea-foam fabric of her long dress draped over her lap, her heart seeming to shrink a little. But Laila had a point. After all the tears Ally had cried in Emilia's presence, she should have known not to count on Chip being here. So, what gave?

Whitney strolled over from her turn with Aggie on the dance floor, stopping at Laila's side and tugging at her arm. She wanted her mom to come dance.

Laila reached out a hand and squeezed Ally's shoulder, her lips pressed into a sympathetic line while resisting Whitney's distraction a moment longer. "Don't think bad of the bride, okay? Maybe you're not the only one wishful thinking."

Ally opened her mouth, ready to assert that she had no "wishful thoughts" when it came to Chip Overton. But the restrictive lump in her throat, the one that grew every time someone mentioned his name, said that was a lie.

Either way, her chance for debate disappeared along with her sister, who swept Whitney into her arms and carried the child back inside.

Ally pulled her gaze absentmindedly away from her sister and onto Adrian Ramos. The man sat two empty spots away—and with Laila and Whitney gone—she had a clear view of him staring at her sister's swaying back.

Ally's lips parted in surprise, mixed with a need to question his line of sight, but he erased that option with the shift of his gaze to her, his raised brow and unperturbed expression seeming to say, *What of it?*

She chuckled to herself and shook her head. With Ramos's distinctly masculine features and glowing bronze skin against the contrast of his bright white shirt, a number of women here seemed happy to have him around. Heck, in any other timeline, Ally would have been happy too.

But she'd had her turn at ill-fated attraction and still couldn't imagine looking at another man the way she had Chip. Besides, Ramos's presence came with a depressing reflection of Harlow's current state of upheaval, the entire town anticipating the Syndicate's next move.

She wanted to keep her distance from anything to do with the ugly violence she'd experienced just weeks ago. Even if Ramos did insist he only stayed in Harlow because he liked the place.

No one truly believed him.

He'd come as added protection. He'd come for his friends.

Ally narrowed her eyes at him but decided to let things be. If Laila proved anything over the years, it was her ability to survive just about any hardship. Dubious men included.

Only with Laila gone from the table, Ally now sat as a remote island between multiple empty seats. Except, unlike an island, she had legs and could escape Ramos's stare-off and the frightful silence of being alone.

So she pushed her chair back and rose, twisting to make her way to the bar, only to stop because another man stood before her.

She didn't dare look him in the eyes, so her attention stuck on his open, white collar and his golden skin in between. The scent of his peppermint and sandalwood cologne made her eyelids want to flutter shut. So she could breathe him in a moment before reality came crashing in.

But closing her eyes would give too much away, so the best she could do was allow his name to tumble from her lips. Less a question. More an inarguable truth.

"Chip."

With just one word, she frowned and dared to lift her gaze to him, where those hazel eyes partnered with his lax cheeks and still expression.

Her breath caught, and her pulse thundered in her ears, halting her ability to question his presence.

It's Emilia's wedding, and he was invited. He has just as much right to attend.

Her attention skipped to the empty chair next to hers. *His chair.*

No way. She wouldn't spend the next hours with him at her side, which prompted her next decision to wide-step around him and power toward her new home for this event. The bar.

She'd seek something harder than the white wine at her table. Stock up on canapés and get chatting with the bar staff. This could work. This could definitely work.

A giant floral arrangement met her at the counter, the bouquet circled by a multitude of violet "Purple Rain" cocktails. Emilia's nod to her love of Prince, an icon in her new home of Minnesota.

Even though the spirits in Ally's newly acquired martini glass smelled a little like jet fuel, the rock sugar around the rim offered a pretty and sweeter balance. She knocked back her first long sip, and a wave of sharp citrus juice and bitter spirits hit her tongue.

Not bad. Not bad at all. She kept her back to wherever she assumed Chip lingered and set to musing at her glass and the surprisingly palatable drink inside.

While she vowed to finish at least three before making her excuses to leave, an abrasive memory took over. Her hiding inside a toilet stall, slamming down drinks to distract from her cowardice and pain. Surely she'd progressed since then.

She could choose one of three options now. Keep drinking. Leave. Or buck up and face Chip with her thoughts. But because she hadn't changed *that* much, she took one last swig of liquid courage before putting down her glass on the counter and marching to where he sat at her table.

"Time to talk." She planted her hands to her hips and tried hard to maintain her newfound maturity through an even tone. "Are you here for the wedding, or are you here to see me?"

His uplifted gaze did nothing to shift the forward roll of his shoulders, and his expression's quick fall prompted an involuntary flutter of her heart.

"One brought me here more than the other." His pause, paired with the sweep of his gaze over her face, hinted at caution and the need to gauge her response. "Though I have an entire other reason for being in town too."

She stared at him a while, maybe just a little sad to hear she wasn't the *only* reason he was here, even though she shouldn't have cared. This being her first proper breakup, she wasn't sure what rules applied, although her focus dropped to the empty chair beside him. *Her* chair. Making it immediately clear that she *did* care.

So, what now? Did she sit down and stew in the awkward silence, allowing him to get on with his life? Just while away this day until they parted ways again?

Screw that!

Not content to leave room for regrets, she flicked her hair from her eyes and set her mind to a direct approach. "What other reasons?"

"Ally"—the long and husky draw of her name on his voice tugged once more at her heart—"my other reason is that I like this place, and I'm staying."

A hard gasp filled her lungs, and she stared blankly ahead, the world around her seeming to freeze, her only redemption being that she'd ditched her drink at the bar, saving her from dropping her glass now.

"But, why?" She stumbled back a little, and he jumped to his feet, catching her wrists like he didn't trust her to remain upright.

Maybe his actions were justified, but the jolt of electricity moving from his hands to her brought a familiar tingle to her body, and the shock of that alone had her shaking him off her. "Please. Don't."

His touch, plus the knowledge that she'd get no escape from him after today, left her heartbroken. Just heartbroken. A life in Harlow wasn't what she wanted for him. Or her.

He had too much potential for this little place. And thanks to the Syndicate, he'd be stepping back into a world of danger. Then there was her knowing that his presence here had at least a little something to do with her. That she'd have to see him day-in day-out and *know* that she loved him but couldn't have him.

Tears pricked her eyes, and she pushed right past, his close proximity already too much. *So much for maturity.* All she could think about was escaping. A hard task given she'd driven Laila here and didn't want to ditch her sister and niece. So now, all Ally had was her hurried steps to the river's edge, and the tiny hope that Chip would not follow.

Forty~Two

"ALLY!"

Chip's voice trailed Ally's brisk escape to her new refuge beneath the sweeping, green vines of a giant willow, the labor of each breath causing her to stop and catch herself mid-cowardly escape.

She rounded on him, hot tears already running down her face.

"You can't stay." She swiped at her cheeks, swearing under her breath at her overwrought reaction. Of course, she'd fantasized about seeing him again, but she hadn't imagined doing so while looking like a half-drowned river monster. "You can't stay in Harlow."

She wanted to push him away, but he stood out of reach, both hands jammed into his pockets. "This is my home too."

"No." Her voice shot out, ragged and pitchy, though some internal monologue screamed at her to get her act together. "Boston is your home. You left here. Ten years ago. This is *my* home, and you're not allowed to ruin it for me."

His chin jerked back a little, like the word "ruin" truly hurt him. His attention fell to the ground so that locks of rose-gold hair tumbled over his brow, that crestfallen image of him beautiful and heart-wrenching.

"I'm staying, Ally." He offered a firmer tone, his gaze hitting her again, though with a steeliness she'd never before witnessed on him. "Regardless of how you feel about me. I'm staying."

As much as she tried to open her mouth in protest, his intimidating and resolute stare turned her heart's earlier flutter into a thundering gallop.

To make this situation worse, he pulled his hands from his pockets and strode closer. Again, she sought to back away. But again, she did nothing.

"Harlow *is* my home." He softened his tone to something less harsh but just as inescapable and matter-of-fact. "I'm one reason the Syndicate is gunning for this place. I'm not leaving these people to fend for themselves."

An incredulous laugh broke past her lips, and she thrust her hands out to her sides, gesturing to the space around her. "And what am I supposed to do? Just lump having you back in town?"

"You could do that." He took another step forward, and she jolted away, his brow flexing in a look that hovered between disappointed and perplexed. "You could get used to seeing my face most days, or... there are other options."

The river's soft lap against its muddy banks filled the silence from her sudden lack of words. She drew a hard breath, centering her attention on the river's damp and earthy scents—trying and failing to find a balance between anger, confusion, and some other emotion she just *didn't* want to face.

"No. No other options." Such flat refusal, marred by her husky delivery.

And in his usual way, Chip remained still. "I'm not leaving."

"Yes, you are." Her mouth bent into a frown, only for her to bite down on her lower lip, the action likely exposing her lack of resolve.

"And maybe while I'm around, you'll come to see I'm fully capable of screwing up my life without your help." A slow smile formed on his lips, forever self-assured even when he wasn't. "And that I'm not my father, either. He says, 'Hi' by the way."

A cold sensation washed down her arms, and her cheeks fell slack, meanwhile the mention of his father had adrenaline tweaking her pulse. Her fear of history repeating now battled against Bill's supposed greeting.

"Your dad, what?" Her breathy tone gave sound to her disbelief.

She and Chip were too dissimilar, Chip far too perfect for a now-unapologetically helter-skelter woman like herself.

"We talked, and believe it or not, without fighting for a change." His eyes softened, and he offered an overly casual shrug. "There are things you don't know about my parents' breakup. Things even I didn't know up until recently. They had other issues besides Harlow and my dad's lack of career glory. So if you're scared we'll make the same mistakes, maybe consider we're all very different people."

A small scoff escaped her, and she shook her head. "You think I didn't consider that?"

His eyes narrowed on her, and he drew out a slow pause, strain apparent over his clenched jaw, as though he fought a wave of hurt and defense. "I have no idea what you considered, Ally. We never really talked this out, did we?"

He raised a brow, daring her to deny his point, but between her running away and then fighting the effects of a concussion, there hadn't been much time to talk.

Perhaps in a sign he found convincing her more difficult than planned, he scratched behind his ear. his chin tilted to the ground, although his gaze still lifted to hers.

"So, did you ever stop to reflect on the fact that my dad is an adult and responsible for his own mistakes? And so am I?" He now held that all-knowing look of his, the one that always seemed to see right through her. "How about letting me fall on my own sword on this one?"

She shrugged, fully aware she'd been too busy trying not to disappoint him to allow room for him to fail right along with her.

And even though she shrugged, her voice still hitched on her next words. "Maybe because I'd be falling too?"

"Ally—"

"I mean, why put speed signs out if we're all supposed to just learn from our own mistakes?" She shot out a manic-sounding laugh, the analogy way too astute for her, her comment on falling also way too honest.

He frowned. "Fair point, but no one will die here, and you're assuming I've inherited my dad's addiction to success. Which, by the way, turns out to be his coping mechanism. Personally, I prefer a slower pace."

"I can't ask you to drop your prospects to be with me."

"Who says I'd be dropping anything?"

"Look around. There's nothing here for you."

"There's you."

"I don't want to be your only reason."

He barked out a laugh. "Jesus, Ally. Don't I get a say here? If all you can see in me, and all that's holding you back, is my career potential, then you're no better than my dad."

Her lips parted at the comparison between his dad's beliefs and hers. "Except he made you feel you weren't enough, but in this case, I'm the one who's lacking. You deserve someone more worldly. More like you."

His stare latched on to her, and he gave a small shake of his head, stepping in impossibly close. "I don't like it when you talk about yourself that way. You're not guileless or simple minded, you're not anything but brilliant to me. I see your frustration at the world around you, but maybe that's just because you do and see things differently, which is another thing I like about you. You're creative and fun—more fun than I've had in a long time—and you're so many things that I'm not. You're everything I need, Ally. Do you understand? And despite what you think"—he wrinkled his nose—"I have no desire to date a female version of myself. *Gross.*"

A laugh broke through her at his joke. "I hadn't thought of it like that, but I get your point."

"Good." His smile inched higher. "Can you hurry up now and get the rest of it too? So we can get to where we're supposed to be. Together."

"I…" Her voice cracked, and she pursed her lips, unable to truthfully say she *did* believe all those nice things he'd said about her.

"Why can't you see?" He let out an exasperated sigh and turned away, face lifting to the sky in a way that only made her feel more clueless. "Fuck it, Ally, you might not want to hear it, but I love you. Every time you say that stuff about yourself—even when you just *think* it—you hurt yourself. You hurt the woman I love. The woman I *chose*. And so, you hurt me too."

Chip wasn't a swearing sorta guy, and her lips pressed tighter, repressing the wild storm of emotions swirling within her and threatening to break out. And the bit about him loving her... about choosing her. She'd known all that but hearing it... hearing it was another experience altogether. As was the prospect of turning him down after all he'd just said.

He spun back around, the stern creases over his forehead indicating she was the only one his words surprised. "If you won't speak, then at least think on this question. Do I make bad choices?"

Though tears welled in her eyes, she still shook her head.

And he chose me!

He marched over and cupped her cheeks, the tender act adding to the sting in her eyes. "I know you don't believe me yet, but we don't have to be the same to make this work. Your fresh perspective makes you an asset, not a liability, and I don't intend to do all the thinking for us. I want the arguments and clashes of opinions. I want a partner. Ally, I want you."

Unsure how he'd wrangled control over this conversation, a small chuckle broke from her, and her first tears tumbled free. But once again, he was right.

He didn't generally make bad choices. And even if she couldn't believe his glowing views on her, to her, he *was* perfect. In every way possible.

So as much as she sought to again think he was more than she deserved, his words about not even *thinking* self-critical things rose to stop her.

He's changing me already.

While she could maybe lay off herself, accepting him back into her life meant accepting that this all could fail spectacularly. It meant accepting the chance of yet another heartbreak.

"But you'll grow to hate me." The words rasped through her throat, designed as a deflection that now inadvertently exposed another painful belief.

He gave an easy shrug and touched his forehead to hers. "And maybe you'll hate me. I'm still willing to find out."

His gaze held for a weighty beat, lips curling higher until sheer laughter rippled between them. A new hush took over, and he stroked her cheek, vying for her full attention. "Ally, I'm all in. How about you?"

More tears fell, and she blinked them away to give him a quick nod.

He chose me.

Time I chose him too.

Her heart felt suddenly lighter, and not a single moment had passed when she hadn't wanted him. Not in the weeks apart, especially not now he stood before her—*in Harlow*—his refusal to leave an admittedly compelling reason to at least give this love a chance.

His lips collided over hers, stealing her ability to form another thought, save to absorb the sweet support of being pressed to him, his hands cradling her head while he dominated this kiss.

But she clung to him, too, the space beneath her chest feeling fuller than ever, even as new and happy laughter pushed for release.

The need for air eventually pulled them apart, and his gaze held joyful and bright, his lips parting as though he sought to speak. She knew what he had to say, and frankly, she wanted her turn to talk. So, she clapped her hand over his mouth and chuckled. "I love you, too, Chip Overton."

She dropped her hand to find his lips pushed into a broad grin. Though he drew in to snare her with another kiss, a loud cheer broke from the flour mill's direction. Thinking those cheers were meant for Blaine and Emilia, that something particularly fun had happened at their wedding, she glanced over to find the attention of about two hundred wedding guests turned to her.

Instant shock jolted her out of Chip's hold. He turned to the wedding party, his quick laughter feeding her own, as more cheers and whoops broke loose at the crowd's delight at being caught watching.

He grabbed her hand, and though her cheeks burned, she ran with the spirit of unfettered elation—bowing to her captive audience and instinctively knowing Chip would join her.

And he did. Of course, he did.

Only to swing her back to him for one last kiss.

Epilogue

A week later:

Ally stepped aside from Chip's front door and made room for her dad with his arms wrapped around her last box of art supplies. Her mother trailed behind carrying the small rack Ally used to house some of her paints, this final parade past signifying that, as of now, Ally was all moved into Chip's place in Harlow.

On the driveway, Chip slammed the tray of her dad's pickup shut and his gaze caught hers in confirmation. She was his. All his.

His every step toward her picked up pace now, his smile growing until he wrapped her in his arms and swung her around, raining countless, quick kisses about her face. "You're mine now."

She laughed at the cartoonist voice he used. Laughed at the euphoric truth in his words. *She was his.* And he was hers. No more distance to separate them. No more family pressures to keep them apart.

"Well"—her dad's heavy footsteps preceded his voice—"that's us done."

He strolled over and clapped Chip on the shoulder, the strain over his cheeks denoting sadness while the light in his eyes held pride. His little girl had grown up. She'd moved on. And with a guy her parents had loved almost as long as they'd loved her.

"Happy unpacking, Ally Bear." Her mom drew in and caught Ally in a hug. "And don't you two get into any more trouble, okay?"

She slid back, her gaze bouncing between Ally and Chip, her face exuding the same forlorn happiness as Ally's dad. Though Ally had no plans for problems with Chip, avoiding the Syndicate's notice wasn't so guaranteed.

Ramos had already intercepted whispers on the Syndicate's main player, Rudolph Manzinni, repealing his past hands-off approach when it came to Harlow. Mark had gone into hiding, perhaps overseas, the chance of him still seeking revenge not over yet. All while multiple government agencies worked to intercept any and all Syndicate plans.

Chip drew in and hugged Ally's mom. "See you Sunday?"

Her mom stepped back and leveled a wink. "You betcha. It'll be just like old times."

While her mom wandered outside, her dad doled out one last embrace to Ally and then followed suit, her dad's truck soon rumbling out the drive, leaving Ally and Chip to start their new life in this house. Together.

Chip pushed the front door closed and then pulled Ally in for a long embrace, one that took stock of this new reality, the house indeed seeming to hold a reverent quiet.

"You sure we can fend for ourselves?" She smiled up at him, loving the strength his body imbued in her moment of uncertainty.

"We'll do better than that." His hand snaked around her bare waist from under her cropped pink halter top, and he pressed a line of kisses down the side of her neck. "We're destined for greatness, Ally Bear."

She laughed at his use of her mom's pet name for her, as well as one other thing. "Destined, huh?" She leaned back and raised a brow. "I thought you said you don't believe in karma, fate, or voodoo?"

"Oh, I still don't, but"—he dropped another kiss to her lips, then pulled away, his tug at her hand taking her with him—"if there *were* such a thing, you and I are most definitely fated for each other."

"And greatness. Don't forget, we're destined for greatness." She found herself nearly out of breath as he pulled her through the living room and into the kitchen.

"Starting now, in fact." He picked her up, garnering a light squeal from her as he sat her on the countertop, the height and cold white marble a shock. "I have to ask you something, first."

Her heartbeat lifted to a fast drum, but she bit her lower lip, withholding questions she struggled to voice, anyway.

"I want to make all your dreams come true." His gaze searched hers, his open expression hinting vulnerability while his eyes still held a cheerful light. "You know that, right?"

Her mouth ran momentarily dry, but she nodded and answered, "Is that the question?"

He let loose with a chuckle and shook his head. "No. But if you lean back ever so slightly and rummage through that fruit bowl over there, you might just find what I'm referring to. Something that belongs to you."

She narrowed her eyes, and her pulse rose to a loud rumble. Her muscles felt heavy and slack, prompting her to stall any action.

Something small enough to fit in a fruit bowl?

Something meant for her?

Not a *ring*.

I'm not quite ready for a ring!

Her jaw sprung open, and his stare latched to her reaction, the need to escape his notice her motivation to lean back and do as told.

She dug through the wicker bowl, fingers brushing over smooth banana skins and bumpier oranges. A green apple jumped the bowl's edge and hit the counter; she squealed again, scrambling to catch the rolling fruit.

Meanwhile, Chip's lips met her bare tummy, the tender gesture and arousing warm sensation forcing her to stifle a groan. "There's nothing here."

His tongue grazed her belly button, damn near melting her into the white stone beneath her. "Keep looking."

"You're not helping, you know."

His breath tickled her skin through his chuckle, her desperation rising until she took to tossing the fruit out one-by-one, the basket eighty-percent empty before a red envelope lay apparent along the bottom.

Catching the envelope and tapping it to Chip's chest in lighthearted retaliation, she worked out a heavy sigh, followed by a shaky laugh. "Oh, thank goodness. I thought you were trying to propose."

"Wow, don't sound so relieved." He narrowed his gaze on her. "Besides, you haven't opened your gift yet. Maybe I still am."

His attention fell to the envelope in her hand, and hers followed suit, her tummy hardening at his warning. Still, she worked a finger under the envelope's top flap, flicking her gaze up to Chip's expectant stare before prying the contents loose.

"What?" Her heart strained, and tears pricked the lower edge of her eyes. "What is this?"

He jutted his chin to the two pieces of paper in her hand. "What does it say?"

"Prague Vaclav Havel International Airport." Her breath hitched, and she clapped a hand over her mouth. "Chip, I'm going to Prague?"

His eyes glittered along with his smile, and he gave a silent nod. "Hopefully, you'll take me with you."

She laughed and sobbed in one rickety sound and threw her arms around him, her tears quick to splash down her cheeks. "This means everything to me. Thank you. Of course, you're coming."

She clung to him with all her strength, her chest heaving, her joy so sky-high, he could have asked her to marry him now and she'd say, "Yes. A thousand times, yes."

She leaned back and swiped at the wetness on her cheeks, sniffing back another need to cry. "How did you pay for this?"

She lifted her gaze to him, her heart heavy because she didn't want to hear he'd made a huge financial sacrifice to help her realize this dream.

Though the drama with Mark Farro had churned unexpected interest in Stonewall, no deal had been settled yet. In fact, while Chip remained in Harlow building his idea, he had a business advisor juggling deals between tech firms in Minneapolis and Toronto.

His work would stay closer to town, with the plan to garner

investment so that Stonewall would always remain largely Chip's company.

"Ally"—his gaze softened in a sign he had something important to say—"my dad paid."

The weight at her heart lifted, and she pressed her hand to her chest, holding back another wave of tears. "Why? Why would he do that?"

"Because he's sorry." Chip shrugged, his lips rising into a big smile. "He called it a belated graduation gift, but secretly, I think he's starting to like the effect you have on me."

"Oh yeah?" She dipped her chin and caught his lips momentarily with hers. "And what effect is that?"

"You forced me to stand up to him. I guess that's a sign of growing up, right?" A tight look of uncertainty took him over, and he nodded down to the tickets in her hand. "I booked for a year from now. That gives us time to settle our work stuff, but we can always change the date."

She reached out and laid a hand to the side of his head, stroking her thumb over his soft hair. "No, this is perfect. Maybe by then, the trip will double as a honeymoon."

She hit him with her biggest smile, reveling in his light surprised jolt, only for his face to relax into a slow look of knowing. Next, his hands found her lower back, and he pulled her forward over the countertop, stopping once she had no farther to go. "I'd like that."

He dropped his mouth to hers, unleashing a long and sumptuous kiss, his hands sweeping under her top and higher up her back, making it clear where he wanted this to go.

She pulled her lips from him for one quick second to whisper her own heart's desire. "Me too."

His lips met hers again, and he lifted her off the counter, her body wrapped around him and supported in his arms. For so long, she'd wanted freedom and needed love, her lacking confidence and scattered approach keeping her away from both. But then, she'd found her childhood friend—or more precisely, he'd found her—and she'd learned all about what she loved most.

She loved Harlow. Loved her family and her tight community. She loved herself just as she was. And if all that love wasn't enough, well, she sure as anything loved Chip Overton too. And despite all her past misadventures. All those times she'd followed her heart all the way to some other man who was not hers, each awkward failure suddenly made a whole lot more sense.

Because now, Chip Overton unequivocally loved her right back.

THE END

JOIN TO GET A FREE NOVELLA AND EXCLUSIVE KATERINA SIMMS MATERIAL

Building relationships with my readers is one of the great joys of writing, it keeps me from turning into a robot! My newsletters are filled with information on new releases, cover reveals, sales, giveaways, and news relating to my series.

To claim your copy simply go to the "Free Book" page on my website.

www.katerinasimms.com

Also by Katerina Simms

The Love at Last Series:

The Last Heartbeat — Love at Last, Book 1

The Last Place You Look — Love at Last, Book 2

The Last in Line — Love at Last, Book 3

The Harlow Series:

Sapphires and Secrets — The Harlow Series, Book 1

Secret Surrender — The Harlow Series, Book 2

Small Town Secrets— The Harlow Series, Book 4

For latest releases, go to:

https://katerinasimms.com/books

Katerina Simms is a contemporary romance author and an International North Street Book Prize semi finalist; originally born on a sunny Mediterranean island, only to move to the weather-challenged suburbs of Melbourne, Australia.

Tea addict, nature lover, and terrible gardener, Katerina's novels feature vivid modern settings and heart-stirring characters, punctuated with the occasional good laugh. Her romances skirt the edges of women's fiction, and her favorite tropes are opposites attract, slow burn, and heat with heart.

www.katerinasimms.com

How About A Review?

Authors love reviews, and good ones help us make a living, and thus
write more books! If you've enjoyed this book, please consider leaving
a review on Goodreads or your retailer of choice. Just a line or two
would make a wonderful difference!

Eternally grateful,

Katerina Simms